GHOST GOLD

Book II
The Manna Chronicles

By Chris Reynolds

www.AuthorChrisReynolds.com

www.AuthorChrisReynolds.com
Retail Distribution Available through Ingramspark.com

Cover design by Chadwick Pelletier

Library of Congress Cataloging-in-Publication Data
Ghost Gold by Chris Reynolds

ISBN 978-1-7348939-3-9

Contact Info
11932 N Lake Drive
Boynton Beach, FL 33436
www.AuthorChrisReynolds.com

Follow us at:

 AuthorChrisReynolds.com

 AuthorChrisReynolds@AuthorChrisRey1

 AuthorChrisReynolds

 Chris Reynolds The Manna Chronicles
This is A Public Group open to those who want to explore the unusual

Acknowledgements

Many characters in this book are based on friends or people I have met along the way. Thank you for allowing me the leeway to veer from your true nature.

I would like to thank Dawn Alexander, Nancy Smay, Lisa LaPaglia, all who have been instrumental in helping shape the final story and keeping me on point.

Lastly and most importantly, I would like to thank my wife and family for their unwavering support and encouragement.

About the Author

Born in Virginia, raised in Maine, son of a sailor. Father, husband, writer, musician, explorer, adventurer. Attended University of Miami, lived in Coconut Grove, NYC, Connecticut, Chicago, Los Angeles, and Culver Indiana. Currently resides in Boca Raton, Florida.

Too many careers to list and too many encounters to be believed. My life has been a collection of fodder for my stories, texture for my tales and eccentricities for my characters.

For each and every one of us, our experiences are the threads that make up the tapestry of who we are. And what we believe to be true will define our reality.

Most of my published works have been explorations of alternative views of history and the shadowy fingerprints that have shaped events from behind the veil. Some call it fiction. I'm not so sure.

I hope you enjoy Ghost Gold.

Chris Reynolds – 2021
AuthorChrisReynolds.com

Satan's greatest feat

Was to convince the world

That he does not exist

A note from the Author about Book I of The Manna Chronicles

Lost Secret of the Ancient Ones

Ghost Gold is Book II of *The Manna Chronicles*. This book is a continuation of the saga of Maya Harrington and the quest to find her father. The first book, *Lost Secret of the Ancient Ones* is instrumental in setting the tone for the collection.

Quantum physicist Dr. Alex Harrington is shackled aboard the private jet of a powerful and dangerous shadow government. He has a secret they desperately crave and desperately fear. At 35,000 feet, Alex removes the shackles that binds him and simply vanishes as if he had been a mirage. This sets off a chain of events that will endanger the life of his daughter and alter the fate of mankind.

Three months after his disappearance, Maya Harrington is concerned. Her father often traveled for long periods and his communications were sporadic at best. But he has been missing for three months. When a stranger delivers a package containing her father's journal, her concern becomes a deep worry.

Why would someone have his journal. Is he in trouble?

The diary is full of esoteric data ranging from remote viewing, which is an esoteric technique to have one's consciousness leave their body and explore outside of one's presence, to shamanic ayahuasca journeys—from the mysteries of Fulcanelli to ancient ideas of interdimensional travel. Knowing her father's fascination with ciphers, Maya senses there are coded messages within the constructs of his written word. What are they? What is he trying to say? Where is he?

Maya vows to drop everything and find him, and the very next day Robert Vaherees—one of the richest men in the world—offers her a job: Find the Garden of Eden. As an avowed atheist, she believes this to be a fool's errand. But when he includes the use of his company's resources to run a parallel path in finding her father, she accepts the challenge.

From the Amazon jungle to Stonehenge, from Gobekli Tepe to the deserts of the Sinai Peninsula, she uses the journal to follow her father's path as he was trying to unravel an ancient oracle's vision about the coming end of time: The Sumerian Prophesy.

End times, transmutation, other dimensions... The more she tries to deny the alternative realities that don't align with her science, the more she comes to see that the quest to find her father, the quest to find the Garden of Eden, and the mysteries of the Sumerian Prophesy are all converging. And at the heart of the intersection is a mysterious powder called Manna.

Known as the Philosopher's Stone, it has been the enigmatic quest of alchemists across time. Chased by such notables as Aristotle, Stephen Hawking, the ancient Sumerians, and Sir Isaac Newton, Manna is the mystery powder found in the Egyptian Book of the Dead, the Bible, and the Dead Sea Scrolls.

Revered by the Egyptian Pharaohs, concealed within the ancient mystery schools and hoarded by secret societies across the pantheon of time, this ancient powder is believed to unlock the secrets needed to cross the veil of time and space, secrets Maya becomes desperate to unravel so she can find her father.

What becomes patently clear is that there are powerful people who want this ancient secret, and they will stop at nothing to get it. It is the lynch pin that will usher in their new world order.

For more details and to purchase, *The Lost Secret of the Ancient Ones - Book I of The Manna Chronicles* is available online at www. AuthorChrisReynolds.com. Book I can also be purchased on Amazon. Welcome to the Quest...

Are these dual eclipses crossing the last great empire a warning?

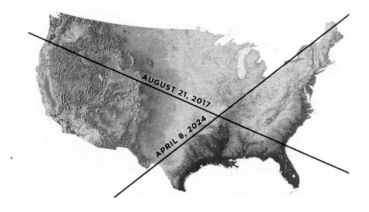

Thousands and thousands of ancient Sumerian cuneiforms tell the stories of a rogue planet called Nibiru. Written over seven thousand years ago, they called this returning celestial body "The Destroyer."

This planet supposedly has a highly elliptical orbit that swings well beyond the edge of our solar system into the icy depths of space only to return to the inner solar system approximately every four thousand years. Sowing mayhem and causing destruction, the ancient Sumerians proclaimed that the asteroid belt as we know it was caused when Nibiru destroyed a planet and sent debris into a fixed orbit around the sun. Further, at one time this destroyer is deemed to have moved so close to the planet Mars, it ripped away its atmosphere.

Legends? Myth? NASA has scoffed for years at such an idea as an unknown planet attached to our solar system. That is until July of 2017when they discovered the planet DeeDee, with its highly elliptical orbit, a planet that is now hurtling towards the inner sanctums of our solar system.

The United States has defied all statistical norms with its seven-year back-to-back eclipses. Are these celestial manifestations a coincidence? Are we in the crosshairs of a celestial bullseye? Can the world stop what is coming…

Most people on this Earth subscribe to one of these two viewpoints shown below. And thus, what you believe to be true, will dictate your life.

- Chris Reynolds

The universe is too organized to be a random series of events that results in life, love, and compassion. Like gravity, God influences all things.

- Anonymous

"Modern culture rejects belief in a great cosmic plan. We are not actors in any larger-than-life drama. Life has no script, no playwright, no director, no producer—and no meaning. To the best of our scientific understanding, the universe is a blind and purposeless process, full of sound and fury but signifying nothing. During our infinitesimally brief stay on our tiny speck of a planet, we fret and strut this way and that, and then are heard of no more.

Since there is no script, and since humans fulfill no role in any great drama, terrible things might befall us, and no power will come to save us or give meaning to our suffering. There will not be a happy ending, or a bad ending, or any ending at all. Things just happen, one after the other. The modern world does not believe in purpose, only in cause.

If modernity has a motto, it is 'shit happens'.

- Yuval Noah Harari

Welcome to the World's Greatest Mystery. It has everything—clues and ciphers, red herrings, and consciously enigmatic jokes. There are villains, victims, and heroes littering the plot lines, along with ancient books, inscrutable monuments, and strange persons that flit along through the ages as if they had a purchase agreement on eternity.

- *Fulcanelli*

At the back of this book there is a bonus Prologue for Ghost Gold. Why at the end at not at the beginning? Let me explain.

The last chapter of Lost Secret of the Ancient Ones 'Book I The Manna Chronicles' and the first chapter of Ghost Gold 'Book II', are a continuation of the same scene as Austin reveals to Maya the discovery of a lost cave by his great grandfather over one hundred years ago. There is a prologue at the end of this book which describes how Wynn Lambert came about this discovery and the ancient wonders his family has kept secret for over a century.

Since Ghost Gold is written both as both a standalone story as well as a continuation of Maya Harrington's quest, the prologue is a transitional chapter for those that have read Book I. Though I encourage everyone to read Lost Secret of the Ancient Ones, it is not required to enjoy the adventures that unfold in Ghost Gold. The prologue is both informative and entertaining but is not germane to the over-all action. I did not want to confuse those who are new to the adventure.

Book III – due out in 2022, 'In the Time of Noah 'will encapsulate the current UFO phenomena but will take on new and highly unorthodox twists as Maya and her teams encounter beings in this saga of the Manna Chronicles.

Welcome to the journey!

CHAPTER 1
Maya Harrington - Pacific Palisades

Maya stared at the muted television screen. The President of the United States was making his way to the podium, ostensibly to announce his decision to support Israel's claim to the Temple Mount—something she knew that was going to ignite a firestorm around the world. Sitting in her friend's room, the image dredged up all she had been through over the last four months. And along with it, a reminder of the danger she was in.

A miracle had happened. Her friend Austin had been in a coma for over fourteen years and suddenly awakened—and she found herself here, curled up in a chair at his home in California. The elation of his awakening had temporarily quelled her worries about those who were hunting her.

She replayed all that had happened over the last few weeks, which triggered something from deep within to bubble to the surface. Whether it was intuition or something else, suddenly the puzzle that had eluded her for weeks fell into place.

"As above, so below. It's not about alignments or stars, it's a warning..."

The revelation answered a thousand questions. She stared off into an imaginary distance, wondering... *How had I missed something so obvious?*

"As above, so below is a warning? What do you mean it is a warning?" asked her friend.

"What?" She saw the quizzical look on Austin's face, not realizing she had said this aloud.

Maya looked at her childhood sweetheart. He was thirteen when he had the accident that left him in a coma. The accident she still blamed herself for. He was now a fully mature twenty-seven-year-old man. Tall, dark-haired, handsome, but lean, because of the years in the coma. He still had the same naivete that had fascinated her all those years ago, but now…

She recognized his emotional maturity still had a lot of catching up to do. Still, at the age of twenty-seven, he was finally getting a chance to live his life.

She did not want to burden him. And besides, how could she possibly compress the last few months into a simple explanation? How could she explain that her father had vanished and was likely living in another dimension? Maybe even the mythical Garden of Eden? Or that there were powerful people after him, who in turn, were after her? People that had tried on four separate occasions to kidnap her and only because she had unlocked the secret of the ancient ones, was she able to literally vanish when being held hostage in Cairo. And now they were more desperate than ever to find her and learn the secret.

Am I putting my friend and his family in danger by being here?

As she deflected by reciting an unrelated half-truth, part of her lamented that the last cache of Sacred Manna known to exist had been lost in her escape. The ancient powder had propelled her across the dimensional realm of space and time. Getting more was the only thing that would allow her to find her father, and she did not have a clue where to begin looking.

"It's from the Egyptian Book of the Dead," she said softly, without much conviction. "It's incredibly old. It's the idea expressed in Einstein's unified theory of the universe, that from the smallest particle to the largest galaxy, everything is in a geometrically expanding proportion. A repetitive, doubling of configurations. Quantum mechanics continues to affirm this idea, but the Egyptians had figured it out at least sixty-five hundred years ago."

Of course this was not it at all. It was something altogether different, something so complex, and so esoteric, that she needed to give it a deeper look. To further explore the implications, thus she felt it best to let it go for now.

Austin got out of bed and turned off the television. "I want to show you something."

2

Maya followed him into the living room, curious but still distracted by the revelation that continued to blossom within her mind's eye.

While he was going through a cabinet full of photo albums, she stepped to the French doors to take in the view. Above were cobalt skies, blue as blue could be. But down below, at the base of the mountain, was a thick grey fog that hugged the coast.

This brought back memories of her childhood. The pungent smell of dirty socks that hugged the beach during the June gloom, her friends… But these memories were always punctuated by her mother's sudden death.

She swallowed once, and then a second time. Thoughts of that fatal car accident always left her with a lump in her throat. Wiping away a tear, she turned back as Austin laid an old leather box on the center island.

"Pull up a chair."

She suppressed thoughts of her deceased mother and sat next to him as he removed the lid to reveal an odd assortment of artifacts. She was surprised to see a solid gold rod covered in Egyptian hieroglyphs. It sat atop yellowed newspaper clippings, penciled drawings, rubbings, an old map, and a worn leather journal. He handed her the largest of the clippings.

"Read this. Then I'll explain."

It was an article from the *Arizona Gazette*, dated April 5, 1909. As she began reading, a tingle caressed her skin. The article described the discovery of an ancient Egyptian temple complex found inside the Grand Canyon.

Explorers for the Smithsonian Institute, G.E. Kinkaid and S.A. Jordan are responsible for the discovery. Egypt and the Nile connected to Arizona and the Colorado. One of the greatest mysteries of our time.

She read through it twice before laying it back into the box.

A cave in Arizona? Could this tie into our discovery in Guatemala? Did Egyptians really come to the Americas over three thousand years ago?

Before she could ask her first question, Austin punctuated a point.

"It's all bullshit," he proclaimed, handing her a second article.

3

The Yuma Carrier, July 12, 1908. Two men identified as Mr. Timothy Carruthers and Mr. Michael Fottrell were found dead, apparently crushed by a rockslide. According to a witness, it was fast and furious… It went on to list next of kin, their state of origin and a few other innocuous details.

"I don't see the connection."

"These were the men that found that ancient cave. Not Kincaid and Jordan, if those were even their real names. Carruthers and Fottrell were murdered, and then their bodies taken to another location so there would never be a connection. And I am sure those men in the first article did the killing, or at least directed it."

His face had flushed red with anger causing her to wonder what changed.

"And you know this… how?"

"My grandfather was there," he said solemnly. He lifted the leather notebook and, tapping a finger on the cover, said. "The whole story is here. But that is not what I want to show you. It was your statement, as above, so below."

Now she was even more perplexed.

He lifted the rod from the box. It had to be worth hundreds of thousands of dollars, maybe even priceless if it was real.

Why would they leave it unprotected in a simple box? There must be a bigger story behind this. And as if Austin had read her thoughts, he proceeded to fill in the blanks.

"My grandfather amassed a huge fortune that has been quietly passed down to each generation from my father's side. Only our immediate family knows the truth."

The revelation answered a question that she had wondered about as an adult. How could the Lamberts afford such a beautiful home overlooking the ocean and also carry the cost of Austin's medical expenses over the last fourteen years?

Is this how…

Shifting his gaze to the gold object, he suggested. "Consider the original news article. You can imagine the things he may have found. But this… using charcoal rubbings he had it translated.

"As above, so below—the talismanic magic of the astral energies is brought down to Earth. Its spirit infused into the sacred architecture, harmonizing thoughts, and the hope for man. As above, so below," Austin said as he read aloud the translation of the hieroglyphs.

Transfixed, Maya felt her eyes sparkle with heightened awareness. She began extrapolating different permutations. "May I?"

Astral energies. Here. Again.

She had recently returned from Guatemala where her team had uncovered an ancient temple in an underground cavern, which led to a new line of investigation. Astral energies—the influence of celestial bodies that emit undetected cosmic rays over our planet.

The object was heavy and cool to the touch. She ran her fingers over the glyphs.

"Can I look at the rest?"

He complied, and she examined each of the drawings one by one. The first was a view of a canyon peak from the vantage point of a river. Examining the intricate details, she commended his talent.

The next drawing appeared to be from a ledge looking in towards a cave. Its entrance was adorned by carved obelisks that framed each side of the opening. This caused a current of excitement to run through her and she found herself taking deep gulps to fuel her racing heart.

Just like the one we found in Egypt. Same illustration of the blue lotus, same height, same spot. That block had hidden a cache of the sacred powder. Could there be more Manna hidden here?

Less than a year ago, Maya was completing her doctoral thesis about an advanced race of humans she dubbed the Master Builders. The evidence suggested they had laid out a geodesic grid of one hundred and forty-four sacred sites across the globe prior to the pole shift of 10,500 BC.

At the time, her father, a quantum physicist who worked for a defense contractor, was looking into alternative dimensions as a path towards the possibility of time travel. He was away on another of his protracted travels where his communication was always spotty at best. She had grown concerned at the inordinate length of time that had passed without contact. And that concern blossomed into deep worry when a stranger left her father's personal diary with the bartender at a pub she often frequented.

Why would someone have his diary? Is he in trouble?

She had vowed to drop everything and search for him. Yet the next day she had been offered an unimaginable opportunity, and it had come from Robert Vaherees, one of the richest men in the world.

"Seek out those who are the Master Builders. I believe they are connected to the ancient Garden of Eden."

This rankled her as an atheist, but he sweetened the pot. "You can form your own team and use all of our resources to look for your missing father."

Alternative dimensions, her missing father, the Garden of Eden…as she and her team sojourned upon their quest, these things all converged, all roads were connected. And the intersection rested upon the lost secret of the ancient ones. The Sacred Manna of the Bible, the revered Mfktz of the Egyptian Book of the Dead.

With clues from her father's journal, she came to understand what the Sacred Manna was and how it could be used. And most importantly, she understood it was now the only vehicle that would reunite her with her father. And as far as she knew, the last cache of the mysterious powder of the ancient ones was gone and she had no idea how to get more.

And now… *a window of hope?*

She no longer believed in the idea of random beneficial events. Her mind, once rooted in nothing but provable science, had taken a tectonic shift towards embracing the idea that there were roads called destiny and hers had been paved long ago.

There's a total of twelve drawings, all Egyptian in design. What had the article suggested? That the Smithsonian explorers linked this to the time of Akhenaten and Ramses.

Is this further evidence of what we found in Guatemala? Did Akhenaten's Royal House of Gold actually migrate to America and give rise to the Incan and Mayan empires?

"I see I've struck a nerve," Austin finally interrupted.

She stood up and stretched her arms high overhead. Walking behind him she wrapped him in a big hug. Her thick mane of blond hair tumbled around his boyish face and she nearly squeezed the breath out of him. It was a reflexive moment as she continued sorting out her emotions.

All my life I used the thought of Austin, a long-lost love, to push away any and all romantic inclinations. But now, here, have I been fooling myself? Our lives have traveled such different roads...

"Why don't I fix us some tea," he suggested. "We can sit out on the deck and I'll tell you Grandfather Wynn's story."

Outside the air was perfumed with the scent of wildflowers. With two steaming mugs, they sat basking in the morning sun. Maya stared at the mist-laden fog below, noting the occasional opening that revealed faraway hints of beach and ocean. The vapor swirled with its inexplicable dance of thickening, closing, lightening, opening...

"My grandfather was in a saloon in Flagstaff in 1908 when two men came in from the desert. He overheard them talking about finding gold and decided to follow them when they left..."

Austin unfolded the story of how his distant relative ended up finding the cave that held all the artifacts he had collected.

"He was a prospector but had never really had any success. And when he heard about gold, and the river being so unusually low, he could not help himself. He wasn't a claim jumper mind you. I think he was hoping to strike up a vein of his own near where they had located theirs."

She thought there was probably more to it but kept quiet as he continued.

He went on to relay the part about seeing the cave the two men had found and the realization he would need to hide when they came back down the path. This led him to a cliff face with cuts in the wall, which he climbed up to find what he deemed a viewing area. "That is when he saw a second cave on the other side of the river. A cave that Fottrell and Carruthers knew nothing about."

There were two caves? Maya had a sudden premonition, a connection that seemed arbitrary at best.

The cave from my ayahuasca dream journey? But she said nothing, wanting him to continue.

Reiterating from the journal, Austin explained the discovery. He told her about the gold and the jeweled vases, which would become the

7

source of his family's immense wealth. Then he handed her the worn leather notebook as he continued to narrate.

It was heavy, reminding her of her father's journal. The pages were travel worn and creased. Jammed with notes, drawings, and speculations, she flipped through the diary and landed on a series of illustrations that elicited a strong reaction. A sudden nausea passed over her, setting her nerves aflame. The images rang an intuitive bell of imminent prophecy and her brain would not allow her to dismiss anything.

The images were so lifelike. A mushroom cloud leaving millions of dying bodies. An insidious plague sweeping over the land, far worse than the recent COVID-19. And most dreadful, a giant shadow passing over the sun that turned the blood in her veins to ice.

Her limbs became shaky as she held her breath. Recalling her father's warnings that there were those ready to cast man into a giant conflagration, a deep and distinct shiver suppressed the warmth from the sun. She could not continue to ignore the threat that the world was facing. She shook off apprehension as Austin continued.

"He made two further trips until he was sure his mare Bessie would not be able to carry anymore. He loaded her up, waited until darkness, and left."

He paused. She finally spoke. "Did he ever go back?" The idea of making a trip to find this place was germinating.

"He did, months later. When he returned, the area was closed. Literally off limits by government decree. And to reinforce that message, he spotted armed soldiers patrolling the foothills and pathways."

Soldiers?

"What was in the other cave, the one mentioned in the article?"

"He never got inside. Like I said, the place was closed to the public."

There was a long pause, she weighed the gravity of the moment and the thousand avenues of conjecture that ran off in so many directions.

"Getting back to the story, my grandfather had a bad feeling about those guys who showed up. Looking to avoid them, he went south towards Yuma and never returned to Flagstaff. It was in Yuma that he came across the article of the two dead men. He knew it was fabricated.

He had overheard Fottrell, and Carruthers say they were going to go north to Denver. That was in the opposite direction."

"Do you think we could find this place again?" Currently this was the only avenue she had to finding more of the Sacred Manna, and thus, finding her father. Though slim at best, right now it was all she had. A glimmer of hope.

"I have his map and the details are in his diary..." Hesitantly, he added "I think Wynn was hoping one of his relatives would try again in the future."

"Did they?"

"My father tried before he passed away, but he had no success. There were government warnings posted everywhere. *'Do not enter. Restricted area. Trespassers will be shot.'*"

CHAPTER 2

Johnny 'JW' White Feather
Wild Horse Mesa, Colorado

Under the big sky of Colorado, the lapping waves rippled reflections of Mount Blanca. JW stood on the porch and watched his grandfather, who was chopping wood along the lake's rocky shore.

Nascha was old, but spry. He had a timeless quality. His creased face was framed by hair as white as snow. But his eyes... they were as clear and sharp as a hawk. They could still cull through even the slightest deviation from truth. JW had learned this the hard way when he was a teen.

Returning the cell phone to his pocket, Johnny White Feather processed the conversation he'd just had with his old friend Maya. Something grandfather had asked him a few months ago now came back to haunt him. *'Are you sure what is best for her is what you want? You may not like it.'*

He recalled the conversation when his grandfather Nascha questioned Maya at the end of her dream journey. And how she had morphed into a childhood sweetheart named Austin Lambert. And now that same person has come out of a long coma.

And what... she's now rekindling the flame?

Grandfather was right, he did not like it. But he blotted out the jealousy to focus on her revelation about the discovery in Arizona. Specifically, on what she felt were harbingers of doom.

Why is this happening. Why now?

His intuition had been fencing with a sense of impending dread for the last few days and this simply amplified that feeling.

"Good morning, Soaring Eagle," Nascha smiled, using JW's new totem name as he approached. It had been granted to him recently by the elders and it caused a small hint of pride to show itself.

11

"What's on your mind? You seem all puckered up about something."
JW laughed, his pride wounded.

"Much," he professed, wondering what to bring up first.

"I just spoke to Maya. As I told you, the boy she morphed into when you took her on her dream journey has come out of his coma. And he revealed something to her from the previous century."

"Is it relevant to the quest to locate the other realm that you and your friend have undertaken?" he asked, now adopting his mantle as shaman.

JW noted the subtle change. The eyes that now sparkled like broken glass, and his tone that had soothed like wild honey, now had a directness that cared not about trivial matters.

"Yes." JW assured. "Remember the cave Maya saw while being pulled along by the river in her dream journey?"

JW knew that Nascha had been her spirit guide and seen all that she had seen, including that cave high on the cliff. He acknowledged this with a slight nod.

"It seems her friend's grandfather located a cavern that by all evidence, was used by early Egyptian settlers who had come to America. Perhaps even from the age of Akhenaten in the second millennium before Christ. Have you ever heard of anything like this?"

There was a soft breeze coming in from the lake that wrapped them in cool moisture. Nascha closed his eyes and began to rock back and forth. JW knew to be patient. This was how his grandfather tunneled through memories, whether they were his own or those of humanity's collective in the Akasha.

"I have heard this story before, years ago," he began. "Originally by a diviner named Slim Spurling.

"Years later I was at a conference on the Flower of Life and Sacred Geometry led by a fellow named Drune Melchizedik. I tried to keep up as he lectured, but when he started using metaphors of the great pyramids touching the four corners of the American Southwest... well, I was lost," he chuckled.

"For some inexplicable reason this jarred my memories of Spurling's tale. So afterwards, I made it a point to meet Mr. Drune Melchizedek and asked him if he had ever heard of such a story. I was amazed that the man took such a keen interest in my question. Drune began reciting from memory.

"A few years ago, an old man came to me with an amazing story. He said something Egyptian was connected to the Four Corners. There was a mountain inside the Grand Canyon called the Temple of Isis and explained that it was once written about in the *Arizona Gazette,* but later was dismissed.

"According to this man, he had met a Havasupai Indian that claimed when he was a young man he had found tiers of mummies in a cavern. At the head of each were copper cups and broken swords. After examining some of them, he had concluded that the room may have been a warriors' burial site."

Nascha stopped his recital and stared out over the lake. JW followed his gaze and together they watched a large bald eagle swoop down fast, timing its plunge perfectly, and then rising up towards the sky with a large fish in its talons.

"Life, death. One feeds the other," grandfather whispered under his breath. Reasserting the wizened mantle, he looked his grandson in the eye.

"I questioned Drune at great length about his story. He says he knows it is true, but he never confirmed why. I got the impression that his comments about this mysterious man were a misdirect. I think he was the one who had actually been in that cave. You should find this man."

JW's eyes widened. This direct comment was so unlike his grandfather, usually his suggestions were so opaque. He logged the info as Nascha stood. The conversation had come to an end. He looked up the hill and together they watched a brood of wild horses crest the ridgeline.

"Such majestic animals," he said softly, pulling his collar tight against the fresh nip in the air.

CHAPTER 3
Layla Thibodaux - Greenwich, England

Layla and Tavis were passing though Greenwich on their way to Stonehenge when the phone rang. Layla answered it on the first ring. It was Maya.

"Hey girl, how's that boy of yours doing?"

"Getting better every day," Maya assured. "How you guys enjoying Europe?"

"Awesome," Layla replied.

After some light banter, Maya launched into the discovery Austin had revealed. She did not get into the images that still left her unsettled, but instead directed the conversation towards a ray of hope, explaining that there were two caves.

"One was apparently sealed by the government, but the second one... I think it may still be filled with artifacts and maybe even some Manna."

Maya paused, as if hesitant to say what was on her mind.

"What's the problem then?" Layla asked, as she placed the phone on speaker so Tavis could hear as well.

"There was an article in the *Arizona Gazette* that goes into great detail about the two men from the Smithsonian Institute who supposedly found the first site. Kincaid and Jordan. They were interviewed, showed the journalist some of the artifacts and the article was quite thorough.

"But in 1909, the government closed this area to outsiders and the Smithsonian suddenly denied that there was ever anyone named Kincaid or Jordan. And the Institute claimed this was all a hoax.

"We know it's not a hoax because Wynn Lambert was there. We know that this area was closed to the public for dubious reasons and that it is still closed more than a hundred years later. I checked. Why would they cover this up? It's the discovery of a lifetime."

"Hey Maya," Tavis chimed in.

"Is my girl treating you okay?"

"Competitive to a fault," Tavis said. "My masculinity has taken a few hits, but she has more than made up for it in other ways."

Maya could only imagine the salacious grin on his face.

"We're returning to New York on the weekend and I will elaborate further. Don't really want to get into it over the phone other than to suggest, as in all things, you must follow the money.

"In this case, who are the principal funding sources behind these world-worthy institutions? The Smithsonian, the British Museum, to name just a few. There are countless stories about ancient discoveries and artifacts that were collected and yet, once those from these hallowed institutions show up, they simply turn facts into rumors that drift into myths and then legends, but the evidence… vanishes. There is a story of a man who had verifiably been employed by the Smithsonian, who on his deathbed claimed he was tasked with dumping large quantities of items from the museum into the deepest trenches of the Atlantic Ocean. And how one time, out of sheer curiosity, he opened one of the containers prior to dumping to find the bones of giants—actual giant humans. Dozens and dozens of them.

"One has to wonder, who gets to write the history books?"

Maya skirted over her nascent understanding of the Hidden Hand. Plumbing what little she knew of their depth and reach. And wondered…

The line had gone silent. And though Maya had a hundred questions, she realized he was right. An open line was not the place for this conversation. Not in the day of endless snooping by the deep state. So she drew the conversation to a conclusion.

"Austin is going to need a few more weeks of physical therapy and I need to get back to business. Let's round up the gang and meet back in New York. How about dinner Monday night?"

♓︎♎︎♎︎♏︎■︎〰︎

Maya Harrington

After the call, Maya's thoughts returned to the idea of a greater organization behind the control of conventional institutions. This led her to wonder about how when Sir Walter Flinders Petrie had found the

Cave of Hathor in 1904, he had journaled that under the floor there were tons of a mysterious white powder which years later he had identified as the Sacred Manna. And how once the Royal Academy of Science became involved, it vanished.

What happened to that powder? Who has it now? A more mischievous thought emerged. *If it still exists, can we steal some?*

CHAPTER 4
The Elder - Uzbekistan

"How ironic that we should meet here, in the shadow of the fabled tower of death," the bearded man chuckled softly. The two men stood in the shadow of the Kalyan minaret, the ancient Islamic tower that was seated at the center of the village of Bukhara in Uzbekistan.

"Yes, my friend," replied the younger associate.

"It is known as the tower of death because during the emir's time, criminals were tied up in sacks and thrown from the top. It is one of the few buildings to survive the rule of Genghis Khan," the elder man reminded the other.

Outside, beyond their small gate was the main square. There was no one around as winds of change swirled across the bleak landscape. Snowcapped mountains ranged in the far distance but here, inside the deteriorating courtyard of a once great and noble house, bleak was the predominant shade.

"My ancestors have lived here for many hundreds of years, back to the eighth century," continued the associate. "Then our city was the center of an expanding Islamic kingdom which prospered as a trade and intellectual center for Central Asia. It was destroyed by Genghis Khan in 1219. But once again, it will play a part in the rise to dominance of Islam."

Both men stood solemnly, the pale sun casting shadows of the infamous tower over the top of the crumbling walls and into their courtyard. Their breath steamed in the cold air and the elder man pulled his sashed garment a little tighter. He adjusted his thick woolen headpiece, so it covered the tops of his ears.

"You have secured the packages?" he asked, flicking dandruff from his grey beard.

"See for yourself." The underling removed a drab olive tarp that covered two oversized suitcases. "As promised. The little dictator

19

has delivered us two tactical nukes. All it took was money, a lot of money."

"And you have made all of the arrangements? You are sure they will be delivered without suspect?"

"Yes, my esteemed brother. All the arrangements have been made. They will meet the timeline that you have commanded."

The old man hesitated. He stared off into the distance, admiring the rugged peaks, but his eyes—they seemed to fill with desire.

"Just remember, they must be stowed at their final resting places by the date we have instructed. This will change the world."

The young associate could only imagine what was to come. He was proud to be part of the demise of the Zionists and help shepherd in the return of the Mahdi. He saw the logic in their placements but wished they could extract a greater revenge upon the other Godless lands of sin, greed, and corruption.

"It shall be done, my brother."

"Praise be to Allah," replied the elder. "Now go in peace."

◆〜〜〜〜〜〜〜〜〜〜〜〜〜

Hans Richter - Gulf of Aden, Somalia

The rusting hulk of the aged freighter was wedged hard upon the sand beach, long forgotten and now a permanent fixture of the shoreline. Subject to only time and erosion she had been stripped years ago of anything of value, even the pirates no longer cared about her.

The locals, fishermen who worked this coast, stayed well clear of the rusting hulk. People had disappeared, and they said it was cursed, the djinn having taken it over as a den of evil.

The whitecaps that slapped the shore had pushed chunks of tangled driftwood up against the rusted hulk, giving further proof of her desertion. But inside a different picture was presented. The ship was a weapon hiding in plain sight. The overhead satellites of the western intelligence agencies saw nothing but an aged vessel, but within hummed a modern laboratory, with pressurized clean rooms, centrifuges, air-conditioning, and comfortable crew quarters.

"How is production commencing?" queried the tall man of Arabic origin.

"On schedule," affirmed the German. "We just completed tests on twelve subjects we had collected from farther up the coast. We infected two of them, and then placed the other ten in sets of two, at varying distances and approximations from the infected. Within twenty-four hours, they had all died of massive hemorrhaging. Blood spewed unabated from every orifice in their bodies. It was gruesome, but effective. We will run our field test very soon."

"Airborne, lethal and contagious?" asked the Arabic man, needing to be sure of his confirmation when he reported back to his leadership.

"Very." Hans replied, the lethality defined by his one-word reply.

♦ ≋ ♏ ≋ ♓ ♎ ♎ ♏ ■ ≋ ♋ ■ ♎

Maestro's Consigliore - The English Countryside

Concealed below the opulent country estate was an enormous cavern that was the command center of The Maestro. He was the elusive head of a secret cabal that wielded influence over much of what happened in the world.

His reach extended into every intelligence agency, criminal enterprise, and clandestine organization anywhere in the world that mattered.

Presidents, dictators, theologians, they all knew and understood that there were powerful forces that pulled their strings, but none had any real idea of who or where lay the head.

"Good morning, Maestro," his consigliore said with deference. He was one of only three individuals who knew the depth and extent of his master's reach. He had been witness to those who thought they could betray the Maestro. Those memories kept his loyalty honed to a razor's edge.

The room was a dichotomy of old and new. The vast subterranean cavern, whose ancient walls had been hollowed out eons ago, were contrasted by floors covered in the world's most expensive carpets. The walls were adorned with art from history's greatest masters, and alcove after alcove displayed the finest sculptures ever made.

Statues from Ancient Sumer and Babylon, sculpted marbles from classical Greece, bronzes from the Roman Empire, and lost and forgotten works once only viewed by Pharaohs adorned the space.

So great was the collection, that it would make the most jaded curator blush with envy. But no one knew it existed, and they never would. Much of what was deemed lost to history, was here.

"Maya Harrington has reappeared," he reported. "We intercepted a burner phone that was calling Layla Thibodaux. Here is a transcript." He handed him a sheet of paper.

"Give me the top line." Maestro growled in a low voice.

His consigliore had been responsible for watching her for months, following her and driving her forward. Directing events that his master expected would lead to her father. Then she inexplicably fell off the map.

"Well sir, it seems the caverns buried back in 1909 have caught her attention and I believe they will be attempt to visit them."

"That place was cleaned out decades ago. There is nothing left to find."

"There's more." His tone suggested this was not quite right.

Maestro gave him a furtive glance.

"What?"

"There is a second cave."

This unexpected revelation brought a stillness, and the consigliore could see the thoughts weighed heavy on Maestro's brow.

"She believes there may be some of the Manna she has been seeking and is making plans to try and retrieve it."

"That cannot happen."

The aide understood.

"Is there anything else?"

"A minor thing." Exercising his nervous habit of twitching his fingers, his aide explained. "It appears that Mr. Wiley discussed with Ms. Harrington how certain well-known institutions are being used to conceal certain discoveries and that their public persona of beneficence is but a cover. Specifically, he suggested that she 'follow the money.'"

"Hmph," Maestro grunted, then shifted topics. "Where are we on phase two of the virus?" The world was in the throes of a global pandemic, something that had been engineered. But this was only the beginning of the horrors to be unleashed.

"We are launching a test run on an outlying Canary Island. A dozen children have been inoculated under the guise of a flu shot. It will test our vaccine in a real-world situation.

"A terrorist event will damage the airport to the point of non-usability and there will be ships off the coast to prevent unintended spreading of the virus. It will happen tomorrow night."

"Good," Maestro said approvingly. "And the other thing?"

His consigliore knew he was referring to the two nuclear bombs that they were smuggling into place. And that his plan to create a Middle East conflict of biblical proportions would be unleashed during the second phase of a much more virulent global pandemic. This would serve as the one-two punch to devastate the world.

"The one for Tehran is in place. The one set for Tel Aviv is a bit more problematic. The Israeli safeguards are proving quite daunting."

"Get it done," he said with a disdainful wave of the hand. "Anything else?"

"Mann is meeting with the politicos this morning. They are being given their latest marching orders."

Charles Mann and his minions were busy orchestrating the coming elections in America. But the next President of the United States was going to become so embroiled in a never-ending series of crises, that it really didn't matter who won.

"One last thing," Maestro demanded. "Get eyes and ears on Maya Harrington."

CHAPTER 5
Maya - Per Se Restaurant - NYC

Maya was the first to arrive and checked on all the arrangements. The private room off the main dining area was quiet and had large windows overlooking Central Park. The table was set for five. She had the waiter bring wine and chill it while taking a glass for herself.

She was fidgeting with anticipation, fussing with her clothes. She paused for a moment to look out at the lights that marked the roads and footpaths stretching through the park. She found herself humming a blues tune from Preservation Road, a band that Layla had made her go see down in Boca Raton.

Tornados down in Texas – And flooding on the coast
The fires in California – This year they are the most
I look across the land – so much at once seems odd
Are we suffering from the – Wrath of God?

What a mess we have made. She considered the drought out west, now in its fifth year, and the never-ending fires in California and Australia. And of course, the viral pandemic that was affecting every corner of the planet.

As the gang trickled in, she greeted each as if they had not been together for a lifetime.

"How is Nascha?" she asked JW, while embracing him. At six-foot six, he had to lean down into her grasp, which caused his long black ponytail to fall forward over his shoulder.

"He's fine, still an old coot. He gives his regards."

"And you two lovebirds?"

This caused Tavis's pale skin to blossom to a rose color, while Layla simply let a knowing smile play across her lips. They were a living dichotomy of yin and yang. The luscious dark skin of her best

25

friend contrasting against the pale coloring of her Scottish paramour. But both were in that special harmony of simpatico.

"Hey Rex, how's the travels?"

Maya knew that this had become a point of frustration for him. Rex was an accomplished remote viewer who under her father's tutelage had mastered the art of freeing his consciousness from his physical body to roam, collect data and return to his physical self with the information intact.

When Maya learned of his talent, she convinced him to give her lessons. Her skill advanced much quicker than the normal practitioner, likely because of the aptitude inherent in her father's DNA.

Though Rex had years of experience, when he had combined traces of the Manna with his remote viewing technique, it hyper-elevated his skill and propelled his consciousness across space and time. Something he had not been able to replicate since the Manna was seized by the enemy.

"The thrill is gone," he said using the phrase from a song to convey his thoughts. In this case, the fabled words of BB King.

She smiled, along with his Texas twang and signature cowboy hat, it was a quirk of his she had come to appreciate. At the ripe old age of thirty-one, Rex was the oldest member of her team. And they were the only two amongst the group who had learned the art of remote viewing. Though Rex's practice encompassed many more years than her own, she was the only one other than her father to have made a physical quantum jump. Which, of course, was what had saved her from her kidnappers.

As the group finished greeting one another and the wine was flowing, her closest friend took her hand and leaned in with a whisper.

"How are you coping with destiny?"

Maya knew the gravitas that lay behind Layla's question, but she was not ready to get into it. Not yet anyway. She had chosen *Per Se* because of its exceptional food, its convenient location and most importantly, because of this private dining room.

After small talk, a few bottles of wine, some more talk, and once the dishes had been cleared, Maya steered the conversation towards business. There was old business and new business. A lot had crossed her mind over the last couple of weeks. And a lot of her preconceptions had changed.

"Please close the doors," she asked of the waiter.

Once he had departed, she cleared her throat, and slowly paced the room. The revelation about *as above so below* was so large, she was going to need to set the tone with some preamble. She could not just spring it on them. She decided a little review of where they left things off when Austin came out of his coma was in order.

"When we took our little break, we had been reviewing The Sumerian Prophesy," she began. "We know that both it and The Prophesy of King Shulgi were written as warnings, meant to foretell the signs heralding the final days of man. What we've unearthed in the last twelve weeks shows that humanity may have already entered man's fatal season."

The room quieted into rapt attention.

"Let's take a look at the parts of that ancient document we feel sure about." Maya proceeded to read the prophesy.

"'Whereas the man of years and days, of eternal life, has marked the appointed time, and the appointed hour, and the appointed place, through the markers of the kesil and the kimah. When aligned with the triad of infinity, after the final empire is crossed by shadows, then those true Sons of God will come to witness the glory.'"

Tavis leaned forward. "The man of years is the biblical patriarch Enoch," he said. "And Layla has made an excellent case that the final empire crossed by shadows is America. It will be crisscrossed by the eclipse that occurred in 2017 and the one coming in 2024..."

Maya nodded. "We know Robert hired you to decipher this prophecy in hopes of finding a dimensional doorway or a celestial window referred to as the Lion's Gate." She paused, knowing what she was about to say next would upset Tavis, but she hoped he would come around to her thinking. "I think we have it all wrong."

As she expected, Tavis's expression moved from disbelief to dismay and then rejection. She had articulated in one simple statement that all his work to date had been for naught.

As she waited for the proverbial air to clear, she opened another tab on her phone.

"After this I looked, and there before me was a door standing open in Heaven. And the voice I had first heard speaking to me like a trumpet said, 'Come up here, and I will show you what must take place after this.' Revelation 4:1.

These are the words from John of Patmos. It appears that he was transmigrated up to Heaven, given a glimpse of the future, and then came back to Earth again to write the final chapter of the Bible. Revelations of end times."

Rex rubbed his chin. "Do you think he is just another dimensional traveler? That he knew how to work the transmutative aspects of the Manna? That would make at least five people in scripture with that knowledge."

Maya nodded. "It is amazing how an alternative view of the Bible reads so differently," she said while making eye contact with Layla, a devout Christian, making sure she was not trampling on her friend's sacred ground.

Layla gave her a smile, the wattage reassuring to Maya.

With emphasis of certain words and the cadence of her tone, Maya was setting the stage. Knowing that she was changing the direction of the quest for which they had been hired, and in all likelihood changing the direction of their lives.

"Getting back to the prophesy," she continued. "Consider this line: *'The time of change will be contested as the Lion sets to prowl. For she seeks this as fate."* She paused. "Then there is a similar line in the King Shulgi prophesy written a thousand years later. *'The Lion will prowl the rift to the place assigned by God…'"*

She said nothing and looked at each member of her team. Her friends. She was letting the silence build to a crescendo.

"All my life my father has called me his little lion. It was the password he had used that allowed us to unlock the code in his diary. We now know he discovered the secrets of the Sacred Manna and by all accounts we have discerned that he is alive and well but hiding in an alternative dimension within the Garden of Eden. What if we have misinterpreted the meanings of these prophecies and that they do not refer to a celestial window? What if these things are all connected to a hope that can be only acquired by using the sacred powder?

"What if I am the Lion—the one who is supposed to open this Gate? This door for humanity's transmigration?"

She understood that the statement was so large, and so self-grandiose, that each of them would react differently. But she also knew that with all they had gone through they could not deny the possibility of truth that was buried in her statement. Still, even for her, it was Earth-shaking to believe.

Maya also knew Layla had understood this the minute the light had gone on in her eyes two weeks ago, even before she had figured it out for herself. Hence the original question she had whispered in her ear.

"Destiny's child," Layla chuckled, breaking into their collective moment with a mix of amusement and awe.

"Well, Simba," JW asked, gathering the steam of levity. "Where do we go from here?"

And then it was over. As if from out of nowhere, the Simba reference allowed the alcohol to take over. Rex, followed by Tavis, started singing, 'aweem away, aweem away, aweem away, aweem away…"

Layla joined. "In the jungle, the mighty jungle, the lion sleeps tonight…"

"Alright, alright," Maya laughed, putting her hands up in mock defense. She had a second point to discuss but could see that it would have to wait. "I guess that's as far as we're going to get tonight. We'll talk about this more in the morning."

CHAPTER 6
Maya - 86ᵗʰ Street Apartment

They had agreed to regroup at the apartment Robert had supplied which was being used as their basecamp of operations—a two-bedroom brownstone on the Upper West Side. At one time, this six-story building had been the home of the founder of Gimbels Department Store. The building was now broken into floor-through apartments, and Maya and her team occupied the fourth floor.

Maya had gone out and procured the basic staples preferred by most New Yorkers—coffee, bagels, lox, and cream cheese. Outside, the rain continued to fall. Inside, she continued to putter.

One by one, they began to arrive. Rex came in with JW on his heels. A few minutes later, Tavis and Layla filled out the team. Any shades of hangovers had been packed away. After they had worked through ample cups of coffee and an army's complement of bagels, the small talk died down and Maya took charge.

"As above, so below..." she said. This saying had appeared on multiple occasions during their quest, and like most enigmas, always left them with unanswered questions. And based on the revelation that came to her in California, she thought she now understood.

She knew they expected the conversation to pick up where they left off the night before, about her, destiny, and their quest. And eventually it would—but the tapestry she was weaving was much larger and one had to see the forest to appreciate the trees. It might be the reason for—and the anchor to—the truth of an end time.

"We have assumed that this is a reference to objects on Earth affiliated with celestial bodies. And in one sense, I am sure that they are. Certainly, most of the sites referenced in my thesis confirm this."

For a brief moment, she thought of the greatest example of monuments emulating the Heavens. The three pyramids of Egypt were perfectly aligned with the three stars of Orion's Belt and inexplicably, the bends and turns of the Nile River was an exact mirror of the outline of the Milky Way. It was the key to her thesis of the Master Builders. A key she still did not fully understand, but she let the thought pass and continued.

"But I believe there is much more. When JW and I went to the Peruvian jungle to meet an Amazonia shaman my father had seen, he revealed that my father had used the same phrase and left him with a cryptic comment. *'When you understand this, you will understand everything.'"*

Opening her father's notebook, she showed them the first page that contained two triangles, bases parallel, with one pointing up and one pointing down. The phrase 'As above, so below,' was written between the horizontal lines. She flipped to the journal's last page and again, turned it so all could see. It bore a large Star of David.

"The triangles on the first page when pushed together, create the six-pointed star of the last page," Layla said, a dawning of understanding spreading over her face.

"Correct. And I think it is the key to comprehending what my father was trying to say," Maya affirmed. "Let me explain. The six-pointed star was not used by Judaism as a Jewish identity until the Middle Ages. At the time it was considered very controversial due to its connection with their Egyptian oppressors. Ancient Egyptians used this icon to symbolize the lotus flower and it also was used to represent the heart chakra.

"The lotus blossom is the active ingredient in creating the transmutative properties of the Sacred Manna. And this is a key component of our collective destinies," she said. Her eyes locked with Rex, since only the two of them had any experience with the Sacred Manna and fully understood the power of the blue lotus blossom.

"The last twelve weeks have changed my view of science and tested my beliefs about other worlds. We have all confronted undeniable proof of alternative dimensions, but to what extent do they exist?"

She paused to look at each person in the room. There were a few coughs and some shuffling of feet, but she saw no outward expressions of objection, so she continued.

"From all that we have learned, it seems we are living in a multidimensional world. Our five senses interact with the three dimensions of our physical plane and we are constrained by the fourth dimension of time."

"The ayahuasca experience argues the probability of a fifth dimension of spirits, which is free from space-time constraints. If you recall in Genesis 6:22, Enoch was transported up to Heaven and then returns to warn Noah of the coming flood. After that there is no further mention of him in the Old Testament. But in the Book of Enoch, rediscovered in the Dead Sea Scrolls...

She lifted a copy of the tome that she had set on the table and tapped her finger on the cover. At the onset of their quest, JW had suggested this book as a reference guide in their search for Eden. She had never expected to take what was written inside literally, but after unraveling her father's diary, she could not deny its resonating truth.

"Enoch describes his translation from Earth up to Heaven and goes on to give extensive detail about the seven Heavens. The abode of Angels and God. I believe these are seven additional dimensions.

"That would give us three on the physical plane, a fourth dimension of time, the fifth dimension of the Akashic record, and the seven Heavens. Twelve in total."

"For years, astronomers have speculated that there could be at least ten dimensions in space," Tavis said by way of agreement. "So why not twelve?"

"Twelve seems to be a major platform of God." Maya smiled with a thank you nod. "There are twelve signs of the zodiac that God placed in the Heavens. The twelve months and twelve hours round out the increments of time. There are the twelve signs for every twelve years in the Chinese zodiac. There were twelve tribes of Israel and twelve apostles and so on? Twelve is an important number in the Bible."

"Okay?" Layla asked. "What's the connection?"

"I'm working up to that. What if in pre-dawn history there were no separating dimensions? Therefore, no beginning and no end. The Egyptians allude to an early age when man walked with the Gods, they called this Zep Tepe.

"And as the dimensional walls formed and separation became the norm, which I think may be represented by the two triangles coming apart from each other, there were ways to traverse for the increasingly few who knew the secret. Those who had been given the secret of the Manna.

"Bringing this back to the idea of a pending end of time. What if the merging of the two triangles signifies a time when *as above*, will be again be *so below*? The dimensions will re-form into that single unified field, like in the beginning?"

As she pulled fingers through tangles of her thick blond hair, she could not believe how far she had strayed from her science. She paused to read their expressions. Just weeks ago, she would have burst out laughing at such wild conjecture. But no one was smiling.

"Well," JW spoke up. "As you know, when Maya and I were in Gobekli Tepe, we came away with a new theory that explained the enigma of that place. The creation of man was a teachable moment for the hosts of Heaven, and we are all characters in a cosmic game between God and the devil, '*he who collects the most souls wins...*'"

Maya looked to her Navajo friend and gave him a smile of thanks. "Right, so therefore what if the clock of ages is inside the two-minute warning? And the Star of David represents the final unification when God will once again remove the dimensional walls. Or more succinctly, man's time is up."

"And all of God's creatures will be front and center at the foot of His throne..." Layla murmured under her breath.

Maya had considered this and wondered how this large slice of alternative reality would impact her and her friends. *What does it mean? Is it good or bad? How will I be affected? How will humanity be affected? Is this God's will?*

Maya felt her words had charged the room with cross-currents of emotion—part pride in the belief of having been chosen to shape history, part hope, and part worry? But also—a good slice of fear.

The entire world was in the grip of paralysis, not knowing when this pandemic would end or if it would end. What was life going to be like in the future? What was going to be the new normal? How much of this added to the tapestry of what she was feeling? Maya let out a deep breath. Suddenly all that they were up against filled her with trepidation.

JW stood and came to Maya's side. "What can we do?"

She had given this a lot of thought, and all roads led to the Manna. She knew this was shaping up to be the primary focus of their revised quest.

"I don't have a plan yet, but I know we either need to find more of the Manna or we need to figure out how to make some."

For the thousandth time her thoughts skirted along the corridors of wondering how long this powder has been in existence. When did the process get buried until it was just the legend of an ancient secret? *Why? Who buried it? Who knows of it?* Of how the Bible was replete with characters who appeared to have access to its transmutative mystical properties. And of her father's journal which, when deciphered, spells out how to use the Manna to transmigrate.

A smile played at the corners of her mouth. "There is the possibility of a slim path..."

She set out to fill them in on all she knew about the cave Wynn Lambert had discovered and how it had contained a large cache of the elusive powder.

"We need to get to that cave, no matter what!"

◆ ♒ ♏ ♒ ♓ ♎ ♎ ♏ ■ ♒ ♋ ■ ♎

Maestro's Spies - Across the Street

Sitting amongst empty pizza boxes and half-full containers of Chinese takeout, Max Klinger sat listening with headphones. They had not succeeded in placing a bug inside the target's dwelling, so instead they had commandeered an apartment on the other side of the thoroughfare.

The occupants of this apartment had been rendered 'compliant' and Max, along with a partner, were the current rotating team assigned to monitoring and recording everything that went on in Harrington's building.

Eighty-Sixth Street was a wide boulevard that fed traffic from the east and west side of Manhattan through Central Park. But their fourth-story accommodation gave them an unimpeded line of sight, which allowed the use of laser beams bounced off the windowpanes to record almost every word that was spoken.

And from their vantage point, they could also see who came and went from the lobby level door.

"Shit," Max muttered to himself. The rain was creating gaps in the transcript. He tried different ways of painting the beam on various points of the window, but the weather was making his job more difficult than usual.

What they did record was relayed upstream to their boss Victor. Where it went from there was none of their business.

CHAPTER 7
Hans Richter - The Canary Islands

Hans, the German who had worked the lab in Somalia, stood watch on deck as the sea rolled westward chasing the sinking moon. Under a clear night sky, the modified yacht Odysseus launched the first of three Reaper drones to begin the planned assault upon El Hierro Island. At the western end of the Canary Islands chain, it was the smallest and least populated, with a combined total of between ten and eleven thousand residents and tourists. At this hour, only streetlights shone, and alley cats wandered.

The drone housed a package of forty commercial grade mini-drones, each equipped with two aerosol cans with preprogrammed flight and dispersal patterns. Factors such as prevailing winds, climate, and moisture had all been fine-tuned moments before takeoff.

Once their mission was completed, they would continue west until they dropped into the deepest part of the ocean to be lost forever. Contagion would begin showing up before dawn and total extermination was expected to be complete by noon.

An hour after mothership one departed, a second, albeit different craft, also left, and headed towards El Hierro International Airport. Flying over the rocky coast, it crossed the small town of Mediterranean-style houses. Fifteen minutes later it had systematically cratered the runways, effectively rendering the airport temporarily useless for all inbound or outbound aircraft.

◆〰𝍕〰〳♎♎𝍕■〰♋■♎

Young Santos – Survivor

"Momma, wake up. Please momma…" Santos shook his mother who was lying in a spreading pool of her own blood. Everyone was dead. His father, his sisters, and his grandmama.

He ran to his neighbor's house, no one came to the door, so he entered. Everyone there was also dead. "¡Dios mío!" he cried. Rushing back home, he tried the police, no answer. He tried his cousins, no answer. His teacher. On and on, no answer. He went through every number in his father's phone book until...

"Hello. Who is this? Do you know what time it is?"

Santos had no idea this call had landed in New York or what hour it was. He had just frantically dialed number after number after...

The voice that carried across the Atlantic was muffled by tears and a strong undercurrent of fear. It had landed at the home of Dubal Gonzalez, his father's friend from university. The voice of the young child came across as scared. Very, very scared.

After the boy managed to convey the horrific situation, Dubal took down the number and then set out to call the local FBI and make sure this was not buried; he contacted a friend who worked for the local media with connections to larger outlets.

By sunrise, word had gotten out and people from the Centers for Disease Control and Prevention in Atlanta were on their way to the Canary Islands as the world's media swarmed, trying to get the story.

Mothership three had cleaned up any residual boats that had tried to escape before a maritime quarantine could be put in place, but these were far and few between. There were no survivors, except for twelve children. The few that had not been killed, would soon be quarantined and their blood sent for examination.

♓︎♎︎♎︎♏︎

As the Odysseus steamed east towards Morocco, Hans thought of Russia, their orthodox church, and the coming Christmas mass in December. He had his orders and would be ready.

He once again considered Revelation 6:7, and his part in the coming drama.

'*When the Lamb opened the fourth seal, I heard the voice of the fourth living creature say, "Come!" I looked, and there before me was a pale horse! Its rider was named Death, and Hades was following close behind him. They were given power over a fourth of the Earth to kill by sword, famine and plague.*'

"Plague," he grinned. A fourth of the world shall die by plague.

CHAPTER 8
Maya - Remote Viewing the Cave

The following morning, Rex entered the foyer of the Eighty-Sixth Street apartment. Yesterday, Maya had given him two distinct tasks. One was to research the ancient mystery schools to find a connection to this powder and the lost wisdom associated with it. And the other was the reason he was here. To help her locate the cave in the Grand Canyon through remote viewing.

"Hey Rex," Maya acknowledged when he entered the room. "Can I get you something to drink?"

"I'm good," he said, laying his hat on the credenza.

"Have a seat," Maya said. They were alone in the apartment and Maya wasted no time getting right to the point.

"We need to go on a journey—together."

"Journey? That's the word of the day?" he smiled. He knew that she was referring to the out-of-body experience of remote viewing. But she seemed so eager and the smoldering emerald of her eyes was so intense, they begged he tease her at least a little.

Truth be told, had she been able to read his mind, it would have revealed that though he considered himself a seasoned viewer, he was a little jealous at how far and how fast she had come along. Certainly, much faster than he ever had. He had just been at it longer.

"Yes," she said emphatically. "But this time I want to do it together."

She hesitated, and a cloud passed over her eyes. "Have you ever remote viewed with a companion before?"

In fact, Rex had done this hundreds of times when working with her father. They had done extensive experiments with every aspect of their craft. And because of Alex's advanced abilities, he consoled himself that Maya's rapid learning curve was likely due to her inherited genes.

"Yes, your father and I have done joint viewing plenty of times."

This caused a momentary pang of grief to cross Maya's face, which Rex suspected was a reminder of how much she missed her dad.

"That's good. I want to visit the cave Austin's grandfather found. I want to see if there is any proof it might have been used by the ancient Egyptians and if so, see if we might find some of the Manna there."

His own breath quickened at the prospect, but he tempered it knowing excitement made remote viewing more difficult.

"What leads you to think that?"

She opened her phone and showed him pictures she had taken of Wynn's artwork. In an instant, he made the connection. It looked strikingly similar to the Cave of Hathor. And the *pièce de résistance* was the image of the blue lily embossed on a panel at the exact same place as they had found the bag of Manna in Sinai.

"This can't just be a coincidence, right?" Maya looked to him for confirmation she was on the right track.

He rubbed his palms together. The hope of revisiting Alex in Eden and learning his secret was a lust that had consumed him since that one brief moment before he had been yanked away in the middle of their conversation.

"Let's see if we can't remote view that cave," he told her. He took a notepad and pen from his backpack and re-examined the photos from Wynn's diary.

They closed their eyes and within minutes, his breathing was in tandem with hers until the only thing he sensed was that space between his upper lip and nostril. The sole point of focus.

Rex was the first to free himself. Looking down at Maya, he balanced the precarious edge of not wanting to leave until she was ready, with the death knell of conscious thought that would snap him back into his body.

He saw Maya's spirit rise, it mirrored the experience he'd had when doing this with her father. And like before, they were able to acknowledge one another.

♦♒♏♒♓♎♎♏■♒♋■♎

Maya - Rio Colorado, Arizona

Maya felt no whoosh, no sensation of movement or taste, touch, or feel. One minute she was in the apartment in New York, and the next, she was cognizant that her consciousness was on a rocky ledge. Rex was next to her and it felt as if every one of her thoughts was transparent. She could sense every one of his feelings and words and assumed he could sense hers.

Staring at their surroundings, the red cliffs and the painted face of thousands of years of erosion suggested they were in Arizona. Or more specifically, looking into the canyon carved out by the ever-flowing Colorado River. She was curious about the water level, and in an instant was down by the river.

I need to be careful what I think.

The water was higher than expected. She realized it was the Hoover Dam, up near Vegas. It would maintain an even flow which did not exist in 1908. Rex joined her as she studied the landscape and made note of the river and logged its bends and turns. This information would be crucial for their return.

Out of curiosity, Maya willed herself to find the side canyon where Wynn's diary noted he had left his mare, Bessie. In an instant she found herself within a U-shaped offshoot of the river. But it was not as he had described. It was no longer a long wide sandy shoal, but a remnant strand of beach hugging the right side of the cliff face.

They returned to the ledge and ventured into the cave. Though it was dark, she had come to learn that in the theta state of consciousness, light and dark had different variables.

If there are no vibrations bouncing off the cornea of my eyes, how is it I see?

Instantly she was back in the apartment. And within moments, so was Rex.

"Shit," she muttered under her breath. She was still getting a handle on the intricacies of remote viewing.

"Flow, don't think," he admonished her. "Let's go again, but this time, just try to observe."

He had warned her about this during her lessons, but the criticism still stung.

43

Before re-engaging, Rex grabbed his notepad and made a series of entries.

Maya was fidgeting—eager to get back to the cave.

"Ready?"

After she succeeded in closing off all external thought, Rex was already waiting. Instantly they were back at the cave. This time she paused to take in every detail—including the two obelisks carved into the sides of the entrance. Previous research was leading her to conclude these monuments were somehow linked with the process for the making of Manna.

Entering was eerily reminiscent of their Egyptian foray into the Cave of Hathor. And what they had found there caused her hope to soar that they might find more of the Manna here. It had all the same images painted on the walls. The priest holding the cathode tube containing the familiar snake, Hathor's Cow Orb headdress, and rounding out the related pantheon were the Anubis-headed dogmen, who she now knew were the guardians of the secret. Protectors of the process for making the Sacred Manna.

Finding more of the Manna was their mission, learning the process of replicating this age-old secret was their holy grail. Echoes of Wynn's notebook reminded her. *'There were vases full of powder that he had dumped out.'*

Maya began a thorough inspection of the room. It appeared untouched since Wynn Lambert had departed. There were still shelves containing lidded vases, and a small fortune of gold artifacts that must have been here for thousands of years.

Maya moved to the image of the Blue Lily and guided her consciousness behind the familiar panel in the wall. Expecting a repeat of what was found in Egypt, instead she found a beautiful lotus blossom made of a crystalline material, as if it was carved from a giant sapphire.

Huhhh, she sucked in metaphorically. She knew the sensations of the body did not accompany remote viewing. It was merely conscious thought. But with a feeling of lightness and the sensation of a quickening pulse, she could not contain the euphoria.

It's the same as the vase Sir William Flinders Petrie found in Egypt over a hundred years ago. She recalled reading his journal and visiting the Sinai—her father's diary had led her there.

According to his journal, which his nephew David Hudson had let her read, it had the same shape, color, number of described petals and was rife with similar hieroglyphs. Some appeared to be fired within the crystal structure while others had the visual appearance of floating. She committed the images to memory, intuitively comprehending their importance.

As her focal point shifted to the greater room, she saw Rex was talking to himself and had a big shit-eating grin on his face. Looking around, she saw why. Though over a hundred years had passed since anyone had been here, there were still piles of the powder Wynn had poured from the emptied vases. And except for his occasional footprint, it was still here laying unmolested.

Rex's excitement was so loud against her spirit, that together their hopes soared. Within the elation, her penchant for fearing the worst led to the idea of security, guards, and patrols. But nothing happened. They remained rooted where they were. This was a good sign.

Maya telepathically suggested they find a suitable route back to this place and together they scoured the river, the towering buttes and easily recognizable reference points that they could use if traversing from the canyon floor.

When they returned to the apartment they discussed everything including the best options for going in, the choices vacillating between horseback or by helicopter.

"The easiest way would be by helicopter and rappel down to the ledge," Rex suggested. "But of course, this would add additional eyes to our discovery."

"Yes," she said contemplatively. "But since the area is closed by the government, it's likely they'll have included a no-fly zone."

In the end it was decided Rex would head to Flagstaff and do some snooping, casually check local companies, and find outfitters for their journey. From what they had seen, the best option had not changed since 1908. Go in on horseback.

Maya was going to run out to California to get copies of the maps, the journal and to make sure she had Austin's blessing.

Across the street, their conversation was being recorded and passed up the line to those who would determine what happened next. The chain eventually would find itself to the top. To someone most were not even aware existed—The Maestro.

CHAPTER 9
JW – NYC

Remembering to follow up on his grandfather's suggestion, JW called the Flower of Life Institute in Phoenix and spoke to a woman named Maria, asking her if she knew Drune Melchizedek. After explaining that his grandfather is a shaman and suggesting he had once met Drune who told him about a cave he had seen hidden in the Grand Canyon, she guardedly acknowledged knowing the man.

Maria said that if and when she heard from him, she would give him JW's number.

JW sensed from her tone that Mr. Melchizedik was quite reclusive and there was no telling when his message would get relayed. Still, Nascha had said he should reach out to the man. Now he could check the box.

With a shrug, he tied his hair back into a ponytail and brought his focus to bear on the other tasks that had been assigned to him.

The reality of end times, he thought. How do I separate fact from fantasy and confirm our hypothesis?

He was tasked with two projects. One was to seek empirical evidence of end times and the other was to try to get a handle on astral energies. And of course, thanks to the internet, this was a little easier to accomplish than verifying end times, so he started with astral energies.

Based on the ancient subterranean cavern he, Tavis, and Maya had discovered in Guatemala, there was strong anecdotal evidence that the ancient grid of the Master Builders was linked to astral energies.

Rubbing the stubble on his chin, he stared blankly at the computer. The blinking cursor waited. He let his mind wander, opening his thoughts to what his Shaman—Grandfather—had taught him. The Akasha and attunement to universal vibrations. It defied everything science taught and what bubbled up were the comments that had spilled unconsciously from his mouth when they were deep in that cavern in Central America.

"The twelve dimensions flow from the twelve signs of the Mazzaroth. The master harmonic tunes the Earth-bound frequencies with the astral energies, and their ruling spheres. But only the pure of heart will understand the wisdom, As Above, So Below."

The memory of that experience still freaked him out a little. He had no idea of who or what had taken over his thoughts. However, since then his intuitive cognitions seemed to be increasing daily.

Earth-bound frequencies, astral energies, and ruling spheres? Soon he found himself buried in a labyrinth of websites trying to find everything he could about this triad of celestial elements. The picture that formed was a tapestry of new age data and hard science, the latter surprising him. Deciding to get a baseline of understanding, he found an article on the subject that intrigued him.

What resonated was the experience in Guatemala where someone had placed a replica of the pyramid of Chitzen Itza on the giant map on the cavern's floor. Chitzen Itza was a place of human sacrifice, and it created a dark area around the glow of the grid. Something similar was alluded to in this article as 'Dark Places.'

"The Earth is wrapped in a network of inter-connected energy lines recognized and marked by ancient cultures in the Americas, Australia, Asia, and Africa. These include the St. Michael-Apollo energy line that runs from Ireland to England, through France, Italy, Greece, and on to Mount Carmel in the Holy Land. In China, these energy paths are studied under the science of Feng Shui that sought to correct and equalize the flow of Earth energy through the landscape in a most balanced and beneficial way.

The ancients believed that the cosmic flow of energy came from the Heavens. And that through architecture they could create environments of capability and cooperation, or hell's dark mirror. 'Dark places' are those which through strategic architecture were designed to inhibit the flow of energy. These were thought to produce melancholy and other psychological anguish.

Research has shown that there are areas and sites that have extremely high levels of electromagnetic energy. These sites stand out as nodal points in a network. Energy from these nodal points flows to all other parts on Earth's grid."

What does the grid do? What is the nature of celestial energy?

He thought about remote viewing, auras and biofields. Were they connected? Did Enoch use the Earth's electromagnetic energy as a variable when he defined the sites where these mega structures would be constructed? Is there a secret code to Earth that was now lost to us? How does it impact the inhabitants of this planet? He continued reading.

"Everything that exists on Earth is but the transient form of appearance of some celestial agency. Everything terrestrial has its prototype, its primordial cause, its ruling agency in Heaven... the surface of the Earth, where the mountain peaks form the stars, the ocean's answer to the Milky Way.

Earth energy receives its power from the Heavenly bodies and the planets are the poles that transfer the energy from the universe and our galaxy to the Earth below."

He came across an article about pillars, obelisks, and cosmic energy, and his skin began to prickle. He and Maya had seen evidence that there was some unknown connection with obelisks and the process for making Manna. This compelled him to dig deeper since their prime mandate was to either find more Manna or figure out how to make it.

"Scientists have found that when an obelisk is placed in the ground or upon a base of similar material used to make the pillar, depending on the size, all living plants and agriculture thrive for hundreds of yards or even miles. Like the chlorophyll that plants extract from the sun, cosmic rays, when secreted into the ground, create a balance of harmony that causes life to flourish."

He sat back in his chair and rolled the tension from his shoulders.

What about humans? Can astral energies effect our emotions or how we think?

He considered the book of Habakkuk in the Bible and the prophet's vision of end times. *'All I see is strife, brother against brother and neighbor against neighbor...'*

He considered the state of division in America today fueled by politics, as well as the riots breaking out all over the world. *Are astral energies behind this? Has the Hidden Hand succeeded in manipulating the grid to promote darkness and angst?*

That voice that had ignited his intuition was leaving him with a feeling that somehow recovering the Sacred Manna and understanding the grid were related to countering this threat.

But how?

CHAPTER 10
Collin - Lake Garda, Switzerland

Collin sat in the visitor chair fantasizing about his future. He was ensconced within the protected walls of a converted castle, nestled along the shore of Lake Garda. Sporting a wide grin and ruddy complexion, he thought of the promise of renewed health, vigor, youth, and... Soon his thoughts turned to lust, sex, perversion, and only degraded from there.

The special clinic was known by few and only served those who belonged to 'The Brotherhood.' The secret organization had recruited his ancestors long ago. More succinctly, they only catered to the highest echelon followers of The Maestro.

In acceptance of his absolute and undisputed authority, their leader promised wealth, which most of them had already achieved or inherited. He promised power, which most could contrive, but only a few understood how to use. And the ultimate allure—he promised a greatly extended life of youth and vigor. This was the ultimate hold he claimed upon each and every one of them. And today it was finally Collin's turn.

"Good morning, Collin," the doctor said in a clipped British accent. The man looked to be about forty, but then again, he could be ninety. The thought increased Collin's excitement.

"I am John Grillo. Do you have any questions?"

"Sort of," Collin mustered. "I know we are not supposed to discuss this outside of this building and I understand why. But, well, I'm sure I'm not the first to ask. Can you tell me anything about the process, what it is or how it works?"

This entire understanding was based on faith and trust. Granted, though they were not allowed to discuss it amongst themselves by penalty of expulsion or worse, he had seen the results in two of his colleagues and was quite envious.

Shit, Wilson is banging some twenty-five-year-old model from Paris and he's over ninety. And she can't get enough.

Thinking maybe he had made a mistake, maybe he should not have asked, he meekly backtracked. "I mean, if you can't, I understand. It's just that damn thing curiosity, she's never satisfied." With a weak smile, he quietly folded his hands in his lap.

"Sure," the doc said in a conspiratorial wink. "What we are going to do is feed you the milk from your mother's tit."

The tone was ripe with English humor. Collin wondered if he was merely deflecting.

"You see, within the breast milk of young mothers is the enzyme telomerase, we call it the fountain of youth. Telomerase has unique anti-aging properties. Within a healthy body our cells are programmed to divide a set number of times over a lifetime. This process of division and replication is fixed at birth.

"Like a software program, it is encoded in the RNA. We refer to this as the junk DNA, but this is where science is so god-awfully wrong. There is more going on in human RNA than the world has even begun to understand. At least the world beyond these doors," he added with haughty pride.

"The verse in Psalms where the Psalmist claims God knows every hair on our head and the appointed day and hour of our death... the science within our individual RNA would partially affirm that statement."

Collin thought it unusual that a man of the Brotherhood would be quoting scripture. But whatever, he didn't care, he just wanted to be young again.

"Each cell continues to divide ad infinitum until you begin to reach the back end of its program. That's when things start to turn. Where the deteriorating weight of time begins to manifest itself in the human body. The division potential of your cells is controlled by caps at the end of your DNA strands. Think shoelaces with plastic tips," he explained.

"These caps are the telomeres, and with each division throughout your life, a little piece of plastic tip gets clipped off until there is nothing left. Then as each cell fails to replicate it dies, there is no replacement. This is why our skin, our organs, everything about us ages. Some cells hit the end of their program sooner than others, but ultimately enough will stop replicating and it's lights out.

Collin fidgeted in the chair, his fear of death had grown more worrisome over the years. He had let his hope of this moment cover his anxiety, but now, here... he tried to follow the doctor's explanation.

"By properly adjusting the application of our telomeres we can reverse the process of the diminishing shoelace caps, and instead begin lengthening them."

"If I might be so bold, haven't leading pharmaceutical companies figured this out as well? I mean, there are trillions of dollars to be made."

"I assure you, they are trying," the doctor said with a blank expression. "But they lack the secret sauce. First, we mix in the compound Adrenochrome, this is used by many well-aged actors and actresses to preserve their youth. It's not illegal, but it is quite expensive."

Collin knew many wealthy friends who were addicted, but this did not really answer his question. There had to be more. His disappointment was apparent.

"That's it?" he asked.

Dr. Grillo paused for a moment, then lowering his voice, he parted with a secret.

"Each time one of you are sent to us, we receive a package from The Maestro with the patient's name. The envelope contains a select dose of a fine white powder that when used in our procedure, amplifies the process by a factor of ten thousand times."

"What's in the powder?" Collin asked.

Grillo's face went from blank to stony.

Have I asked too much?

Grillo let out a deep breath and looked into Collin's eyes. With a crook of a grin, they came to an implied understanding. *'What was said here should never be repeated.'*

"Now let's get you into the lab and take you back to funky town. Within a month, you'll be chasing young girls who will want to be caught."

CHAPTER 11
JW with Maya - Pacific Palisades California

Maya and JW arrived at the Lambert residence, in part to ask for copies of Wynn's maps, drawings, and notes. JW was a little hesitant because he knew Maya was still wrestling with her feelings for Austin, and truth be told, he was still wrestling with his feelings towards her.

"This is the friend I told you about," Maya said after embracing Austin. "The brother I never had." JW flinched at the familiarity as he feigned a smile that hung like a cheap suit.

He noted that Austin was handsome in a boyish way, and that for someone who had been in a coma for the last fourteen years, he seemed to have an air of good health.

Mrs. Lambert entered the room, gave Maya a hug and introductions were made. "Please, call me Merryl."

JW studied the woman. Considering the years of stress she had absorbed, he thought she was quite attractive. She led them out to the terrace. It was a beautiful California day and Merryl had laid out a sumptuous spread for her guests.

JW was surprised at Austin's insatiable curiosity, as the man peppered him with questions about growing up on a reservation, his tribe, anything, and everything, maybe trying to drink in some of the life he had lost.

"It's a miracle," Merryl said as she continued to marvel aloud at how the medical establishment was so stupefied. "It's what they are all saying. Unheard of, unprecedented, miraculous. Me, I just say, 'thank you, Lord.'"

Eventually, JW got a word in.

"I have been doing a lot of research on astral energies," JW told Austin. "I understand your great grandfather found an artifact that relates to the subject. Could I see it?"

"Mom, can you get the box, please?" Austin asked.

During the pause, JW looked beyond the Santa Monica mountains to the cold, blue waters of the Pacific Ocean. A sailboat paralleled the coast, and far out on the horizon he could see the smudge of Catalina Island.

When Merryl returned, she laid the scuffed leather box on the table. Austin lifted the lid and removed the gold artifact.

"'*As Above So Below - The Talismanic Magic of the Astral Energies are brought down to Earth, its spirit infused into the sacred architecture, harmonizing thought, and the way for the souls of man. As Above, So Below.*' It is the interpretation Wynn had journaled."

"May I?" JW asked. As he marveled at the synchronicity of these ancient words showing up here and now, he studied the object. It was heavy, and cool to the touch. Perfectly balanced, it felt as if it contained its own lifeforce. He continued his discourse on astral energies.

"According to what I have found so far, astral energies seem to be some form of cosmic dynamisms that are emitted by various celestial bodies. There is research that implies they affect all life on Earth. They can be amplified, modified, and directed though architecture or by placing structures on key nodal points of the Earth's lay lines."

JW went on to explain, mostly for Austin's benefit, about lay lines, nodal points, Maya's grid of the Master Builders and how they were still trying to understand how this fit into everything. He tiptoed towards the reason getting to the cave was so important to their research.

"This cave..." Austin interrupted, looking deep into Maya's eyes. "The one you saw from your dream journey is our destiny. Mine and yours."

Maya started to speak, but he was not finished.

"The path was laid down centuries ago when my grandfather came upon that special place. Are you really going to ask me to not be part of 'our' quest?"

"No," she demurred. "I would never exclude you from our destiny. I am simply here to assess if you are physically able to make the trip. We are leaving in two days and will be on horseback, roughing it for at least a week."

Austin reached across the table and laid his hands on hers. "How can I prove to you I am ready?"

"Let's take a hike," she suggested.

The event that caused Austin to fall into a coma when they were children was a fall down the side of an incline where he smashed his head on a cliff. It was only by providence that the bluff stopped him from sliding over the edge to a sure death.

It was a chance to put that awful episode behind them forever.

"You guys go," JW said. "I'm a little jetlagged. I'm think I'll head back to the hotel to take a nap."

◆♒♏♒⚥♎♎♏▪♒☉■♎

Maya

It was a strenuous hike to the top of the Highlands. As they trudged along the fire road, Maya saw a lot had changed over the years. She also noticed that Austin's breath was labored even though he put on a brave face. She felt bad but it was why she had suggested the hike.

There was no way he would be able to endure a lengthy foray through the canyons, and if she had allowed this to happen, inevitably it would put them all at risk.

She felt a sadness, knowing how disappointed he was going to be, but she was going to let this play out, hoping he came to the right conclusion on his own.

When they reached the top of the hill, Maya stared at the place where half of Austin's life had been taken away from him. It was here that he fell and ended up in a coma for fourteen years.

"Are you up for this?" she asked with a heavy sigh. A dullness filled her chest as she thought back to the things she had said. Or at least the timing. She could have waited until they had made it back up to the top of the slope.

Destiny's child.

The thought reminded her of Layla. This allowed her ache to fade. It also reminded her that the event was a thread in her tapestry, likely planned long ago, before time had even started to unfold.

Now that they were older, the hill seemed so much easier, like a simple gradient. They climbed down to the ledge and together peered over the side.

In her dream journey she had fallen into a raging river that carried her to the shores of Eden. But in reality, there was no water, no raging river, just a long drop to more scrub, more brush, and more jagged rocks.

Austin stood next to her rubbing his thumb over the ring she had given him so long ago. "Neither time nor distance shall come between us," he murmured.

"I am not going to join you on this trip. I understand why you wanted us to hike up to here. Thank you for letting me be the one to make the decision… but when I am able, would you consider another chance?"

She squeezed his hand in hers. The familiarity of their past, the first love of their childhood was now moving towards a platonic friendship. She just hoped that he would not cling to the past.

◆〰♏〰Ж♎♎♏■〰♋■♎

When they returned to the house, Merryl was glued to the television. From her body language, Maya could see that something had happened.

"What is it?" Maya asked as she tried to follow the banner running on the bottom of the screen. A cold shiver started from deep inside and worked its way up her spine.

The news out of the Canary Islands was amped at full throttle across every crisis news network, but little information was actually being revealed.

'A hard quarantine has been enforced until the virulent nature of a deadly pathogen can be determined…'

Maya's eyes were glued to the screen. The unfolding images caused her to gasp. It was not so much what they showed, but the emotive they elicited. It echoed how she'd felt the first time she had seen the drawings in Wynn Lambert's diary. There was something about this event that resonated within her.

Is this the work of the Hidden Hand? The start of the catastrophic events that we were warned of?

She called JW, who answered on the first ring. "Have you seen the news?"

"It is starting," he said.

"I'm gonna Uber to the hotel and then I am going there." She was about to set off on another remote viewing excursion—something that was becoming a fixture in her life.

◆〰♏〰⚹♌♌♏∎〰☽∎♌

Maya - The Canary Islands

Maya returned to the hotel and, after checking in with JW, went to her room. She insisted on being alone, as the presence of others was simply one more distraction that made the process of remote viewing that much more difficult.

Her instincts were that this was the work of the Hidden Hand. She could not explain it, she just knew. She also knew that the scope of their quest was continuing to grow and thwarting the efforts of those who wanted to create a New World Order for their own gain was part of her destiny. She knew for them to have any chance she was going to need more of the Sacred Manna.

She cleared her mind the way she always did, creating tunnels for each stream of thought and deliberately focusing on the mental masonry of blocking off each stream of distraction until her mind was blank.

She could feel sinews deep within being metaphorically freed from her husk, until the moment came when she was floating above, looking down. She let her intentions take her on an instantaneous leap to the other side of the world.

Below was an ocean and above, the sky was red-tinged by the approaching dawn. There were small fishing boats pulled up on the sand beaches, protected by a manmade breakwater. The town was made up of whitewashed buildings with barrel tile roofs, anchored by a modest church and its silent bell tower.

There was little movement, though she had seen a huge white CDC ship anchored offshore. Maya let her intent guide her, having come to understand the words her father had taught to Rex, who had taught her.

'Don't think—flow.' It was a tricky balance to avoid cognitive thought that pulled you back too quickly while trying to guide one's intent.

Drifting through the various buildings, she saw bodies everywhere, lying in pools of blood that appeared to have evacuated from every orifice and opening. It must have been sudden, for very few had ever made it out to the street. It was one horror after another. She fought to keep her emotions steady as the revulsion of this atrocity unfolded. She had learned in the past that dwelling on an emotion was a distraction that would snap the remote viewer back into their physical body.

Are there any survivors?

Energy follows thought and she found herself upon the CDC ship where twelve children had been contained in a clean room with workers in biohazard suits tending to their needs. She let her spirit flow throughout the ship and came upon two people in the mess hall. Tired, weary, and staring into their umpteenth cup of coffee, she listened.

"This was no accident," the elder woman said to her male companion.

"Why do you think that?" His body language gave no challenge, though his question did.

"The airport. They wanted to make sure nobody left. That the contagion was contained."

The man rubbed his stubbled chin. "Is this a test run?"

Though Maya's state was that of mere consciousness, the cold familiar feeling of dread returned. She squeezed her metaphorical eyes tight and when she reopened them, she was back in the hotel.

She flashed to the images that Wynn Lambert had drawn over a hundred years ago.

Can these be connected? Is that even possible?

Intuition said yes, her gut said yes, and her rational mind knew, fate was rapping. Actually, not rapping, but pounding hard upon her door.

CHAPTER 12

Rex – Flagstaff, Arizona

This was the third helicopter company Rex had visited. After his two previous failures, he decided a different tact was needed.

Red Rock Aviation, said the faded sign, weathered from the sun and the ravages of time and dwindling fortunes. This was one of the smaller outfits in the area that catered to the tourists.

It was off season, too hot in July and the middle of the week, so it was slow. Inside the small reception area, the ceiling fan pushed around the tepid air and a television played a looping news station in the corner. Behind an old chipped counter sat a man in an unzipped flight suit, drinking coffee with his head buried in a local newspaper.

"I see it's standing room only, must be giving something away," Rex said by way of hello.

The man set the paper down and gave him a toothy grin.

"How can I help you?"

"You the pilot or the desk jockey?" Rex asked in an affable manner. Offering a backhanded compliment to the man. No desk jockey would wear a flight suit on a day as hot as today.

"Well, as you can see... " he smirked with open arms. "Both."

"Good thing I beat the crowds, then," Rex jested, looking to set the man at ease with light banter. "I'm only here for the day and was wondering if I could get a three-hour tour."

Rex saw the man's ears perk up at the prospect of a potential customer.

"Your name ain't Gilligan, is it?"

This set the tone. Once the business of business was settled, Rex was told to wait inside the air-conditioned room as Donny Paulson, the piloting desk jockey, went out to prep the chopper.

When he returned, Rex had unfolded an old survey map.

61

"Do you know any history of this area?" Rex placed a finger on one of the restricted buttes. The pilot looked over the old survey map but said nothing. Rex pushed a little harder.

"Why do so many of the bluffs have Egyptian names and why are the Tower of Isis and the Tower of Sett off limits? The map gives no reason for restricting this area."

"I'm not really sure why that area is closed," Donny said. But he was quick to shut down any idea of crossing into that space. Apparently, locals had been warned.

In the end, they agreed to follow the river as far south as they could and circle some of the buttes outside of the restricted perimeter. Rex was hoping for more, but he would take what he could get and glean whatever information availed itself from the aerial recon.

Crossing the concrete tarmac, shimmering waves of heat swirled sand across the open space. Inside the EchoStar 130, Rex put on the headphones and immediately, the wash of rotors was replaced with sound-suppression quiet. Once they cleared the TCA, Donny dropped the nose of the chopper and they took off like a Labrador on the hunt, heading south until they came to the rim of the canyon.

Rex had served in the Marines for two stints before joining Advanced Dynamics. Choppers were second nature to him. And as nonchalant as Donny had acted, he was an excellent pilot.

"It's beautiful," Rex admired. The plateaus were a patchwork of splits and crevices, shadowed ravines and rock faces striated in red. Below, the tumbling river cut a blue-green ribbon that meandered through the wash.

"Does the water level change much around here?"

"Not since the Hoover Dam," the pilot said, thumbing over his shoulder.

"Do hikers or horseback riders ever go into the canyon?" This was becoming the likely route they would need to take, and his heart raced a little in anticipation of an answer.

"As I recall, there's an outfit called Hitchin Post Stables that used to lead trail rides into the canyon. Not sure if they still do it or not." Then he muttered "It's the damn insurance companies."

After two hours, they were nearing time to turn back. Rex knew he had gotten Donny to flirt beyond his comfort level as he cajoled him to occasionally dip into the restricted perimeter. As he pulled the craft up over the rim, a flash of sunlight off metal could be seen deep within the restricted area.

"Did you see that?" Rex noted Donny's shoulders bunch and his hands grip the levers a little tighter than necessary.

"I know two pilots that had been quite casual in obeying the warnings about these parts," he said. "They were visited by government officials. Neither ended up in jail, but both had their licenses suspended and paid a fine." Donny concluded with a mention that it was a fine he could not afford.

Rex wondered who would be flying through this space and continued to pepper Donny with questions all the way back. But Mr. Paulson had pretty much become a dried-up creek bed. Still, the tip about the Hitchin Post Stables turned out to be a good one.

CHAPTER 13
Rex - The Canyon

Rex waited in front of the Southwest Airlines baggage area with the engine on and the A/C blasting. When Maya and JW emerged, he smiled and helped stow their gear. He was glad that it was only going to be the three of them. He had worried Maya would cave and include Austin. Unknown dynamics were just one more variable they did not need to worry about.

"I have six horses arranged for a week," he said as they pulled away from the curb. "I also informed the owner not to worry if we ran up to ten days or so."

He had given the stable owner a general overview of the proposed trip but certainly not the specifics. He recalled the owner's quiet relief once the liability waivers were signed, and a handsome sum of cash had exchanged hands. Rex could have argued the size of the required deposit, but they were the only game in town.

Once that had been completed, Rex had returned to the hotel and remote viewed the south rim. He located a switchback that would lead them down to the river in about three to four days' ride. It was still possible to pick out pebble-strewn washes on most parts of the watercourse, certainly this would be no problem for trail horses.

They would need to be alert in case the dam let out a water burst, which they did periodically. But even this, he did not leave to chance. He had checked the public listing. Dam sluicing were advised well in advance so the rafting companies could take advantage of the action and more importantly, so tourists would not get swept away. There was nothing on the calendar for the next three weeks.

♦〰♏〰♓♎♎♏■〰♋■♎

The following morning, they met up with Chuck Thomas, the old Jamaican cowboy with whom Rex had negotiated. Once Chuck was sure these people knew what they were doing, the old cowboy took the lead, followed by Maya and Rex. JW brought up the rear. They passed the sprawling ranch house, continued on through a nearby field, and soon were approaching the towering pines.

"The Bill Williams Trail is about hour more," Chuck called back.

The three amigos had chosen the old Bill Williams Trail the night before at the Hotel Monte Vista. It was the best entry point to the south rim of the canyon. From there they would pick up the route Wynn had detailed in his journal.

Once they came to the trailhead, Chuck wished them good luck and a safe journey. He promised that if they did not return within ten days, he was sending out a posse to come rescue them. "Via con Dios," he muttered in a soft prayer as the three rode south.

♦ ≈ ♏ ≈ ⋊ ♎ ♎ ♏ ■ ≈ ♋ ■ ♎

The weather was mild, about eighty degrees. After two hours of riding, Maya saw a train passing in the far distance. This was their first marker. Maya's hopes of retrieving some of the powder they had remote viewed in the cave gave rise to the promise of seeing her father again. The anticipation amplified the longing she had to reunite with him.

It was time to turn off the trail and find the south rim. The rest of that afternoon they saw no other riders as they plunged deeper into the tall, wooded forests.

The trail was marked with weathered trees that rose from out of the Earth to brush the sky. All the while, animal trails crisscrossed their path.

Maya enjoyed the quiet solitude. Walking on pine needles released a smell that reminded her of Christmases long ago. A rabbit ran across the trail in panic, startling her and the horses. Hot on its heels was a fox, who hesitated at the sight of humans. Good for the rabbit, not good for the fox.

"Lucky wabbitt," Maya laughed.

Once they passed the unmanned fire tower at Woody Mountain, they began a gradual downward passage. Butterflies flittered amongst the wildflowers as bees busied themselves. It was an idyllic retreat from the pressures they had left behind.

The first day went as planned. As the sun hung low and the shadows stretched long, they arrived at Chocolate Falls. It was so named because of the brown soil which frothed like running chocolate as it crested over a multitude of shelves that cascaded to a russet-foamed tumble.

Here they pitched the tent and watched as the red-streaked clouds vanished into ink. Stars burst forth with the randomness of popping corn.

◆〜♏〜⯎♎♎♏■〜♋■♎

JW - Deep in the Canyon

The south rim of the Grand Canyon was a spectacle of peaks and valleys. And erosion from wind, water, and time. Striated colors of every hue were punctuated by green patches of forests that clung to any flat ledge they could find. Wind whistled over the stone and JW took off his hat to enjoy the soft breeze blowing through his hair.

It had taken them another two days of moderate pushing to get beyond the tourist sites, reservations, and public roads. On the third day they crossed into the restricted area. So far there had been no signs of human activity other than random signage with increasing degrees of warnings. Some were not so subtle.

Warning: You Are Trespassing and Subject to Being Shot.

JW knew they were close, maybe two days' ride. As the distant glow of a new day teased the high shadows and parried the stubborn pools of night, they packed the horses and set off for the switchback.

It was noon when they reached the dismount point. The sun was high, the shade elusive, and the temperature had a mean streak to it.

They had a total of six horses, and it was nearly a half-mile of tight turns to the bottom.

"I will take the horses down one at a time," JW said, leaving no room for discussion. "Rex, you follow, and Maya, wait topside until we bring the last one down together."

Rex followed on the first foray and was keeping watch on the horses below while Maya held station in the unbridled heat above.

By the time JW had come up from his fourth trip, he was bathed in sweat, breathing hard, and needed a chance to rest. His legs ached, and the thought of two more trips did not sit well. But he did not like them being separated. Only by completing his mission would they be back together again. So after a canteen of water, and ten more minutes of rest, he took Marilyn, the mare with the golden mane. He cinched the pack, checked the strapping, and started down for the fifth time.

Contrary to intuition, down was far more arduous than up. The strain on the front quads and the need to pick each step carefully was time-consuming and left no room for distraction.

Marilyn was not typically used as a pack horse and she had shown her distaste from the minute they set off. It was one of the reasons he had chosen her as second to last to be led down.

"Easy girl, I know you enjoy being the center of attention," JW cajoled. He bribed her with handfuls of oats every few steps. At one point, loose scree caused his feet to go out from under him and he landed hard on his rump. Marilyn let out a toothy nay, mocking him with laughter.

He could choose to be angry or choose to laugh. This was the secret you learned on the reservation. Joy, anger, happiness, sadness, these were choices we made a hundred times each day.

"Come on Marilyn, you old movie star," he chuckled, choosing laughter.

They still had the most treacherous part of the path in front of them, and he was extra careful, relieved when the incline flattened out.

Once he reached Rex, he saw that he had stripped the animals and was letting them cool by a pool of water.

JW was glad to see that Texas twang was backed up with a little ranch knowledge and the fundamentals of equestrian care.

"One more time," he said looking up the side of the canyon.

Socks, so named because of the white leg markings that contrasted against the rest of the chestnut gelding, was ready, willing, and able. JW could see the horse knew that anywhere had to be cooler than this and no doubt could scent the water below.

"Okay Maya, last one. I'll lead and you follow behind." He was glad this was the last horse. His legs were wobbly, and his stamina almost spent.

As they descended, the accumulated vestige of a dozen trips had loosened the rocks. Hooves clapped and an occasional parade of small rocks would go scurrying past.

Between Maya and Socks, a small pile broke free and in so doing, disturbed the shade of a rattlesnake. With its tongue darting in anger, its rattler sent fear through the steed and in an instant of pure panic, the horse bolted dangerously down the hill.

JW barely had time to see what was happening when the horse's front legs collapsed on the loose gravel and Socks pitched forward, landing on top of him and throwing his body to the ground. JW's head was slammed into the Earth and in an instant, he saw trails of light, then darkness.

◆〰♏〰Ж♎♎♏■〰♋■♎

"Is this what you are looking for?" the man said, offering a flower to him. But JW did not understand. He cast his thoughts about as he took in a world that was dreamy, its edges blurred. The searing light had been replaced with a mirage. He was confused—shock dulling his senses.

"This is the man you must talk to," Nascha told him. But it was not real—Nascha was not here with them in the canyon. It had to be a dream.

"It's too late," stepped up another man. He was old, had a long white beard and carried a V-shaped branch in his hand. JW somehow knew this was Slim Spurling, the diviner who spoke to his grandfather before dying twenty years ago.

"They left nothing for you. But of him, they do not know." He pointed to the man offering the flower.

His head hurt and the blinding light was returning. His growing pain replaced the fog of his dream. Opening his eyes, he saw that his legs were trapped under a collapsed horse. He forced the adrenaline of reality to return and pushed his body beyond human strength.

In his peripheral vision he saw Rex bounding up the path, breathing hard, worry lines beading like sweat. JW freed first one leg, then another. Wiggling the toes inside his boots, his cursory examination yielded relief. Nothing was broken.

With a wobble, he stood. What he saw broke his heart. The exposed break of the horse's front right leg had ripped through the skin and protruded like a jagged shoal.

JW took a knee by the wounded animal. With words whispered that only the fallen horse could hear, he calmed his spirit. JW closed his eyes and began rocking to a silent rhythm. He began to recite a prayer in his native language. Socks let his head rest and his body stopped quivering. His breathing was no longer labored, and he too shut his eyes.

"Rest my friend, I will be with you in our memories."

No one said a word as the two men removed the supplies tethered to the animal. Maya gathered up stuff that had been thrown free.

Rex and Maya took what they could down the hill.

I will bring the rest of the stuff," JW said softly, letting them know he would join them below in a bit. Ten minutes later a single shot rang out.

That night they made camp on a spit of rocks less than ten feet wide. Hemmed in by the sheer cliff on one side and the ever-flowing water released from the Hoover Dam hundreds of miles away, they were in a precarious place.

But the clear sky did not portend rain and there were no planned bulk releases for the rest of the month. With solemn introspection, JW considered Socks' death, their quest, and inherently understood the daunting task ahead of them. But he was committed to Maya and their undertaking.

◆ ≋ ℳ ≋ ⵋ ♎ ♎ ℳ ■ ≋ ♋ ■ ♎

Maya – The Cave

When morning arrived, Maya's mood had overtones of somber reflection. The horse's death was a reminder of the fragility of life and how fast things can change.

They continued along the south side of the river, which was characterized by a steady trail of tumbled stones firmly packed from years of flowing water, making the trail mostly hazard free.

They made good time and expected that they should be near their destination by nightfall. Maya continued to check their landmarks. The buttes with Egyptian names were clear. Based on Wynn's entries in the diary, it would not be long before they would need to keep a sharp eye out for the stairs. He had mentioned they were naturally camouflaged. She found herself humming as the possibility of retrieving some Manna pushed away any remaining melancholy from the events of yesterday.

As the late afternoon sun graced them with shadows from the wall of the south rim, Maya heard a loud noise that was alien to their locale. Her skin prickled, and a tight ball formed in her stomach.

"Listen," she said with a hushed exhalation.

"Quick, grab the horses and press into the shadows as close to the wall as you can," JW said sharply, his voice carrying alarm.

A Bell Helicopter come tearing around the point mere yards above the river. As it raced past, Maya noticed there were no markings of any kind and prayed they had not been seen.

Continuing up the river, the chopper showed no signs of deviation. Maya was left to wonder... Why hide below the canyon unless looking to avoid radar detection?

Who are they, why are they here and do they know of the secret cave?

Maya's anxiety took off like a rocket. Something did not feel right and the timing...

When the echoes of rotors had faded with distance, there was nothing left to hear but the tireless coursing of the river.

"I think we should go and check the cave," Rex said.

Maya had a bad feeling about that helicopter and looked to JW for his thoughts. His silent nod placed them all in agreement.

"Okay, let's rest the horses while Rex and I journey to the site."

They found a spot and sat with their backs to the wall. They closed their eyes and began their individual processes of transition. Maya laid brick by mental brick to close each tunnel of thought...

Floating above their bodies, Maya took one last look at JW, who was minding the animals. With intent defined, Maya found herself with Rex standing in front of the cave. They knew right away something was off. The obelisks on each side of the door remained untouched, but the sensation of awe was no longer present.

Upon entering, the two had different hopes and worries. One hope was dashed while the other one was preserved. Everything was gone.

The bowls, the errant powder, the utensils, nothing left. The place would have smelled of a bleach cleaning if their olfactory senses worked while in a dream state.

Damn it! How do I find my father now?

Maya's anger that a ready supply of Manna had been taken and robbed her of her only chance to find her father was infuriating but she put off the speculation about who had done it for the moment. She willed herself into the secret chamber and found a surprising comfort to see that the sapphire blossom still remained.

Maya exited the cave and from the vantage point of the ledge, looked out over the river. She considered if one could see the other cave. In an instant she was there, standing before a pile of rubble.

Is this the cave Carruthers and Fottrell saw? It was purely an illusion, but she felt as if her heart was racing... Fueled by anger at those who came before and those who just left? Likely all of it.

The remains of any evidence, such as the Anubis-headed men carved into each side of the opening, had all been removed. Had it not been for the level floor that was by all appearance manmade, there would be nothing to suggest anything had ever been here.

Rex appeared at her side. And as if their thoughts were telepathic, they opened their eyes to see JW watering the horses.

◆ ♒ ℳ ♒ ⊬ ♎ ♎ ℳ ■ ♒ ♋ ■ ♎

They continued down river. The shoals were not wide enough to walk side by side and thus each was isolated within their own thoughts. By the time they entered the general vicinity, they had all gone down different paths of the who, how's, and whys of those that came by helicopter.

Maya's fear of the pervasive presence and inexplicable knowledge of what she was starting to refer to as her enemy caused her to beat down every trail of how they could have known about this cave. The only path she could not dismiss was her call to Layla from a burner phone when they were returning from Scotland.

Does this mean all our phones are being monitored?

Her nostrils flared in anger and she found herself grinding her teeth. This led to the next possibility.

Have they bugged the apartment?

She fought to bring the roiling inside her under control, so she stopped, dismounted, and let the horses take a drink. Her only thought was to get to that cave as soon as they can. Maya took out her copy of the diary. Wynn had done extensive drawings of the spot where the steps could be found. Lining up visual references, she knew they were around here somewhere.

She started scanning the face of the cliff at and around eye level. Her breathing quickened but she found nothing that looked manmade. She paralleled the wall as frustration mounted. Fifty feet from where her horse was being watered, she stepped around a pile of driftwood and then she spotted something.

"Look." Her voice carried triumph. The others came to inspect, and she contrasted the cuts in the rock with the ones in Wynn's drawings.

"Imagine, after a hundred years of wind, water and erosion, it's as if he drew this yesterday." The elation of finding the cuts in the rock was quickly tempered by the knowledge that what they had come for was gone. Taken by whomever was in that helicopter.

"Let's set up camp and then we can climb up and see if they left us anything," JW suggested. They set off downstream, walking the horses. It was not long before they found the vent Wynn had used.

Maya had been correct that the water level had encroached into the ravine, but there was a spit of beach that followed along the wall to their right. The deeper they entered, the wider it got. About one hundred and fifty yards in, there was a soft sanded area that was maybe twenty feet wide and fifty feet long, more than ample for a campsite. And as if God had been waiting for them, there was abundant driftwood, which would make good kindling for a fire.

At least one thing is going our way, she thought. Then she considered that if the water came rushing in, they would be trapped.

"Do we need to worry about the river?"

"I checked the dam's release schedule," JW assured. "There is not a planned release until Labor Day weekend, and there is no rain on the horizon. We should be fine."

CHAPTER 14
Maya - Wynn's Cave

Starring up at the cliff face, shade and shadows revealed crags and crevices in the changing light of late afternoon. Anticipation and anxiety fueled the adrenaline now pumping through Maya's body. All her senses were heightened. She saw a lizard dart along a piece of deadwood. Fear formed a dry metallic taste in her mouth. And she felt the sweat beading on her forehead.

"Here goes."

Packing rope, water, and pitons, Maya began her ascent. Wearing gloves, she was still careful to check each handhold for scorpions or worse. The cuts were marvels of engineering. Deep enough for a foot to be comfortably inserted, they were chiseled a few inches in, and downward-cut for handholds.

Once she reached the top, Maya stopped to catch her breath. Her heart was pounding a mile a minute. She was relieved nothing was lurking in the handholds.

Maya proceeded to hammer hiker's pylons into the rock, secured the rope, and dropped it to the floor. This would allow them to clip a safety harness with a fast latch that would catch them if they slipped or fell backwards.

"All set," she yelled down." As they proceeded to climb, Maya kept an eye on the pylons, leaving nothing to chance.

JW was the last up. Being big had its benefits, but not when dangling from a rope or clinging to the side of a three-hundred-foot wall. Maya's hands were sweating, and she kept licking her lips in anticipation. Once JW had made it safely onto the ledge, Maya hastened to the cave.

◆〰ℳ〰〰⟊⟊ℳ ■〰♋■⟊

JW was relieved they rushed in ahead of him. He wanted time to think, feel, let his intuition have some free reign. He knew the helicopter that passed over them was exiting. And their dream journey had confirmed the culprits had scrubbed away any evidence this place was ever a source of the sacred powder.

Still, he did anticipate the look of victory when Maya brought her trophy out into the sunlight. She had confirmed the crystal vase was still there when she and Rex had remote viewed the cave after the helicopter had passed.

And as if the thought conjured action, Maya emerged from the opening triumphantly holding the sapphire blue crystal.

Shaped like a blue lily, the sun's rays refracted the facets with colors of the rainbow. It created a cascading halo that washed over her. And through the corona of light, he could see her eyes held both elation and puzzlement.

"What?" he asked.

"Look, inside. Orion has been embedded into the crystal."

The constellation of Orion was another one of those enigmas that kept cropping up in their quest. And here it was again. JW had come to accept coincidence was more like divine intervention and this was one more affirmation.

She handed him the piece, which was larger than a softball but smaller than a soccer ball. He held it up into the sunlight.

The entire flower was translucent. And yet within the structure, suspended in the glass was an array of images. Dominating the arrangement were the familiar outlines of the stars of the Pleiades. Orion's Belt.

"What do you think it is?" JW handed back the crystal blossom.

"My first impression is that like Petrie's discovery in Sinai, this place was where the sacred powder was manufactured. And 'this'" she said tenderly holding the lotus, "I think is somehow related to the process, or the formula, or something along these lines."

JW considered her point, and considered the fragile nature of the item, and the rough journey home.

"Then I suggest we photograph it. Just in case."

Maya took her phone and began a series of shots and videos. Close ups with a bent towards each glyph, an all-encompassing video stream that captured the refracted rays of the sun.

When they brought it back inside, the symbols radiated with a particular glow. JW was reminded of the cavern in Guatemala and how the paint on the walls had interacted with the energy from their lights.

But his focus shifted to the larger room around him. This was his first time inside the cave. He was overwhelmed by the striking similarities to the cave they had entered in Sinai.

Touching his lips in thought, he wondered *How is this possible? Could they all be connected to Akhenaten? This cave, that cave. The temple dedicated to the manufacture of the Sacred Manna?*

"I think your assessment is correct," JW said contemplatively as he continued to look at the intricacies around him.

"This is likely where they made the sacred powder. The giveaways are the two obelisks framing the entrance. The more I research astral energies, the more it becomes clear obelisks are used in the process."

◆ ≈ ♏ ≈ ♓ ♎ ♎ ♏ ■ ≈ ♋ ■ ♎

Maya sat next to the fire, its blaze warding off the chill. The horses had been fed, and so had they. The topic of conversation centered on two themes. How knowledge of the cave had been exposed and what was the meaning of the lotus crystal's symbols?.

It was a freewheeling, anything-is-possible banter. They bounced around, subject to subject. Looking up through the narrow heights of unscalable walls, they saw an explosion of stars glowing. The sky was clear and light pollution was nonexistent.

And dominating the view directly over their head was Orion's Belt. The classic three stars supporting the purported sword on a strap.

"Do you remember the three wise men from the Bible?" JW asked. "Legends linger that these ancient magi were represented by the three predominant stars of Orion. Historically, the magi were Sabeans, star watchers who had scanned the Heavens for a thousand years, waiting for the sign of the coming Messiah.

"Imagine father teaching son, teaching their sons, and so on for a thousand years. There only job was waiting and watching. Then one day there is an astrological alignment in the sky, and they set forth for

Bethlehem. And surprisingly they bring three gifts. Gold, frankincense, and myrrh. Why would a new baby need these things?"

"And you have a theory?" Maya asked. She had come to know his cadence when leading to a point and appreciated that though his words were sparse, his observations were solid.

"Well, yes I do," he said with a smile.

"What if these magi…"

Maya became disconcerted when he stopped in midsentence. Worry replaced his easy smile.

"The water," he pointed, suddenly distressed.

Maya looked towards the river. The water was rising fast and already the narrow spit of shore at the opening was covered. She rose on stiff legs, her lips trembling as the realization that the water was coming in so fast the exit was no longer viable. They were trapped at the back of a horseshoe. The water level continued to rise.

The wall behind them was the only reason the current was still manageable. There was nowhere to go but up.

"Dammit," she spit in anger. "This is no accident." Somehow their enemies had managed to let a massive torrent of water get released from the dam upstream. And the thought that they could exert that much control over the dam simply raised her anxiety another notch and increased the omnipresent feeling about the depth of their enemies' reach.

"Quick, over here," Maya said making eye contact with Rex. "Start digging a hole. We need to save the vase."

Rex did not question her and got on his knees and started excavating a hole.

She wrapped the crystal artifact in a blanket and then got on her knees and aided in the digging. The width of the beach was shrinking quickly. Once they had dug down about four feet, she placed the object in the hole, carefully concealed it with sand, then small river rocks and then packed it with more sand.

She hoped by placing it deep enough, the flood would not dislodge it and that they would be able to retrieve it in the future. She scratched the wall with a small stone, marking it for future reference.

JW and Rex began untying the horses, but it was too late. The inflow of water was too deep to overcome and the closer they got to the opening, the stronger the current. Foot by foot, their sanctuary was rapidly disappearing.

"On the horses," JW barked.

Maya took the copies of Wynn's diary and scattered the pages as a safety precaution. Whoever was behind this could not use these documents. She tucked her phone deep into her pocket as the water continued its steady rise.

"It has to abate at some point," JW offered with very little optimism in his voice.

Maya stared at the rising water, hope being drown out as it grew deeper.

Amongst the roar of water, a new sound appeared. It was clearly manmade, and it grew in intensity until it was so loud, it drowned out the rising tide. From above, a light appeared. Blinding in its intensity, she could not see beyond the muddled haze of illumination but discerned there was a helicopter hovering above.

A candle of hope flickered but she knew instinctively they were leaving the frying pan and into the fire—still, they would live. But for how long?

Like a hand from Heaven reaching down to them, a basket attached to a line appeared. The water was now up to the horses' bellies and they were getting restless, scared, and rightfully so. They were trapped.

"Rex, you go first," Maya insisted. "I'm going last." Before JW could argue she explained.

"If this is a kidnapping, I'm not letting them abandon you here."

Her voice left no room for argument and her logic could not be disqualified.

After each had been hauled up, with sadness she said her goodbyes to their faithful steeds and climbed into the basket.

CHAPTER 15
Layla - New York City

The buzzer announced the arrival of Father Book and Ron Tobias, the journalist the priest wanted Layla to meet. With the door ajar, she waited as their visitors climbed the three flights of stairs. Father Book gave her a paternal peck on the cheek, and she introduced Tavis to the two men. In turn, Book introduced Ron.

He appeared to be in his late sixties, glasses, a full head of graying hair. About five-foot-ten and generally fit. She considered her preconceived notions of career journalists. Either they were whiskey-drinking, chain-smoking, barrel-chested caricatures, or they were the field-hardened, slim-framed war correspondent types. Tobias was more typical of the latter. "Please, have a seat." Layla directed them to the couches.

"Ron was a reporter for the *New York Times-Chronicle* for over twenty-five years," Father Book began. "He has written a number of books that range from the missing weapons of mass destruction in Iraq to the attempted coup of the sitting president. It was his research into the operations of the bipartisan deep state and the back tracking of their power structure that has led me to believe his information may be of some use to your own investigations."

"When did you leave the *Times-Chronicle?*" Tavis asked.

"After the 2016 election," Ron said, removing his glasses and wiping them on his sleeve. "For most of my career I felt that I worked for the preeminent news organization in the world. That is until the age of a non-globalist president. Overnight the *Times-Chronicle* threw out all the rules of fair reporting.

"Now do not get me wrong. I am no fan of the man sitting in the oval office. And a lot that is negatively reported is justified. But this is more about political bias than it is about truthful reporting.

"When I learned that György Sorensen had acquired a significant stake in the paper, something that went unreported with no fanfare, I set out to research the man. I was wondering if there was a link to the hardened editorial position of the organization."

"And...?" Layla asked, sensing he had something significant to share. She knew who Sorensen was, he was often in the news.

He handed her a bound document. "I suggest you read it. Sorensen is a front man for your enemies. He was a Nazi collaborator. He made his fortune wrecking third world economies putting hundreds of millions of people into poverty. Everything he touches turns to misery. He has hundreds of NGOs set up, all with a focused aim of destroying the United States."

Her eyes widened. The shock that such a public figure was actively working against the interests of his adopted country seemed far-fetched.

He handed her a second bound collection.

"He is a minion of the Rothchilds, who have controlled both sides of every war since the seventeenth century. Nothing significant happens in this world that is not approved by them first."

The room had gone quiet while Tavis and Layla perused the two copies. Amidst moving lips, frowns of consternation, and faces hit by surprise and shock, the gravity of the evil they were up against weighed like a damp cloak.

Layla looked up and started the train of questions, which ran on for miles.

CHAPTER 16
Maya – Military Air Base

The man in the silver flight suit closed the door of the hovering chopper. Maya's final image was of the five horses floundering in the rising waters. They were trembling in fear. It was now seared into her memory. She prayed quietly and vowed to avenge their deaths.

The helicopter ascended to the top of the rim and turned towards Flagstaff. It was manned by a team of three. The pilot, the one now seated next to JW, who had attended the bucket lift, and a third man in dark glasses who sat in the copilot seat all said nothing.

"How did you know we were stranded?" JW asked the strapped in man.

Maya saw the nod from the front passenger. Establishing who was in charge.

"We got a report from a geologist crew that had seen you as they were returning from one of their surveying trips," he explained.

The chopper that had passed by two days ago. It was a bullshit answer, but she kept these thoughts to herself.

There was no further conversation for the next hour until up ahead, Maya saw the lights of a military airfield. When they landed, five armed men politely escorted them into an air-conditioned room. They were relieved of their backpacks and in all probability were being searched at this very moment.

She knew she should be scared or at least deeply concerned, but her anger seethed to the point that there was no room left for any other emotion.

Maya pulled out her phone, saw two bars, and quickly emailed all the photos of the lotus blossom to Layla. After which she deleted the photos and the emails. She cleared the trash can as a further precaution. She dropped her hands into her lap and covertly slipped the phone back into her pocket just as the sunglass man who had been in the front seat of the helicopter came into the room. He was with two soldiers who were dressed in military fatigues.

Maya and company were instructed to stand and put their arms out by their sides where they were professionally patted down and searched. Each was relieved of everything in their pockets, including their phones, wallets, and sunglasses.

The military men departed with their possessions. Mr. Shades, the name JW had given to the leader while they were waiting, invited them to sit. He took up a chair and placed it in front, looking at them. Crossing one leg over the other, the man introduced himself as Dan Malanga.

"I guess we got there in the nick of time." His tone hinted of savior, but his grin said gotcha.

"No doubt," Maya agreed. But what she was thinking was, *you orchestrated that flood, you bastard, so go screw yourself!*

Her intuition at the first sight of the rising waters was affirmed. These people had the power to open the dam, commandeer part of a military installation, take away everything they may have discovered, and act as if they were their saviors.

"We are lucky you found us," she said, showing no fear." I would not even know how to begin to thank you."

Pricks. We're still one step ahead of you.

"Perhaps..." he offered with a note of seriousness. He did a poor job hiding body language that read victory. "You could explain why you were so deep into a restricted area."

"Curiosity." She knew this was all theater. They would either release them with a warning or kidnap them. It did not matter how she answered.

Dan peppered them with question after question. This went on for hours. Eventually the randomness and lack of cohesion became obvious. He was wasting time. She considered that he was probably waiting for the soldiers to hack their phones and copy everything and was glad she had deleted all the photos.

But if true, it was a little worrisome. Though they were using relatively new burners, Maya could not recollect every text, call, or email that was now in the possession of her enemies.

It brought some small satisfaction that she had had the wherewithal to delete the photos, emails, and trash can. Unless they did an actual forensics dissection, the vase would remain their secret.

With the questions beginning to slow, Maya killed time by studying her surroundings, counting rivets in the ceiling, wondering about old water stains and rust in the corners. The room was a classic World War II corrugated barracks with a rounded roof and rectangular windows near the top.

It was dark outside, well past midnight. Eventually the soldiers came back, and their personal items were returned. A soldier whispered into the ear of Shades and she saw the curl of his lips. She assumed his easy manner rested on the unwarranted confidence that his three captives had discovered nothing.

"Ms. Harrington, Misters White Feather and Rexford... do not, and I mean *do not* let the U.S. Government find you in that restricted corridor again." His voice had turned ice cold and there was no mistaking this was not theater.

This comment surprised her. She did not expect to simply be released.

What's their game?

They were hustled to the airport where two men in black suits shadowed them to the door of their flight, bound for La Guardia.

CHAPTER 17
Maya - NYC

The big black sedan pulled up to the front of the building on Eighty-Sixth Street. It was the final in-your-face F.U. that had Maya totally pissed off.

It started at the airport in Arizona where each had been assigned to middle seats in the back of coach. They were intentionally placed rows apart from one another. When the flight landed at LaGuardia, two men were waiting at the top of the jetway. They hustled them to a car and delivered them here.

The message was crystal clear: *'We know who you are, where you are and who you associate with.'*

Somewhere between the cross currents of anger and fear, Maya picked through the confusing web of motive. She thought back to the attempts these people had made to capture her.

First someone tries to kidnap me in the Amazon, then they are successful in Peru, and now, they had us under full lockdown in Arizona but set us free. Why?

Her mind played out every scenario. There were only two things that she could conclude. Either they had changed their minds, or there was more than one group interested in her. And if that was the case, then who?

"Get out," scowled their escort.

♦ ≈ ♏ ≈ ♓ ♎ ♎ ♏ ■ ≈ ♋ ■ ♎

"Madness, the world has descended into total madness."

They entered to see Layla directing her lamentations at the television screen.

"Where's Tavis?" Maya's nerves were rattled, and she was stressed. Her first concern was for her friends. That they were safe and accounted for.

"He's at the library," Layla assured her. "Everything okay? How was Arizona?" Layla's query unleashed a litany of woes punctuated by Maya's overriding concern about their adversaries knowing this apartment was their base of operations.

Could they continue to speak freely or was the place bugged? Maya considered the dangers and the worst-case scenarios. It was her new reality. It was a new reality for all of her team.

All the while, hovering in the background was the flat screen television hanging from the red brick wall. It continued to pump out its gloomy glow of troublesome events from around the world. Troubles that had the fingerprints of the Hidden Hand smeared all over them.

"The Middle East is on fire because of the Israelis' decision to retake the Temple Mount..." The announcer's voice reported in grave tones.

"Iran, with the backing of Russia, has moved a brigade of modern tanks and guided missile systems into Syria, and they are threatening Israel. If they do not back down from the retaking of what was once the place of Solomon's Temple, war is inevitable..."

And on top of all that, the act of terrorism in the Canary Islands was the most frightening. Authorities did not know who controlled this weaponized virus and as of today, still had not been able to identify how they would contain the wildfire if it were to be released into the general population.

Her thoughts turned to God. Only a few weeks ago she would have laughed at such superstitious folly.

Was the Coronavirus just a preamble? Or maybe he allowed the first pandemic to happen so we could prepare for something much worse...

Turning from the television, Maya gathered Layla, Rex and JW around the large farmer's table. It was late afternoon, and the sun was streaming in from the western horizon. The dust motes were shuffling along on invisible currents and Maya heard the imaginary strains of Tom Petty's *Free Fallin'*.

With a head full of worry, her eyes traced the grain lines embedded in the old wood planking. And for whatever reason, this caused her to recall the landlord's mention that both Robert Downey, Jr. and Tom Cruise had lived here at some point in the past.

What stories these floors could tell.

She considered that both actors had gone on to be quite successful. Clearly, no one had handed their careers to them. Her train of thought was so discordant to everything that was happening, it became the knife she needed to cut through the veil of despondence. Her mind was growing clear and hazy outlines of a plan began to form. She was about to change the game.

We can sit around feeling helpless, or we can go on offense.

"Layla, did you meet with Father Book?" she asked, sitting up. "Was the reporter any help?"

Layla retrieved two bound books sitting on the credenza. The first was titled, *György Sorensen.* And the second, *Rothchilds, Illuminati and the New World Order.*

"I'd start with Sorensen," she suggested.

Maya flipped through the pages. The book was divided into subsections and had an essay feel to it. Headlines such as, Sorensen and Madame Secretary Rape Billions from Russia, Sorensen Operation S.O.S-Secretary of States.

"In a democracy it does not matter how many people vote, only who counts the votes."

The deeper she dug, the more lurid the headlines. The darker the truth, the greater the sense of evil. There was no doubt this guy was a bad dude. Wringing her hands, she blew out a series of breaths. Trying to relieve the growing anxiety as she placed a name and face on her adversary.

"Can you set up a meeting with Father Book?" she asked. "Also, did you get the photos I sent?"

"Already in the archive," Layla affirmed.

Back in March at the onset of their project, Layla had created an encrypted web-based storehouse of all their findings, photographs, and documents. It was also a secure communications hub.

"Good. I have an idea." Thinking that the possibility of being bugged was more than likely, she suggested. "Let's step out on the back porch." After closing the apartment door, she set out to illustrate a rough idea of her plan.

"It's time we go on offense…"

CHAPTER 18
Maya - Café De Paris- NYC

It was a few minutes after two o'clock. Maya noticed the lunch crowds were returning to the office. Even the bureaucrats at the United Nations who worked just down the street had to go through the motions of justifying their existence.

The bustle of passersby's comingled with blaring horns, chattering voices and a host of other distractions, and all converged to form the tapestry of another day in New York City.

Maya was the first to spot the priest out on the curb and waved him over to their table. "Father Book, it is good to see you again."

Maya had met Father Bohdan 'Book' Halibshuck only once—in Boca Raton when he had delivered a letter from her father. The fact that Book and her dad had been friends since college gave her enough of a comfort level that she used his preferred nickname. In fact, she was so comfortable she skipped the social preliminaries and went right to a question about the Sons of Jared.

Father Book had acknowledged the last time they met that he was a member of that ancient secret society. An organization dedicated to fighting the enemies of God who are under the control of dark spirits.

"If we are battling forces that the Sons of Jared refer to as the Celestial Mafia, would that make you Elliot Ness?"

With a raised brow, Book hesitated to smooth down the whiskers on each side of his mouth. Maya could see it was a diversionary tactic. Something he had likely developed over the years as he sought a proper response.

"Well, I guess we're not here to talk about the weather, are we?"

Smile lines crinkled around his blue eyes. Adopting a more serious tone, he leaned in.

"I can see you have a million questions, and I have just over an hour. So how can I be of service?"

"What do you know about the Lion's Gate?"

She was testing him. Would he answer something about a cosmic happening as was their previously held belief, or would he allude to her assumption that she had a big role to play in man's destiny? Or nothing at all? His choice would answer a lot of needless questions.

He took a deep breath, exhaled, and relaxed back into his chair. "So, you figured it out," he beamed. "And you understand the secret of the Sacred Manna. Your father hoped you would."

"Yes," she said with a slight nod. She was glad that he had chosen door number two, for it affirmed what she had come to accept. The randomness of the people that surrounded her, was maybe not so random after all.

"So my father was aware of my role all along..." The tone was part statement, part question. His reply came in the form of a confirming smile.

She smiled back and hopscotched to a different topic.

"You know that in the Book of Job, Satan and God engaged in a little side wager. God let Satan have his way with his loyal servant to prove a point, but Satan was given limitations. So I wonder..."

Pools of sunlight slid over the tables as rays peaked out from the patches of blue. The fast-moving clouds gave evidence that a storm was on the horizon. Maya considered it a metaphor for what was coming.

"If I am to be an instrument of God's will, is my enemy still free to do with me as he chooses? Or are there rules? Will God protect me and those who are part of this quest?"

The conundrum of why suddenly they were no longer trying to kidnap her was a scab she continued to pick. But by implication, she had widened her worldview about their enemies. She connected them to the cosmic game.

With thoughts hanging in the air, Maya considered that a normal person would view these changes as erratic, worrisome, or maybe even dangerous. But after all they had been through over the last twelve weeks, this had crushed even the most dearly held walls of convention. It was a good question, and Book tilted forward.

"Free will and the laws of physics are generally constraints that hem us in," he told her. "But that is not to say that sometimes incredible coincidences won't occur. And sometimes, the paths of others cross our own at just the right moment in time.

"Have these been set by the one who already knows who needs to be where when…" Father Book let his voice trail off. Maya would need to come to her own conclusions.

Maya thought back to the large Indian who had waited on them on the Amazon ferryboat. He showed up at just the right moment.

Ordained or arbitrary?

"Don't tempt fate. You are not invincible. God has given you a clever brain, a group of good friends with diverse talents, and you have a gift, which is your edge over the enemy. They do not know the extent of your remote viewing. Keep that weapon a secret and never relax your security."

This was not the answer she wanted. She had hoped to be told she had an invisible shield. But right now, she did not have time to dwell on her disappointment.

"You have seen the news…"

Subtly shifting to her next topic, Maya set out to explain about her friend Austin, his role, his great grandfather, and the powder that the Hidden Hand snatched away just a day before they arrived. This led her to pull her phone out and scroll through the photos of drawings Wynn created over a hundred years ago.

"Disease, nuclear war…" Her voice trailed off, vocalizing the dread that was steadily building inside of her. She handed him the phone and he viewed each picture more carefully.

His lips formed barely audible verses of scripture. Finally, he looked up and confirmed her worst fears.

"What has been foretold—it is starting."

His comments affirmed what she suspected he already knew. She reiterated both the prophesy of King Shulgi from 2024 BCE and the Sumerian Prophesy before that. She further explained how they believed the eclipse of 2017 was the trigger to the seven years of tribulation outlined in the Book of Revelation in the New Testament of the Bible—an apocalypse that would culminate in a colossal inferno of end times events in 2024, just a little over three years away.

She led him to her conclusion that for some inexplicable reason, she was being guided as the Lion, the one who was to open doors for mankind. Accepting of, but uncomfortable in, *'the role of hope for the world.'*

His body language never rejected her ideas, his attention never wavered from her comments.

"How do I do this?" Maya finally asked.

This was the crux of the meeting. Seeking a path. There was a soft plea in her voice, a hope that maybe he could fulfill.

If he is not rejecting my theory of being chosen by God, then he would have to assume he is part of all this as well…

His expression changed and she waited, expecting an answer.

"Our adversary has a plan to reduce the world's population to under five hundred million," Book told them. "They have made this spectacularly clear for all to see when they anonymously erected a Stonehenge type monument in Elbert County, Georgia, which is known as the Georgia Guidestones."

Maya made a mental note to look into this. As he continued, she could not shake the idea that the recent global Covid-19 virus that had killed so many people might be part of their handiwork.

"As I mentioned to you the last time we met, our organization is very old and we have informants in almost every hall of power throughout the world. We have learned that our adversaries have planned a two-prong attack, which, from your photographs, would seem to have been foreshadowed by Wynn Lambert. Nuclear war and plague.

"I am not talking about the pandemic currently sweeping the globe. I am talking about the plague we witnessed in the Canary Islands. We do not know when or where this horror will be released, but it will—and it will make this current virus look like child's play. "

"And?" The heat of fear and worry flushed her face with fever.

"As far as nuclear threats, we are stymied. We are hoping that with your talents, perhaps you can help us find out where and when this might occur so we can attempt to stop them." His tone had gone from one of assurance, to a plea of his own.

Maya made no comment. She was at the point where she fully embraced her role that was linked to her destiny. "And from what little I have gleaned—you think György Sorensen is a good place to start?"

He nodded.

"You mentioned to Layla a few months ago that my father was helping you in exposing the Hidden Hand. I am not sure if you know, but one of my colleagues, Tim Rexford, used our last bit of Manna and visited my father on the other side."

A knot of sorrow gripped her as she considered the loss of any known chance of reuniting with her father. The fact that Rex had met him and not her, only made the wound feel deeper.

"Tim Rexford." Book smiled with familiarity. "He was like a son to your father."

"Yes," she agreed, as if it was common knowledge. "Getting back to the Manna, you knew of the hidden cache of powder in Sinai, and I assume you know it was taken by the enemy. Do you know of any more anywhere?"

His body language said it all. Disappointed, she asked her next question.

"Do the Sons of Jared have knowledge of how to make it? For us to be successful against such a powerful adversary, we are going to need more than just my remote viewing." She sat back hoping, pleading with her eyes. Expectancy was in the air, its palpitations felt tinged by unseen forces.

"Our resources are very old and our achieves very deep," he said in a low whisper. "I personally have never partaken of the Sacred Manna, but many of the Sons of Jared have. I will ask the Elders to scour our network for information and I will get back to you.

"As far as any powder that may remain, when Professor Hamid told you back in Egypt that this was the last known cache on Earth, as far as I know, he was telling the truth."

This landed like a thud that concluded their lunch.

"Please see what you can learn from György Sorensen," he said. Then, with a weak smile, he changed the atmosphere. "Our organization is very old and very secret. But we have a long history of knowledge and resources. I will find someone somewhere who will be able to help you."

CHAPTER 19
Maya - Searching Sorensen

Maya returned to her own apartment on Sixty-Fourth Street. She found comfort that her old friend, Big Bird was still sitting in the window keeping an eye on her. Sesame Street's studios were in the building across the street and for years the giant yellow friend had been a fixture.

If they know about Eighty-Sixth Street, then they know where I live. If they want to kidnap me, they will. Her rationalizations toggled between the practical and the probable.

She decided the back of the apartment would be better for remote viewing. It had less street noise and was quieter than her combined living room and kitchen.

There was a small window by the side of her bed that looked into the shadowed courtyard below. Hemmed in by the residential buildings on Sixty-Fourth and Sixty-Fifth Streets, it was typical of New York.

City code required the space behind these buildings to remain open to fire escapes in case of an emergency. In all the years she had lived here, Maya had never seen a soul down there. She liked that she could open her window, let in fresh air, and yet it was private and predictable.

She settled into a cross-legged position with her back below the windowsill. Her goal was György Sorensen. It was getting easier and easier to slip into the theta state. The experience was addictive like no other drug on Earth. Total freedom from the physical world.

She set her intentions and began the process of inhalation and exhalation, focusing on the space between her nose and upper lip. One by one, she boxed each errant thought until that sweet sensation of release set her spirit free.

Staring down at her body, her breathing was steady and then her thoughts were whisked through the ephemeral world of spirit to another place.

It was an office, it was night, and sitting alone, at an ample desk in a plush room of what looked to be a London townhouse, sat the eighty-year-old man who had crushed economies by shorting weak currencies, causing millions and millions of people to be thrust into untold poverty.

A man who had aided the Nazis in rounding up Jews as a teen. The man who had seized control of one of America's main political parties in 2003. And the man who was the public face of the New World Order. From all she had learned, even with a net worth north of thirty billion dollars, he was just middle management.

She arrived at a very auspicious moment. Mr. Sorensen was logging into his computer. Maya hovered over him watching as he entered a complex password into the field. She committed it to memory.

Who is he writing to?

Energy follows thought and she was sucked into the email and came out on the other end. It was a room full of servers, a dozen monitors and keyboards. It was a complex relay center.

An elderly woman of eastern European appearance saw the incoming email, transferred it from one system to another with a flash drive, and then forwarded it. Maya followed it the same way. This time she found herself in an Arabian bazaar and a bearded man was reviewing the message on a smart phone.

None of his communication is direct. He uses a cut out. Added security?

She read the message, but it was written in such a way as to be rendered unintelligible.

The cactus in the desert is ready to bloom, but unleavened bread will not rise. TM would like to know when we can eat.

She returned to the initial Sorensen location and explored it more in depth. It was one of his homes, not a traditional working space. She inserted herself into his files but found no smoking gun. She tried to track his finances, but it seemed that all within his residence led nowhere. Remote viewing removed all physicality from one's experience, but it did not stop her rising frustration.

She scanned his desk and saw he used an old-fashioned *At-A-Glance* monthly calendar. Something caught her attention.

In three days, he was going to Switzerland for the annual meeting of the secretive Bilderberger Group, and he had underlined an appointment with Charles Mann. She recognized the name but could not remember why.

She knew of this secret society, but only by what was allowed to be released into the press. JW had done research on them as part of his overall look into secret societies.

Who else will be there?

Instantly, she was inside the machine looking at a list of the 2020 BBG Conference attendees. A single name leaped out at her: Robert Vaherees.

Whoa, why is he on the list? Is he a friend of Sorensen?

She noticed dozens of other names. Titans of industry like Gates, Bezos, Fauci and a number of well-known politicians and media types. An idea began to form, which pulled her back to Sixty-Fourth Street. Maya immediately wrote down the username and password Sorensen had used; she knew a good hacker who might find it useful.

♦︎♒︎♏︎♒︎♓︎♎︎♎︎♏︎■︎♒︎♋︎■︎♎︎

It was twenty blocks from her Lincoln Center apartment to their workspace on Eighty-Sixth Street. Walking at a brisk pace, she arrived to find the team all engaged in various tasks, including JW, who nodded with a sigh as she sat down.

"How's it going?" There was a look of frustration on his face.

"I'm gonna head back to the Mesa. I need some help—maybe I can get it from the Akasha. I told Grandfather I would be there over the weekend."

Maya contrasted her remote viewing-directed dream journeys with her ayahuasca experience. She preferred her way better.

"Before you head west, care to run down to Georgia with me? Father Book suggested we visit Elberton and view the mysterious Georgia Guidestones. Sort of our own homegrown version of Stonehenge."

"Sure," he said with a shrug. "Why not? I can fly west from Atlanta."

"Good. I'll leave you to your misery then," she said, and left to make a call.

She stepped out to the back porch overlooking the area hemmed in by buildings. She needed to speak to Robert. When she saw he was on the Bilderberger list of invitees, her ideas for how she was going to go on offense had gained some shape.

Confront my enemy... Shake things up and see what happens!

"Good afternoon, Robert." Maya said, cradling the cell phone against her ear.

"Hello Maya, what a pleasant surprise. How are you? Are we making any progress?"

The progress he was referring was the expanded quest to include finding out more about Manna. She still had some reservations about sharing everything with him. After her escape from her kidnappers in Egypt, the story about the Manna and how her father had discovered its mystical qualities had all come out. But that was a few weeks ago.

After seeing his name in the computer of a known member of the Hidden Hand, those same concerns about why he had hired her resurfaced. And it was in that moment, the name of the person Sorensen was to meet with leapt out at her.

Charles Mann—fu...! He's the person who supplied Robert with our fake passports. Documents that undoubtedly had tracking devices inside of them that had allowed the Hidden Hand to always know where they were.

Suddenly her mouth felt dry. She originally agreed to work with Robert to take advantage of his resources to try and find her father. But she had never stopped worrying if he in turn was using her for the same reason. It was a tightrope she'd walked every day since meeting him.

Tread carefully girl, don't let your imagination run wild.

She fought the quiver in her voice, giving him a bland answer to the question.

"The entire team is tasked with researching the Manna. I will let you know the minute we make any real progress."

Maybe...

"So what can I do for you today?" His voice was light and non-threatening, which surprisingly relaxed her concerns. She actually liked Robert, he was thoughtful and kind, and he had always treated her with respect. It was the damn paranoia and the timing of his unsolicited offer back in March that had cast shade on his motives.

"Well, I happened to see a list of the current invitees to the Bilderberger summit in Lake Garda next week. I saw your name on the list. Are you attending?"

There was a pause at the other end. She could imagine the wheels that were turning. Billionaires were generally pretty sharp, and Robert was sharper than most. "And you would like to be my plus one?"

He didn't mean anything by that... did he? But she found her heartbeat starting to race.

"I would."

"May I ask why?"

Unsure what she hoped to find, truth was her best response.

"Honestly, I don't know why. But there are those who are after me and my father. And... well, I think stirring the pot a little may be revealing."

She could hear chuckling at the other end of the line.

"Ms. Harrington, I do like the way you think. I will have a jet waiting for you Thursday night."

For some reason, her suspicions fell away, at least temporarily as she let her mind wander towards what it would be like to be with him. What if...

Then he added. "I look forward to spending the weekend together."

CHAPTER 20
Maya - The Georgia Guidestones

"God, I hate Atlanta," Maya complained when she and JW became mired in stop-and-go traffic. Their GPS's time-of-arrival recalculated an additional hour onto their two-hour trip to Elberton.

"You seem tense. What is it?"

Maya stared out the window, rubbing her brow. "Something's changed. Do you think they could've made a trade?"

JW glanced in the rearview mirror, then slowed to let another car squeeze in front of them. "A trade?"

"Yeah, like they keep their hands off us and my father stops exposing their secrets. Over the last few weeks there have been no new revelations of the Hidden Hand," she clarified.

"Perhaps," he said, without much conviction. "Or... they feel they have us on a leash and want to see if we can discover the secret process for making the Manna. They have to assume your father has already discovered this."

On a leash... She had no idea what types of technology they could use to track and record them, but she had a pretty good idea of the face behind the trackers.

"Of course. That makes a lot more sense. So what do we know? The dossier on the Rothchild clan claimed their bloodlines go all the way back to Sumer. They believe they are direct descendants of King Nimrod. That means some of the Watchers from the time of Eden could be living among us today, behind great wealth and power. Do you think the Guidestones could have been placed here as a way to taunt God? Kind of like an in-your-face F.U.?"

JW nodded, checking the rearview again. "It's like Jacques said when we visited Gobekli Tepe. As the oldest creation ever known to man, we know these marvels of ancient engineering were placed at the spot where man supposedly exited the garden. And that they are and have always been the scoreboard in the cosmic game between God and Satan..."

"Yes, he who collects the most souls, wins," she said, parroting the words of their friend in Turkey.

Maya considered Adam and Eve being kicked out of the Garden and Satan's role as the final ruler of Earth. The ultimate New World Order as defined in the Book of Revelation. Satan, in his battle for control of the cosmic gameboard called Earth, was the true mastermind behind all the ills of mankind and each was a calculated move, like that of a chess master.

He would want that powder destroyed. For if man could see the big picture, he would not need to rely on faith alone.

"With the Earth currently containing as many as half the total of every human that has ever lived on this planet—if Satan could destroy Earth's remaining inhabitants... would he win?"

JW's eyes darted to the mirror then he muttered, "Shit."

Maya saw the red and blue flashing lights in the side mirror. *What the...?*

Her mind raced through every bad conclusion as JW pulled the car off the road,

The patrol car pulled in behind them and a Georgia trooper dressed in a pale blue uniform exited his vehicle. He adjusted the wide brim of his hat and approached the driver's side of the vehicle.

JW rolled down his window keeping his hands in view.

"Good afternoon officer, is there a problem?"

"Driver's license and registration," he said in a firm voice. "Ma'am, do you have identification?"

"Me?"

"Yes ma'am," he said politely, but with authority.

She bit back her desire to ask why he needed her identification, and they handed over their IDs. Maya watched in the mirror as he took them back to the patrol car.

"What do you think?" She asked JW.

Before he could reply, the officer stepped from his car and approached the passenger side of their vehicle. In one hand he held their licenses, in the other, a large envelope. His gait was casual and non-threatening. Maya put down the window as he approached. He handed both items to her.

"The Sons of Jared are praying for you," he said with an indiscernible expression. He then tipped his hat, returned to his car, and was gone.

Maya's pulse raced at the encounter. *Was he waiting for us? How would he know we were coming?*

She opened the packet and slid out several documents and photographs. She did a quick perusal.

This is Father Book's answer to my request.

She stopped on one photo in particular. It was old and faded, but it sent an electric current coursing through her.

"It's the vase," she said. The background was unfamiliar, but the image was identical to the one they had found.

JW scanned the traffic before pulling out onto the highway. "Let's keep moving."

As he eased onto the road, Maya went through the rest of the packet. There were photos of ancient obelisks, there were sheaths of Egyptian hieroglyphs, most annotated with English notes. On the whole, it appeared as if it the material might be related to the process of creating what here was referred to as the Shem-an-na, which she knew was simply another name for Manna. She knew the 'Sons' had come through for them and found comfort in knowing that there were others around who had their backs.

JW slowed to turn onto Highway 51. "You should probably photograph each page and upload them into the archives. Just in case."

It was a smart idea. After photographing each item, she would fit the sheaf back into the envelope. All except for one. It was different, it was a composite picture of an ancient cuneiform, photographed from multiple angles. The picture itself was old. She took this page, folded it into quarters and placed it under her foot inside her boot.

It was just after 2:00 P.M. when they arrived at the Guidestones. They were literally in the middle of nowhere. Sitting amongst cow fields, the parking lot was a gravel patch hemmed in by a large hedge of trees. There were not many people around, just a few tourists taking photographs.

Maya stepped from the car into a bath of deep southern humidity. Donning dark sunglasses, they approached the polished dedication marker that had an official government feel about it.

'*Let these be Guidestones to an Age of Reason*' read the capstone in classical Greek, Sanskrit, Egyptian hieroglyphics, and Babylonian cuneiform.

She slapped at a mosquito that had landed on her neck, then another. "Fricken' Georgia state bird," she muttered.

JW cracked a smile. "Look at the first commandment—the very top of the list. '*Maintain humanity under 500,000,000 in perpetual balance with nature…*' Most conspiracy theorists consider the purpose of the monument's ten edicts to be to establish the groundwork for a totalitarian world government," JW explained.

"The Ten Commandments of the Illuminati. Each of the edicts can be construed in numerous ways. But consider them from the perspective of a proposed 'New World Order.'

"Replace God and religion with an age of reason. Create a global set of laws and courts, thus one can ignore local officials, or anyone of authority not part of the new world order. The will of the many over the rights of the few, always the totalitarian excuse for individuals who are disappeared or abused."

Maya examined the four-ton granite slabs and took a series of photographs. But with the voracious appetite of mosquitos, intent on feasting on her, she had had enough.

"Ah, to be so sweet and so wanted," JW chuckled. "Let's head back to the car."

Another couple followed their leave. As they entered the parking lot, Maya's instincts bristled. She didn't like the look of these two. They were dressed like tourists, but it was too obvious. They seemed shifty and had an agenda. Her gut was screaming alarm as the woman pulled in close and pushed the nozzle of a pistol into JW's back.

Her body shielded them from the two other people who were still taking selfies at the monument.

Her companion, a man dressed in a NASCAR T-shirt and wearing a Confederate cap, searched their car while Maya and JW were held at bay. He found the envelope, opened it, and showed it to his companion.

She smiled to reveal her tobacco-stained teeth. "So, our information was right." The woman wheezed in a smoker's rasp. "Those Sons of Jared whores were going to meet you here. Let me guess, you were stopped along the way?"

WTF—first the Sons know where we are, now the Hand?

Maya glared. Her palms were sweating, and blood was coursing anger through her veins. Just when she had convinced herself they were not interested in capturing her, they turn up waiting for her.

"Buddy, do your thing," the woman instructed. Her trained mutt jabbed a large hunting knife into the rear tire, to either slow them down, or just to be a prick. Its hiss evidenced that they would need to change the tire before they could leave.

"Adios," she waved. "Give my regards to the priest."

"The priest?" It left her with the same blank expression as JW as they departed like they were the Dukes of Hazzard—gravel flying in a trail of dust.

CHAPTER 21
JW - Wild Horse Mesa

Cresting the sage-brushed hills, JW was warmed by the iconic sight of the old church steeple still hugging the Sanchez Reservoir. He drove past the worn wooden building and followed the shore towards his grandfather's home.

To his left, across the lake, loomed snowcapped mountains, their reflection mirrored on the pristine waters.

"Hello Grandfather," JW said, wrapping him in greeting. His paternal father was now with the spirits, but this man had raised him like his own.

"My son," Nascha said with a warm smile. He directed them to a log sitting by the lake. "I've seen more of you in the last six months than in the previous six years."

His visits had been more frequent since he joined Maya's quest. And after years of wandering without ever finding his totem, his grandfather, bearing the mantle of tribal shaman, had watched the murky waters of his fate emerge.

His totem in the spirit world became clear. Soaring Eagle. *'The one who is most noble and will soar higher than the rest.'*

With this designation, JW could see that Nascha knew the nature of this visit surrounded his path. A path that the will of the Creator set down long before man ever walked the Earth. And because he was keenly aware of Nascha's thoughts, he could see in his beloved relative's gaze that this knowledge was what fueled the glow of his pride.

"I have started the brew," Nascha said. The sun-drenched lines crinkled around his eyes.

"And Wild Joe?" JW was referring to another seasoned Ayahuascaeros in their tribe.

"Yes—he will be with us." Nascha added an odd proclamation without further elaboration. "This journey will be different."

Different? JW didn't know what to think, he had only done this a few times.

They spent the remaining light of day in chit chat, the catch-up banter of family. When Nascha asked about Maya, he must have seen JW flinch, so he quickly moved on.

"Tell me, have you reached out to this man Drune?" there was a subtle shift of his tenor.

"No Grandfather," said half-heartedly. "I put a call into his institute but have heard nothing."

"Ahhh… that is too bad," Nascha said, pursing his lips with a slight tilt of the head.

The winds of late afternoon had picked up and the lake was now tipped in small white caps. The roiling waters caused the reflected mountains to shimmer in the troughs.

"This man Drune," Nascha said, looking up for the roiled waters. "The spirits have said he is a guide, perhaps he is yours…"

The smile in his eyes was telling. JW realized his beloved grandfather saw the truth that he had not made much of an effort to locate this man.

"I will find him," JW asserted, now feeling a little guilty that his grandfather had attempted to help him and in all that had happened, he had given it a weak try. *I will find this man,* he vowed silently.

He began rocking on the old log and bumped his massive shoulders intentionally into his Grandfather. A gentle thump that made all things right again. The wind, the water, and Mother Nature. They all sat together in the harmony of the moment.

◆〰Ⅲ〰⯑⯑⯑Ⅲ■〰☉■⯑

The sun sank into the color of an Indian sky. Soon the stars split the night with diamonds. Wild Joe was down by the lakeside fueling the fire. Each piece of fresh wood caused sparks to rise up into the night, competing for attention with the twinkling lights above.

The ayahuasca was bubbling in an old iron kettle. JW wondered how many times this pot had brewed the sacred potion of the indigenous world. This would be the fourth time in his life he had partaken of the dream journey.

He knew that both Wild Joe and his grandfather had probably lost count of their own journeys decades ago.

Nascha approached. By the vigor of his walk and the tone of his voice, JW knew he was now Shaman, spiritual guide of the Four Corners.

"Are you ready?"

Nascha wore the patient expectation of the tribal Shaman, JW understood he was waiting for him to divulge the route for this journey. The route he had culled, categorized, and defined on the flight west and the subsequent drive from Albuquerque, through Santa Fe and up into the San Luis Valley of Southern Colorado.

"I have gathered many papers and many photos that I believe are related to the essentials in creating the Sacred Manna," JW explained. "What I want to understand is, do I have all that I need? What is the recipe and how do I initiate the process?

"And..." he hesitated as he tried to formulate his grand desire in a simple, concise sentence. "If we are gifted with this knowledge, how can we use this to save mankind?"

JW sensed the warm glow that fused through Nascha, the father—not the Shaman. They walked down to the water's edge, each taking a seat upon logs that faced one another through the fire. The cauldron was bubbling, and the acrid smell of burnt grapefruit permeated the air.

JW's hands felt sweaty with anticipation and there was a pounding in his ears. The Shaman gave each of them a cup and he downed his with a single gulp. This was the best way, for it tasted like hell.

Purging what little food remained in his stomach, JW slid his butt to the ground until his back was resting against the log. His body was starting to disconnect from physical sensation. He leaned back and closed his eyes. Immediately, patterns formed behind his lids. Green triangles, blue squares. As they grew in neon intensity, they thickened, blossomed, and morphed into three-dimensional images of more and more complex patterns. The collage became dense like a million indistinguishable threads that made up a quilt.

111

Soon, all JW could hear was Wild Joe's soft whistling. It was a slow haunting melody that embraced him. It worked its magic and like a tender blade, it reached deep into his soul, setting his spirit free.

Able to roam without restriction or restraint, and unbound by human limitations, his spirit took flight and rose high up into the cosmic pools of light amongst the siren song of the celestial spheres. Through the veil, he raced to another dimension. That of the Manikari and the Akasha. The great vault that housed echoes of every action, thought, feeling or emotion that had ever transpired.

Higher and higher he flew. As the tapestry faded away and the energetic twinkling of a billion points of light beckoned, he saw the iconic stars of Orion boldly straddling the Heavens.

A soft radiant figure of shimmering blue light sidled up next to him and she took his hand. *Grandfather said this would be different.* Anxiety should have washed over him, but instead, he felt no fear and willingly succumbed to her lead. She was taking him back to Earth.

He let the spirit lead him where she will. Casting a final glance at the Heavens, he saw the three dominant stars of Orion began to change, to morph, suddenly no longer the points of light that held up the warrior's sword, but now they had become three animals. *Camels?*

JW struggled to look back but they were diving headlong towards the Earth. From his periphery, he saw that the transparency of these camels solidified and then there were riders upon them. Men of flowing Arabic dress. A female voice spoke inside his head.

'*They are Sabeans, the star watchers of old. These were the Magi of Bethlehem.*'

The blur across time and space deepened. They plunged through a foggy gauze and once through, came to a rapid stop. They were still in space, but it felt dirty, stained, and worn. Hovering in front of them was the blue crystal from the cave. This was followed by the sensation of an adrenaline rush.

Is she showing me the keys to the process?

It pulsed, light flowing in and out, in and out. Beams refracted from each facet of the gemstone. JW stared transfixed, studying the light, its pulse and its rhythm.

The inbound source of light was from beyond. It poured down from the Heavens like a river of energy.

And there was Orion, a force to be reckoned with, standing as if unassailable. He had a sudden thought of the Sumerian Prophesy.

The Kimah and Kesil? Guardians of the Heavens?

Like a lung, the breath of the universe exhaled. The outward dispersion was like a wave. And with each respire, the pulse pushed the stain back a little bit further.

Wisdom, the name he applied to the light being, opened her arms in a wide gesture. Through her power, she manifested two obelisks, one on each side of the blue crystal.

There was an explosion of brilliance as a cavalcade of starlight fused into the tips of the shaped stones. This sent a million little time nuggets manifesting as sparks, pouring into the crystal. It was a steady stream inhaled deep into the bowl. When the torrent stopped, all around them it began to snow. And all around them there were swirls and slurries.

Manna?

There was no time to digest, no time to think, they were on the move again. As the universe had flattened into a two-dimensional realm, the Earth took the appearance of a map. And upon it were placed the sacred sites from Maya's grid of the Master Builders. Beams of light shot up from each and he was confused.

The grid? Orion? The vase? What? What? WHAT does it mean?

The falling snow drifted towards the shafts of light, fueling them with increased wattage, radiance, thickness, and glow.

Then he saw a vision manifest before him. A dark malignant object hurtling through space aimed at his beloved planet. A sudden sensation of fear, and then sorrow overwhelmed him.

Then as suddenly as it appeared, it dissolved as a ripple began to spread outwards from the Earth. The dirty stain of space cleared away like pollution washed by a summer rain.

With the sky glittering fresh, the constellation of Virgo poked out amongst the panoply of stars. In his periphery was Orion. They were drawing closer to Earth and the continent of Europe loomed large. He did not understand.

Spica and the other stars of the constellation Virgo broke free from their tether, as if space could no longer contain them. They fell to the ground and landed in France, where they glowed.

'*The churches,*' said the angelic voice of Wisdom. It was an answer, but it was a riddle. Allegory or guidepost? He did not know. The Heavens smiled at his thoughts, tranquility became a rhythmic tide and peace washed over them.

But the journey was not over, not yet.

The Earth morphed from a two to a three-dimensional image. And the Angel called Wisdom reached out and removed the Great Pyramid of Giza as if plucking a stone from a stream. She lay it over the North Pole. It grew in size until it touched the planet with all four points of its base. One of these being the famous Four Corners of the American Southwest. The angel mouthed something, it felt like goodbye. No, that was not it. It was '*until we meet again.*'

JW gaped in open wonder. Tipping his head back he closed his eyes. Letting out a gasp, he was suffused with a feeling of contentment when he awoke to the low grumble of Wild Joe.

"Now that was definitely different from anything I've ever seen," Nascha's friend said.

JW opened one lid, then the other. Coming out of the dream journey, his brain overcompensated like a compass until it could steady to its true north.

His thoughts repeated the journey and logged each symbol and segment for further analysis.

Two things were clear, they had to get that vase back from the canyon. And he needed to step up his efforts to find this man Drune. The man who had used the metaphor of the Great Pyramid touching points upon the globe when explaining Sacred Geometry and the Flower of Life to his grandfather years and years ago.

CHAPTER 22
Maya - Lake Garda, Italy

Other than a steward, Maya had flown by herself across the Atlantic. She had rested in the private sleeping quarters of the exquisitely appointed Gulfstream. Robert had sent her a copy of the Bilderberger itinerary along with recommended dress for the specific events in which she would be allowed to participate. There were many gatherings, which for her, were mostly off limits.

Nearing approach, she changed out of her Lululemon's into a chic outfit Layla had chosen. As usual, her friend's taste was perfect. Like a chameleon, Maya was now one of the moneyed class.

When they had landed at Comando Aeroporto Lionello Caffarati, the tarmac was jammed with luxurious aircraft. Their abundance was creating a problem. Many were now being diverted to other airports after dropping off their passengers. She had never considered how much wealth could be accumulated by so few. These people had a collective worth in the trillions.

The Grand Hotel Fasano was a long, narrow six-story building nestled upon the shores of Lake Garda. The grand foyer had an old-world charm of dark wooden arches and coffered ceilings that drew Maya's eyes to the expansive lakeside terrace beyond the ornate atrium.

Here the waters were clear, the sky was blue, the air lush and the temperature exquisite. The complex was walled by tall cypress trees, date palms and ample willows that thrived in the Italian Lake District.

The heady scent of money was widespread. Men were smartly dressed in crisp whites and the woman were draped in Gucci and Dolce and Gabbana. Jewels—the value of which could feed a large family for a lifetime—dangled from the young women.

Did men bring mistresses to an event like this?

Probably their secretaries, Maya thought euphemistically.

After checking in and being shown to her room, Maya examined the suite Robert had reserved for her. It was larger than her apartment. She opened the French doors to take in the view of the lake. Below was a large pool and she could see the sun worshippers arrayed in private alignments. Beyond was a pier that jutted out into the translucent waters.

She had most of the day to kill. Robert would not arrive until later in the afternoon, and her first commitment was the conference's opening reception at 7:00 P.M. The Bilderbergers had taken over the Scaligero Castle, an ancient fortress at the southern end of the city. That would be her first chance to assess and engage her enemies. György Sorensen, the Rothchilds, and the group that was enigmatically labeled 'The 300.'

Sorensen was her target. Though he was a billionaire thirty times over, Ron Tobias had referred to him as merely mid-management. And reminded her that the Rothchild family was the octopus and György but a suction cup on a tentacle.

♦♒♏♒♓♎♎♏■♒♋■♎

Maya decided to take a vision hop through the castle to get a lay of the land. This was where the first shots would be fired. This is where she would go on the offensive.

She was becoming so adept at slipping into the theta state that the closing of curtains to block out the sun was more of a ritual than a requirement. In mere minutes, she was looking down at herself, cross-legged, eyes closed and her body's breath a practiced mantra.

She let go and was instantly in the looming shadow of the ancient Scaligero Castle. It was a grey stone edifice whose coloring matched the rock cliffs that protruded out into the waters across the lake.

There were two rectangular turrets designed for archers, both rising up and out of the lake framing each side of the marina. These anchored the lone tower that was the center of the fortress. It reminded her of the prison from which Rapunzel had let down her long golden locks.

The castle was surrounded by the lake on three sides and a moat that bordered a narrow cobblestone street that separated it from a hopscotch of city dwellings that fronted the castle.

On the street were a phalanx of Carabinieri, the local law enforcement. Through her remote viewing she suspected that the guests would arrive by boats that slipped unseen into the marina, whose high walls protected the participants from view of the press and onlookers.

The only point of vulnerability was a small peninsula that extended out into the water beyond the walls of the castle's marina. It was separated by a mere fifty meters of lake and had a clear view of the arched tunnel that boats used to pass under and into the secluded privacy of the aquatic entry.

And just beyond were cliffs that rose from the lake with elegant homes high above looking down on the town. She saw a shadow, and her thoughts drew her to a natural opening at the base of the cliff face. Empty beer bottles exposed a hidden drinking place.

Probably local teens.

She altered her intent and returned to the other building that dominated the point, this perceived vulnerability. She was not surprised by the presence of black dressed militia without insignia or rank. This was the real security. Those tasked by their masters who had unlimited funds to provide protection and to ferret out anyone who should not be there or was no longer welcome.

The latter was of mild concern, for she fully intended to wear out her welcome. Here she would lay down the gauntlet.

Before leaving for Europe, she had made a lot of preparations. One of these was to have Rex waiting for her call. She was going to shake the tree, and using his viewing skills, he was going to gather the fruit.

◆ ≈ ♏ ≈ ♓ ♎ ♎ ♏ ■ ≈ ♋ ■ ♎

Scaligero Castle

"Miss Harrington," Robert said in admiration. "At the risk of repeating myself, you look stunning."

Maya's heart beat a little faster and she could feel herself blush. But she had seen many in the hotel lobby casting approving glances her way. This caused a soft glow which was projected as confidence.

Robert was in a classic black tuxedo. And though the trimmings leaned minimalist, his totality was elegant and relaxed. He was clearly in his element.

But most eyes were on her. She wore a floor length off-the-shoulder satin Valentino gown. She felt a surge of confidence, like a young movie star who knew she owned the room.

"Shall we?" Robert asked, slipping his arm into hers. "The night awaits us."

The hotel was strictly limited to guests of the conference. Security was discreet, but it was there. Without exception, everyone's credentials were checked at various points.

They proceeded outside where dozens of Riva Classics were waiting alongside the quay. Their wooden hulls gleamed with craftsmen's care.

"Mr. Vaherees," waved a man from one of the finest boats on the wharf. "My lady."

Maya stepped into the craft in her long silver gown. The helmsman smiled as he offered a helping hand. They sat in the cream-colored banquette where a bottle of Dom Perignon was being chilled.

Pulling away from the flotilla, the driver maintained a comfortable pace, which abated Maya's concern that the wind would disrupt the effort she had put into getting her hair exactly the way she wanted it.

She loved the freedom of the open water. Reaching one arm over the side, she felt the cool spray glisten on her skin, clean and fresh. While she was relishing the pristine waters, Robert reached into a side compartment. She thought he was going to retrieve champagne flutes, but instead he brought out a rectangular velvet case.

"Final touches on an already perfect masterpiece," he said, and opened the box.

Words stuck in her throat. It contained a diamond necklace that was probably worth millions. She half expected him to snap it closed like in the movie *Pretty Woman*.

"May I?" Robert took the necklace from the box and delicately laced it around her neck. His touch sent a jolt through her. Its tingling warmth contrasted with the cool stones that caressed her skin.

The dichotomy of emotions within—*can I trust him*—versus a growing infatuation, was forcing her to pick a side. She just didn't know which one.

The boatsman kept a steady pace as he followed the shoreline. Robert pointed out various castles on the distant hills and grand estates along the shoreline. The irrelevant banter had the effect of soothing away the social binds of their working relationship. The formality that had been so prevalent in their previous meetings had all but vanished here on the romantic lake of storybook dreams.

He explained who owned each of these luxurious estates and though the family names could be found threaded throughout the history books of Europe, his tutorial offered a little more insight of a personal nature to each of the current owners.

"I never knew you were such a gossip," she quipped unabashedly. She had a pounding heartbeat and a fluttery sensation within. The scale was tipping in his favor.

"The picadilloes of the rich," he said in relaxed repartee. "The older the money, the stranger the twist. Most of these estates have been owned by the same families for so long, there is little origination documentation to be found."

She considered how old the aristocrats of Europe were and how young the American experiment was in comparison. She considered how many of her countrymen's strings were pulled from clandestine gatherings held within those ancient buildings.

As the looming castle drew near, boats began to form up in an aquatic conga line, each dancing unhurriedly into a position of turn. And Maya arrested her longings and set her mind on the task before her. She pulled her phone from a small clutch and sent a one-word text. 'Showtime.'

The castle had been transformed into a lavish tapestry of wealth, power, and entitlement. She knew that high ranking politicos from many countries peppered the crowd of international financiers and famous movie stars. By a grand banister, the recent head of the CIA was talking to a dark man dressed in ceremonial African garb. Tuxedo-attired servants with flutes of champagne were never more than a few steps away.

Maya recognized the movie star Misty Monique who was surrounded by an entourage of admirers.

"She's beautiful," she admired aloud, causing Robert to turn and follow her gaze.

"She is." I have met he once before. Her real name is Reynolds, but she changed it to Monique for the big screen."

"Good evening, Robert," an older portly man said in interruption. "And who is this lovely creature?" His leering eyes fixated on Maya's décolletage.

"Maya Harrington, meet Reggie Balforth."

Maya had an instant dislike for the man. His mannerisms encapsulated everything she hated about grotesque people who thought they were superior, entitled, and immune to the niceties of society.

"Lord Balforth," he reminded.

She thought him a pompous twit as she put forth her hand and forced a smile.

"LORD Balforth is the Exchequer for the Bank of England," Robert explained in exaggerated deference.

"I see, the keeper of coins," Maya retorted in the most diminutive tone she could muster.

He stiffened, whereas Robert fought to swallow a broadfaced grin.

"Well," he said, backing away. "Perhaps we can catch up later."

"Touché," Robert whispered as he drew her in close.

Maya had been partially candid with Robert about why she wanted to join him at this conference. But only partially. Though she did not divulge her sources, she had explained that her intelligence contacts had identified György Sorensen as a member of the group who may have been behind her recent kidnappings.

She further revealed that Charles Mann, whom Robert had contacted to help find these people and provide her and JW with new identification and credit cards, had a relationship with Sorensen.

He never asked about her sources, though Maya suspected he related it to her remote viewing skills. This both comforted her and worried her. Again, she found herself straddling that tightrope.

Robert had said nothing, his poker face remained unreadable. But he neither rejected the idea nor looked at her as if she had conspiracy in her eyes.

They continued deeper into the gathering, and Robert stopped along the way to introduce Maya to influential people. She was impressed at how easily he assimilated, that he knew everyone's names and had a pertinent quip to share with each. But mostly, she was awed at the level of respect that was conferred upon him. Respect shown by some of the richest and most powerful people in the world. It was almost as if he was in a class of his own.

This sent a tingle though her body. The heady feeling of being surrounded by power and being the woman on the arm of someone so respected caused her heart to race and also bolstered her confidence.

And unlike that pompous twit Balforth, she could see that Robert's reputation was not one that was prone to dalliance. The respect she was given when meeting other participants was never feigned.

"Charles," Robert said as they approached a man who was in his early sixties, who looked quite fit and had a slight tinge of grey at the temples.

He turned and smiled a big affable grin that seemed genuine and not forced. She was learning that this was one of the hallmarks of high society, the persuasive posture one could maintain as they politely stuck a dagger into you.

"Charles Mann, Dr. Maya Harrington."

The introduction caused a slight palpitation of breath and suddenly her mouth felt dry. She had the sensation of being exposed. As cover, she deflected into the armor of knowledge.

Showtime...

"I want to thank you for the passports," Maya said holding eye contact. He had bugged them and was a pawn of the Hidden Hand. She wanted him to know that she knew. Her text upon entering the marina was the cue for Rex—she assumed he was now remote viewing the people she met and would trail them to see how they reacted to her confrontations.

She watched Mann slip into a posture of superiority, as if he were playing a game of cat and mouse and she wasn't the cat. For some inexplicable reason, confidence swelled within Maya, which caused her to push harder than was probably socially acceptable.

"You are welcome," he said with feigned sincerity. "Did you find out who was behind your problems?"

Yes you, you son of a bitch...

"Of course." She knew this was not the response Charles had expected and saw it caused a slight twitch which he quickly suffused.

"My father showed me," she bluffed. "Along with the tracking devices that were in the seam of the passports you supplied to Robert. Any idea how they got there?"

He was good, but she saw the shadow of concern cross his face. It was now time for Rex to do his thing.

"Shall we?" She slipped her arm into Robert's and they moved away. On the surface she looked calm, but below, her heart was racing, dragging the metallic taste of fear into her mouth.

"You know I may never be invited to one of these things again," Robert said in a half-serious tone. She had not told him about the passports. She had expected his questions, but he left it alone.

She took a flute of champagne from a passing waiter. Next on her agenda was György Sorensen.

Robert continued to work the room and always introduced her as Dr. Maya Harrington. When he presented her to Prince Charles, someone who seemed to be more than just a casual acquaintance, the man took a keen interest.

"Are you an MD?" he queried.

"No sir, I am an archeologist."

"Ahhh, you don't say. And what is your forte?"

He was either a practiced charmer, which she suspected he was, or he had a genuine interest. She recalled a distant memory of an article that alluded to his 'hobby.'

"Ancient monuments," she told him.

"Dr. Harrington, I envy your freedom." He kissed her hand and they moved deeper into the room.

The soft glow of recognition blossomed, and it had come from the next in line to be the King of England no less. It was quickly arrested when she saw Sorensen holding court in the middle of the grand hall.

Anger blew up like a tropical storm. Strong gusts of adrenaline caused her breath to come sharp and shallow. She knew that face, and suspected he was behind the disappearance of—and the hunt for—her father.

A stupendous chandelier was hanging directly above him. Draped from a ceiling that was too high to estimate, it appeared dim compared to the wattage of this man. He was a dark halo that drew in others, mainly those who feared the exposure to light.

He saw her from across the room and stiffened with recognition. He turned the full wattage of his gaze upon her. There was hate in his eyes and he made no effort to hide the malice, that is, until Robert looked his way. Then like a chameleon, he was all smiles and sunshine. She half expected to see rainbows shoot out of his ass.

As they drew near, she assessed the man. He was in his eighties and had a full head of white hair. There were thick bags under his eyes and his jowls revealed a decadent lifestyle.

From Tobias's dossier, she knew there was a clinic near here where advanced science in the use of telomeres was used to greatly reduce the effects of aging and actually caused one to regress in a trek back towards youth.

She also knew this was a place only frequented by those of the 'Brotherhood.' Its success, advancements, and proprietary secrets were known only by whispers and rumor.

Obviously, Sorensen has never been there...

Armed with ammunition provided from Layla's forays into his digital realm, she had a number of arrows in her quiver. They had learned that there was something called 'the special project,' that loomed on the horizon. Tangential threads suggested it could relate to the events in the Canary Islands but there was no connection to confirm that Sorensen was involved.

He was the only one of the group that their threads labeled 'the 300.' But right now, he was her target. She wanted to find a path to those who ran this 'special project.' And all roads intersected with someone simply referred to as TM.

So far, none of their information circled back to anyone named Rothchild and they were guessing at the 'who' that was within the circle dubbed 'The 300.'

"Mr. Sorensen," Robert said, his hand extended in greeting. It was not an approach of familiarity, but one of passing notoriety.

Poor Robert, he has no idea of the shitstorm he has just stepped into.

Before replying, the aged gentleman turned his attentions on Maya with a withering stare that would cause most to back down. But she held her own.

"The infamous György Sorensen," she said with a confidence she did not feel. She closed the space between them.

"The maker of kings, the destroyer of countries. Nazi collaborator and purveyor of misery. On the one hand advocating for open borders, pushing the 'we owe it to all people to have a chance at a better life' stance. Yet in the same breath, pushing hundreds of millions into deep poverty. Crashing countries' economies for what? Money or just for fun?"

His face blossomed beet red. She did not give a shit. It would give her nothing but pleasure if he had a heart attack and died right here. The adrenaline rush of confronting the man she believed had chased away her father was exhilarating and made her feel reckless.

She did feel bad for Robert, though. This was not the way a guest should act under any circumstances. And certainly not amongst high society. She knew his reputation would be forever damaged. But her calling was that of hope, and sometimes casualties got caught in the crossfire. Sorensen was her enemy, and she had no intentions of dialing back now.

"It would appear you have not been invited to the special clinic here on the lake," she said with a raised eyebrow and exaggerated head to toe inspection of the man. "Maybe you are not worthy. Perhaps this is why you are not in the loop about TM's special project."

The first insult he absorbed as a mere flesh wound, but the second... Any pretense of civility vanished. His nostrils flared at her insolence. But she gave him no time to reply. Before he could utter a single word, she laid down the gauntlet.

"Screw with me or my friends again"—she wagged a finger inches from his face— "and every single secret held dear by the you and your 300 will show up on headline news."

She lowered her finger and moved so they were nose to nose, a total violation of his personal space. There was to be no misunderstanding, this was not a bluff.

"Can you imagine how quickly you and your family will disappear if the release of their darkest secrets were tracked back to you? I am my father's daughter, and he has taught me well."

Those who had been engaged in conversation around them cast their eyes to the floor. Some coughed, others tried to clear the imaginary lump in their throat. None had ever seen someone so young be so brazen. No one had ever openly assaulted this man like she had.

Okay Rex, they're all yours...

"Excuse us." Robert firmly grasped her arm and steered her to the other side of the room. She knew he was mad, and he had every right. It would take a while, but she hoped that eventually he would get past it long enough for her to explain. She had not meant to be so cruel, but she had intended to roil the waters. And roil she did.

"Do you realize the danger you have created? Not just for you and your friends but for me as well?" He was pissed and Maya could literally envision steam coming out of his ears.

"For putting you in this position, I am sorry," she said apologetically. "But for confronting him, I am not. He is a bad man. Evil is the only word I can think of to truly describe him."

Oddly, his strong reaction gave her pause – *maybe he isn't involved with them.* She sensed fear. But at that moment, the chasm growing between them felt uncrossable. As the night progressed, they went through the motions expected of guests at a function. They dined when it was time to dine. And they danced when it was time to dance. But something had changed. Maya wondered if he now considered her a loose cannon. Maybe he was even rethinking their professional relationship.

As the evening wore on, the tension between them grew heavy. But at the same time, her impatience became an itch that needed scratching. Had her actions sent the rats scurrying? Was Rex gleaning any actionable intelligence? It would need to wait. Right now, she needed to manage damage control.

It's time to get off the fence, girl... She needed Robert and the resources he offered if they were to have any hope of confronting such an immense adversary. It was time to trust in her fate, her destiny, and the people providence had surrounded her with. It was time to pick a side, and she chose to trust him and pray it was the right choice.

"Robert," she whispered, as the two glided across the dance floor. "We need to talk. You need to hear what I have to say.

"There is an attack coming. One so horrible it will rock the world. Governments will fall, millions will die, and human freedom will fade into a myth."

They stopped dancing. He stiffened and suddenly they were standing in the middle of the ballroom floor as bodies all around them glided by on classical strains of the orchestra.

The space between them became even more charged as he assessed her. A piercing probe of his smoky gray eyes. She knew if she so much as flinched...

It was a defining moment, and it could go either way. Her heart was racing. Her mouth was dry. She wanted to bite down on her lip but dare not move. She remained frozen. Weathering the storm.

"You don't seem crazy," he said, and she saw his hardened expression soften just a little.

Careful...

"Okay, let's talk."

They moved towards the stairs and ascended, their hands on the sweeping bannister until they were on the landing at the top. Here, doors opened out into one of the tower top landings. The moon was three quarters full and cast a quicksilver light upon the lake.

She needed Robert to understand the full picture and proceeded to explain what she believed to be true.

◆ ♒♏ ♒♓♎♎♏ ■♒♋■♎

Robert listened and found himself standing at a crossroads. Trust she was telling the truth and that she knew what she was talking about? Or cut bait and run? He had never liked the latter. But he was worried. She was picking a fight with forces way beyond her weight class. And by extension, way beyond his own. Was this a fight worth having?

"I assume that you and Rex have used your, um ... special talents to come by this information?"

"In part," she replied.

The soft breeze coming down from the hills had the hint of frangipani. It carried the strains of violins that faded in and out from the grand ballroom below. He did not know what to make of this, and he did not have an answer. He would need time to do what he did best. Assess, evaluate, and act.

As the spike of adrenaline receded, his anger abated, and the storm blew itself out. In its place, the vacuum of volcanic emotion had to be filled. He found himself reaching out, drawn as if in a dream. Rational thought had been subsumed by a more primal calling. Without care or consideration, crossing all boundaries of his personal code of conduct, he pulled her into him and pressed his lips to hers.

She opened her mouth, receptively unleashing a hunger that she did not know existed. Deeply enthralled in the haze of passion, she ignored the vibration coming from her bag. It buzzed again. And then again. And would not cease…it was not going to be denied.

CHAPTER 23
Rex – Remote Viewing

Rex had slipped into the role of dream warrior and was now executing his clandestine surveillance. When Maya moved away from Charles Mann, Rex made him the object of scrutiny.

"Excuse me." The target had politely deferred to those with whom he was engaged. Mann moved across the floor and went out onto the terrace. A casual spotting would see a man out for a smoke. Except on closer inspection, he never inhaled. He retrieved his phone and sent a text.

'MH knows of passports. And more.'

One of the flaws in Maya's expanding intelligence operations was that phones were still a weak link. But not entirely. Rex willed himself into the body of the text and instantaneously found himself in a familiar setting. He was back at the server room, the place where the chain of communication was broken off for anyone tracing members of The 300. It served almost as a perfect cutout.

A stocky middle-aged woman of eastern European descent retrieved the message and typed it into an email.

Where is it going?

From his previous recon, Rex knew this place was in Iceland. It was housed within a greater server farm. One that used the frigid air of the Arctic's edge as an economical form of cooling for the massive amounts of heat emitted from the unending walls of servers. Many cloud-based operations were moving here, Greenland, or northern Alaska.

The question of where, acted as an intention and he was slurped through the path of this latest transmission, which deposited him at an estate. An artist's rendering of Mount Vernon on the wall led him to believe he might be in Virginia.

A man was sitting in front of the monitor, awash in its glow. He had the feel of a sentry. Rex did a quick reconnoiter of the vicinity, which expanded out onto grounds draped in security and surrounded by rolling hills and a soft summer haze.

He returned to the room. The sentry was on the phone.

"Yes sir," the man stiffened at the command.

Rex followed the line to its source. He recognized the man laying the phone back into the cradle but could not remember his name.

The man placed two calls. Familiar with both country codes as he dialed, the first was to a number in Turkey and the second was to Germany. Both conversations were innocuous in meaning but conveyed an urgent need to meet. What caused the metaphorical breath to stick in his throat was the man's closing comment.

"This is a special project. The Maestro expects that it does not fall behind schedule."

Rex had recently discovered a new talent, to will his intent to a place that *once was.* Or in this case, to where a call had been received even though the line was now closed. He had names and faces, but still did not know the nature of the special project.

He opened his eyes, made some notes, downloaded all he could to Layla, and returned to the castle.

Charles Mann and György Sorensen had slipped into a private room and security had parked themselves in front of closed doors. He was fortunate to have arrived at the moment. The feeling of growing chaos was prevalent.

"What is this special project?" Sorensen demanded of Mann.

"I don't know and truthfully, I don't want to know. My task is to steer the helm of America's administrative state and keep her on our course. Yours is to keep an eye on that twat and her merry little gang.

"Specifically," he paused. "You are to bring us her father. Alive!"

Sorensen was scorned. And by his drooped shoulders it was apparent the admonishment had found its mark.

"We beat them to the cave," he said in contrition.

"And?"

Rex was still working with Layla to put together the Hand's hierarchy. He assumed Charles was not Sorenson's superior and that they were tangential based on data collected so far. But he watched as Mann foisted an upper hand.

"We collected a large cache of items, some of them probably priceless."

"And?" he asked yet again.

"And some of these were urns full of a powdery substance."

Rex had not expected this. These were the people behind the cave extraction. He fought the urge to get excited—afraid he would be drawn back to his body and miss something important. But this was monumental. *Please tell me you still have this.*

It was a biomorphic suggestion. Energy follows thought.

"It is safely on its way to The Maestro."

Shit. Who the hell is Maestro? TM? Is TM The Maestro?

"What is it?" Mann asked.

"I do not know. But The Maestro's involvement would lead me to believe it is related to whatever secret it is that Alex Harrington has uncovered, but I am merely speculating."

At that moment, the door opened and a rotund man with thick jowls and a sagging waist entered. Both Sorensen and Mann straightened, as if corporals in the presence of high brass. He half expected the man to tell them, 'at ease, soldiers.'

"Lord Balforth," Sorensen demurred.

No mistaking, he was the man in charge. One who, by all outward appearances, could be easily dismissed, but behind closed doors was a force of nature.

He interrogated each man, asking probing questions and considering each answer. When Sorensen mentioned the 'Special Project,' Balforth was jolted. His momentarily let his guard down and his aura of invincibility exposed vulnerability.

It was Mann who dared ask. "What is this project?"

Scorn blossomed crimson upon the man's face, his voice taking on a shrill tone.

"This is not your concern," he huffed angrily. Then, to reassert his standing he added. "I am running a special op that will be known to all at Christmas." He forced a contrived smile and acted as if he was letting them in on a secret. "The world has gotten a taste, but not the feast."

He looked to Mann "Do your job, get our team back into the White House." Then in an afterthought, he added. "As if it matters who the next President will be."

The door opened and one of the security men stood at attention. "Find the girl," Balforth instructed. And then returned his focus back to Sorensen.

"This is your chance to do whatever you need to find out where her father is. Don't muck it up!"

Rex snapped back into the apartment on Eighty-Sixth Street. He needed to warn Maya. He rushed through the details with Layla, his heart beating so loudly he could barely hear himself talking. With a tightening chest he called Maya's cell phone. Over and over, it rang, and over and over it went to voicemail. Worry was now exasperation. Exasperation soon became fear. The hollow transatlantic sound hummed.

"Come on Maya, answer the phone."

♦ ≈ ♏ ≈ ♓ ♎ ♎ ♏ ■ ≈ ♋ ■ ♎

"Hello." Maya's breath was husky and drawn.

"Maya, they're—I heard them. They are taking the gloves off. You need to get the hell out of there. Now!"

But it was too late. Maya saw four armed guards come through the doors and spread out with guns drawn.

"We need help," she whispered and ended the call.

Behind them appeared the pompous ass, Lord Balforth, but he no longer appeared a caricature of waddle and girth. He had assumed the mantle of leadership and had an aura of lethality.

Every one of her nerve endings seethed at this man's presence.

"Mr. Vaherees," he addressed in a tone that underscored the extreme danger they were in. "It would be better if you followed my men to a safer environment."

There was no room for discussion. Maya saw the red dots of their gunsights quivering on Robert's heart. Maya looked at the fat man. She had grossly underestimated who he was, and from the grin on his putrid face she could see the pleasure he took in her miscalculation.

She had brought this on, and Robert did not deserve to pay the price.

"Go with them." she insisted, suspecting that if he gave any resistance, those infrared sites would send a bullet, and send him to his death. She repeated her request as she took a step back. But he did not move. His determination showed no fear. But she needed him to go. She needed to create space, distraction—multiple things happening at once.

"Please, Robert."

The muscles of her torso tightened as she added separation between them. She retreated farther, drawing her hands to cover her face. She feigned tears and acted embarrassed by her lack of emotional control.

"Not such a warrior after all, are we, Dr. Harrington?"

That's right, you fat turd. You are so predictable.

She knew Reggie had lusted after her when they first met. It was so painfully obvious. So she used this to create a further distraction, and to hopefully get Robert out of the crosshairs. She dropped her purse to the tower roof floor. Taking her hands, she pulled her gown down until it was draped around her feet. Stepping free of the crumpled gown, she stood naked but for the sheer panties that covered almost nothing and the diamonds that glistened against her skin.

"This is what you want, isn't it, Reggie?" she asked, putting another foot behind her. Hoping to gain one additional second, she released the diamonds. As all eyes watched them fall to the rooftop, she leaped into the moonlight.

♦≈♏≈⟩⟨♎♎♏■≈♋■♎

She hit the water, her heels plunging through the surface like a knife. Momentum plunged her far below the surface. But even in the cloud of everything that was happening around her, the cold water, her naked body, her enemies above and the need to escape from the security that she knew was already on their way to seize her, the memory of that embrace with Robert suffused her with a warm glow. It also fueled her resolve.

I'm coming for you Balford, you bastard...

Looking up she saw the lights that shone from above the marina. Shadows of the sleek crafts tied to the docks were blotches on the surface. She needed a boat. She saw a craft idle in through the tunnel, a lone driver likely here to pick up his passengers. She broke the surface, took a deep gulp of air, and set a course to intersect his path, a spot that had to be outside the halo of the sodium vapor lights along the shore. When she felt a modicum of invisibility, she popped up in front of the slowing boat and waved her arms for help.

The man slowed and brought the boat to bear. Fortune reigned as it sidled up between her and the shore. Blocking her from view.

"Grab my hand," she said feigning panic while extending her arm. When he reached for her, she applied her rudimentary knowledge of judo and used the man's own momentum to toss him into the water.

'Sorry…" She pulled herself over the side, gave the man a cursory glance to make sure he could swim, then grabbed the wheel and turned the bow back towards the lake.

As the boat neared the tunnel, men fanned out onto the dock. In moments, a spotlight found the yelling boatsman who was treading the marina waters. Maya turned back to see a man on shore speaking into a radio in alarm. The response was instantaneous. A chain link fence set within a hidden track began to lower from above the passageway—the only thing that separated her from capture or freedom. She gunned the boat.

Lower it fell, faster she went. Either she would escape or die trying. *Closer, lower. Closer, lower.* Impact was imminent, she ducked her body and gripped the wheel. There was a loud crash and the tearing apart of glass and wood. Splinters flew and struck her hands. Then she was free, out onto the open water.

The windshield was gone as well as the pole lights and two cleats off the back. She found the switch for those lights that still worked and turned them off. She saw that blood seeped from wounds on her arm—cuts from flying shards of windshield.

The boatsman had a jacket that lay on the seat beside her along with blankets. She slowed the boat and tied a blanket to steady the wheel. Setting a course towards the far side of the water, away from the marina and away from where she planned to escape, she grabbed the man's coat, jammed the throttle full forward, and leaped from the boat as it roared off into the night.

She was on the lee side of the jutting peninsula out past the marina. A place no one would expect her to be. She swam towards shore, keeping a low profile on the water's surface. It was not long until a small flotilla poured from the marina. She could see other boats, searchlights sweeping the water. Bearing from three different locations that were all vectored away from her. For the moment she had lost them.

She knew where she was headed and began a steady rhythmic stroke towards shore.

◆〰️♏︎〰️♓︎♎︎♎︎♏︎ ■〰️♋️■♎︎

Rex had seen her jump, and he had followed her out into the lake. He now watched as she sat cold and shivering in a cavern below the cliffs less than a half a mile from the Scaligero Castle. The only thing between her and an almost naked body was a wet jacket. Her aura was strong. He had never credited her for the strength she so obviously possessed.

The balls to leap from a hundred-foot turret and the unflinching wherewithal to crash through a closing trap. The woman was a banshee.

She was sitting cross-legged with her eyes closed. Rising up in her dream state, Rex was there waiting.

"Damn, I wasn't expecting you," she shared in their odd theta state telepathy. "But I'm glad you're here. Robert's in trouble."

"I know, they are holding him in a private room. He's being watched over by three sentries." As if he knew her next question, he added, "He is unharmed, and they are not sure what to do with him. Many people saw them descend the stairs and he is too powerful to just 'disappear.'"

"Tell Layla to contact Father Book. We need the Sons' help. And Rex, make sure to tell her I am okay, then come back."

◆〰️♏︎〰️♓︎♎︎♎︎♏︎ ■〰️♋️■♎︎

When he left, Maya wracked her brain. She needed leverage. She focused her intent on Balforth and found herself in a wood-paneled room where four men were ensconced in leather club chairs, drinking expensive whisky, and wearing worried expressions.

She recalled the experiment she had done when she first got a grip on remote viewing and applied the same principle. Get into his phone. It worked.

All around her were letters and words, like random fruit in an overgrown orchard. She struggled at first, and then visualized the field, the rows, the trees, and soon text messages aligned on one side of the grove and emails on the other. All of it ready to be picked.

She was so engrossed; she was startled when Rex appeared inside the phone with her. She logged the info; remote viewing was a field of which she had only a scant understanding.

"There you are," he said, standing amongst the data field. "What is it?"

"It is part of the special project," Maya said, thinking they might have gotten their first break. Back in college, she had studied the ethical aspects of dropping a bomb on Japan to end WWII and her eidetic memory made the quick connection.

"Look—here, there is a satirical reference to a fat man and a little boy."

"And?"

"These were the names of the two nuclear bombs America dropped on Japan. See where this text came from," she told him. He was gone.

Time was skewed in the theta state. So she had no idea how long Rex had been gone. But when he returned what he had to say was the leverage she needed.

"There is an Iraqi who has been tasked with secreting two nuclear bombs. One in already in Tehran and one is targeted for Israel. They are struggling to get the second one placed."

"Okay, this is what I want you to do…"

CHAPTER 24

She watched Lord Balforth reach into his pocket and retrieve his phone. She could see the consternation on his face, annoyed and confused. It was an 'Unavailable' number. But it was not a telemarketer. Definitely not a telemarketer.

"Yes," he hissed cautiously.

"I have a message from Ms. Harrington."

He froze and then demanded. "Who is this? How did you get this number?"

"In ten minutes, she is contacting the Israeli government and providing them with proof that you are attempting to smuggle a nuclear weapon into their country. It is planned to be detonated along with the one you already have at the warehouse in Tehran."

She watched from her theta state as Lord Balforth turned ashen. So much so, that those seated around him froze.

"The Mossad will be given your location." The speaker on the other end paused, letting the tension build. "And The Maestro will be informed it was your lax security that unraveled his grand design. His special project."

"What do you want?" he said with a bit more caution.

"First, apologize to Mr. Vaherees and release him. Second, call off your dogs. You won't find her anyway. Third, mention this to anyone or try to move the bombs, and we will show you the next card in our hand. You cannot beat a Royal Flush. There is nowhere to hide from us. But The Maestro need not know of your failures."

"I see. And then what?"

"And then... we see." The line went dead.

Maya watched with satisfaction as the fat twaddle stood with an angry scowl of indecision on his face. No one in the room dared speak. He walked to the door and opened it. He spoke to one of the guards and she smiled in satisfaction. He had folded.

"Please bring Robert Vaherees to me," Balford said to an attending guard. "Apologize for the misunderstanding and give him whatever he asks for."

♦ ≈ ♏ ≈ ⊬ ♎ ♎ ♏ ■ ≈ ♋ ■ ♎

Maya heard voices. Loose rocks announced that someone was scrambling down the cliff face. She had nowhere to go and could only hope it was her rescue. She had told Rex to find someone, maybe from the Sons of Jared, to gather up some things and bring them to her. Who else would be here at this hour?

Two young men poked their heads in. One hung back while the other approached her.

"Maya Harrington?"

"Yes."

"I am Carlos."

He handed her a duffle bag. She opened it, surprised to see her own clothes. They had obviously been lifted from her hotel room.

"I'm sure they'll fit," he said with a straight face. Her smile eased the tension.

♦ ≈ ♏ ≈ ⊬ ♎ ♎ ♏ ■ ≈ ♋ ■ ♎

It was late and the moon had long since slipped below the black horizon. Revelers were all tucked in for the night and only alley cats roamed the streets, keeping to the shadows as they patrolled their turf.

Maya felt like one of the bedraggled cats. Her hair was wet, and she had a wide array of cuts from crashing through the castle's aquatic gate. Fortunately, the sweatshirt that Carlos had liberated kept these covered.

When she entered the elegant lobby, only the night manager was on duty. She watched him as he gave her a nod. She assumed it was the cue for security—wherever they were holed up—to let her pass.

She had nowhere else to go. She was worried about Robert and she could only assume that Reggie Balforth was more scared of being revealed to The Maestro than he was of her. At least for the moment.

She found Robert's room and knocked on the door. Then a second time. When it opened, fear and tension all fell away. He was still in his evening clothes. She could see his jacket tossed over a chair and on the coffee table was a half empty bottle of McCallan Eighteen.

"Buy a lady a drink?" she asked. She was not sure if she should embrace him or if now, after the heady steam of emotion had run its course, they would simply revert back to employer and employee. She compromised, and placed a hand on his check, gave him a kiss still infused with passion and then assumed the role that she usually played.

"Are you alright?" he asked, closing the door behind her.

"I really could use a drink."

He took a crystal tumbler, placed a few cubes in it, and added a hefty pour.

She took a long deep pull and offered the glass for a refill. There was a pause of quiet introspection. So much had happened, what was important? Their kiss, the events at the castle, the realization that Lord Balforth was a senior member of the Hidden Hand, or the painstaking truth that her fears of a manufactured conflagration were no longer speculation?

He had a slew of questions and she was glad to see his anger had burned itself out. She returned to the topic of nuclear weapons she had mentioned before they were rudely interrupted on the roof top.

"Robert, we need to let both the Israeli and Iranian governments know about these weapons. They need to be stopped before they can be used."

She watched him, perhaps seeing him in a new light, as she ran through the facts. The guards holding him at gunpoint. Lord Balforth's Jekyll and Hyde demeanor, obviously the pompous docile twit was an act.

"In for a penny, in for a pound," he said softly. "The Israelis have a robust delegation here. I will reach out to them in the morning. Are there any specifics that I can pass on? This is not going to be taken lightly."

"Rex knows where the bomb is placed in Tehran and will send me a sketch as soon as I replace my phone."

Robert stood and walked towards the other side of the room. Sitting on the credenza was her bag atop a pile of glitter. The diamond necklace had been haphazardly tossed onto the table. She saw that all her things were there, including her dress, shoes and…

He retrieved the bag and handed it to her.

"They were trying to make amends," he said by way of explanation. "I sensed Balforth was in a compliant mood, so though he resisted at first, I demanded the return of everything including your phone."

She saw a text notification from Rex. She opened it to reveal a detailed drawing of a warehouse with nearby signs written in what she assumed was Persian. She showed it to Robert.

"I assume Rex is trying to give me the location where one of the bombs is located; these must be the names of the closest known streets."

She forwarded it to Robert and put her phone down. "May I use your bathroom to clean up?"

While showering off the night, her mind found its way back to the passion on the rooftop. She had a growing desire to let it unfold. She dried herself off, fixed her hair as best she could and, after rinsing her mouth with water, she stepped naked into the room.

She saw the impact her nude body had on Robert—he was slack-jawed. She moved towards the bed and with a crook of her finger, beckoned him to join her.

CHAPTER 25
JW - Phoenix

The symbolism of his dream journey vacillated between the obvious and the obscure. Technically, JW knew he wasn't any closer to figuring out how one would make the Sacred Manna, but he had no doubt that they would need to recover the crystal vase buried along the Colorado River.

He had spoken to Rex about this and was shocked at the events that had transpired in Italy. At the same time, he was relieved Maya had come out unscathed. He was especially relieved that the Israeli government had been made aware of the nuclear threat and that through back channels had alerted Tehran.

We've dodged one bullet, but plague...

But there was something else that was nagging at his psyche. Something totally unrelated. And something that felt much more ominous. In his dreams he saw sporadic glimpses of a hurtling mass careening through space, which always woke him in a cold sweat. It felt so real.

He shook the feeling aside and set out to fulfill his promise to Nascha. He was going to find this man, Drune Melchizedik. But in light of all the news, he wondered—*is this the best thing I could be doing right now?* He recalled a famous metaphysical point of view.

Be here now...

It was the subtle shift that reminded him to stay on point. He had found the address of the institute that he believed had a relationship with Drune. But the more he researched the man, the more he appeared to be an enigma. Drune Melchizedik had written many books and given many lectures about Sacred Geometry and The Flower of Life, but he claimed no inherent affiliation with these institutes of wellness and spiritual understanding. And JW could not pin him down to a location or even a sure state of residence.

JW got off the highway east of Camelback and was traversing a residential street. It was already over one hundred degrees and he was glad that the road was lined with tall shade trees, appreciative that someone way back when had the forethought to canopy the caustic rays of the Arizona sun.

Cruising slowly, he studied the stenciled markings on the mailboxes. Even numbers on the right, odd on the left. 246 Pierson Way turned out to be a low, one-story putty colored adobe house with a manicured rock lawn and brick driveway. Obviously, the institute was run from within someone's home. He could see only one car parked in the shade, so pulled in behind it.

He knocked on the stout wood door. It had a small, hinged window in its center and someone inside opened the flap. They must have decided he was harmless, he heard locks turn and the door opened.

"Yes?" A Mexican woman asked with nary a trace of an accent.

"Good afternoon, Señora, I am looking for Señor Melchizedik."

She studied him without saying a word. JW had a strange sensation, as if his aura was being probed by an expert. He felt strangely naked in front of her. Finally, she opened the door.

"Please come in. My name is Maria Vasquez, and you are…"

"Johnny White Feather," he replied. "But please, call me JW."

"Ahh," she toned in recognition. "You are the one who called before."

"Yes ma'am," JW confirmed.

The room was warm with relaxed furniture that exuded function over form. Her mannerisms had grace and her smile conveyed kindness. She was somewhere between sixty and seventy, the deep creases that belayed years of toil could not contain her keen clear eyes. She appeared inquisitive, knowing, and always probing. It reminded him of his grandfather.

He liked this woman, Maria Vasquez. She had a special knack to asking, then listening. He tried to bring the conversation around to the whereabouts of Drune Melchizedik, but she kept deflecting with personal questions about his experiences growing up on the reservation, and the teachings of his adopted father, the shaman. This led to Nascha's story about the lost Egyptian cave, and how it had brought him to her doorstep.

She often smiled knowingly and then the next minute a flicker of a question would dart across her face.

"I have heard this before," she said, pushing a strand of hair from her brow. It was no longer thick and dark, which he imagined it was when she wore a younger woman's body, but it was not grey either.

"Drunc and I are friends," she finally acknowledged. "But he is not here."

"Not here, as in not in Phoenix?" he asked, his shoulders drooped slightly under the weight of dashed hope.

"Not here as in, not here." Her lips curled with an enigmatic smile. "Not in Phoenix, not in America, and maybe not even..." She toyed with her cadence.

"I see." He didn't, actually. "And where might he be and when would he be coming back?" JW asked.

It looked as if her thoughts crossed between what she could remember and what she thought prudent to share.

"He said he would be back but did not say when. But the man does not hold himself hostage to a watch or a calendar," she chuckled. "He is distracted by the wonders of creation and often follows his heart simply to see where it will take him."

"And this led him... where?" JW nudged.

"He loves France." She said this as if it was common knowledge.

He did not know what he had expected, but this was not it. "For the wine?"

"Undoubtedly, but he loves the cathedrals. Did you know that all the great gothic churches were built by the Knights Templar? And there is a cluster of churches in the northern part of France that are aligned in a pattern that mirrors the Virgin Mother and her place in the sky."

"Virgo?" His dream journey sprang to mind. "Has he gone to study the symbolism of these specific churches?"

She simply smiled.

Have the spirits sent another pointer? This meeting was not an accident. The hermetical truth was loud in his ear. *'There are no coincidences.'*

"You said he loves France, but is he in France?"

"He once told me, that of all the Gothic Cathedrals, the one that always intrigued him the most was at Auch, near the Pyrenees Mountains."

Is she giving me a message?

It soon became quite apparent her conversation had run dry. The room suddenly felt as if it was running out of reasons for keeping him.

Preparing to say goodbye, JW stood and thanked her for her time. In return, she reached to the small table next to her chair and handed him a recent copy of the *Arizona Gazette*.

"It is getting harder and harder to find a decent newspaper," she laughed by way of goodbye. "I hope you find what you are searching for."

♦ ≈ ♍ ≈ ♓ ♎ ♎ ♍ ■ ≈ ♋ ■ ♎

JW arrived at Sky Harbor International Airport with an hour remaining before his flight back to New York. He grabbed a large coffee and found his gate, taking a seat close to the window.

He replayed the afternoon and vowed to revisit Fulcanelli's *Mystery of the Cathedrals*. There had been something about the alignment of the Gothic Cathedrals that had been built and paid for by the Knights Templar. Those who had discovered something of great importance under the Temple Mount, the catacombs of Solomon's Temple.

He could not recall the specifics, only that they had perfected a technique that had created glass with incredible depth and color. A process that was not replicable today.

Just like the symbols fired within the buried crystal...

With time to kill, he removed her newspaper. The headlines still barked of lingering violence spread across the Middle East. The commentators still aimed the arrows of fault at the President.

Same old shit, different day, he thought.

Having never been a follower of sports, he skipped to the local section. Printed news was a dying breed as evidenced by the scant few remaining pages. He found a local article whose title looked promising.

Ghost Gold and the Vanishing Man
By: Jeffery Booth

He looked at the picture of a man who was the central point of the story. It was captioned, Drune Melchizedik.

"What?" he felt his face soften in amazement. He thought back to Maria's enigmatic smile and then immersed himself in the story.

'Drune spoke about his research and discoveries by making multiple connections between the works of the Anunnaki of Ancient Sumer, the Flower of Life, The Egyptian Book of the Dead, Alchemy, Superconductivity, and the Ark of the Covenant.

He set out to explain that numerous researchers had taken a variation on Orbitally Rearranged Molecular Elements and have tried to create the base elements for zero-point gravity and evolve this to possibly unlocking the secret of the transmutation of matter.'

Transmutation? His breath quickened with the beating of his heart.

'I worked old, abandoned mines for fun, not profit, Drune began. 'In the process of recovering gold and silver, I began to recover something else. I am not a chemist and had no idea what the stuff was. It would flow out of the lead but when I held it down, I had nothing. The mining community refers to this as 'ghost gold.'

Curiosity got the better of me and I contacted a friend who did a spectroscopic analysis. We burned this at obscenely high temperatures.

After 90 seconds, it began to read Palladium, 110 seconds, Platinum. At 130 seconds, these were the mystery metals that I knew were used by the ancients.

Let me explain, in 1990, my uncle showed me the Time Life Book, Secrets of the Alchemist. The book talks about a white powder of gold which was the objective of every alchemist. The Philosopher's Stone.

It was referred to as 'the container of the light.' If you stand in its presence, you don't age. If you partake of it, you live forever. It all goes back to a man named Enoch. Thoth, Hermes, Trigeminus. Same man. By partaking of the white powder, he never died, instead ascended because he was so perfect.

Was this a form of the mythical monatomic gold, I asked myself? My path veered from concerns about wealth accumulation towards unlocking the secret of the ancient ones, the mystical quest for the Philosopher's Stone.'

As he devoured the story, JW made mental notes. Astonished, intrigued, and captivated, he read on as the story continued to unravel hints at the process for creating monatomic gold. It talked about mass sitting on an atomic scale that when mixed with this powder vanished to below zero at extreme heats, and when cooled, returned to its undisturbed natural state. This segued into its perturbations caused by magnetic fields and how it aligns with the human body.

'In our bodies, we have all this junk DNA. There are 30 aspects of the DNA that nobody can figure out what it's there for. And we only use 15 percent of our brain. Why evolve 85 percent of a brain we don't use? It's as if at one time we had a higher state of enlightenment, and then we fell into the state in which we exist now.

If you ask a Rabbi, 'have you ever heard of the white powder of gold?' he'll say yes, we've heard of it, but to our knowledge, no one has known how to make it since the destruction of the First Temple. The temple of Solomon.

For those through history that have unlocked the secret and consumed the Manna, they said you feed it and feed it and it grows and grows and you become more and more enlightened until you reach the point where the light body exceeds the physical body. You light up the room when you walk in. You are no longer of this space-time. You become a fifth-dimensional being.'

At the end of the article, the writer concluded:

'Drune wore a Cheshire cat smile, as if he could read my every thought. I did not see him eat of the bread of light, but he must have.

For he said, 'It is time for me to go. Time to see new worlds and to explore the creation of our father.'

He shook my hand, and while our palms were grasped, he vanished. No sound, no sensation, no whoosh. He was just gone. For the last two months I have tried to find him. I have spoken to those who should know him, I have been to his places of teaching, I have attended the Flower of Life and have read all I can about sacred geometry. I am now left to wonder about this Ghost Gold and the vanishing man.'

Jeffery Booth – June 2021

JW laid the paper down. This confirmed what they already knew or suspected about manna. But this man Drune, Nascha met him how long ago? Twenty years?

They discussed the finding of a sacred cave. He had mentioned something about the pyramids. His mind raced through the information he had accumulated.

The crystal vase, the color blue, Hathor, Anubis, Gold, obelisks, then his thoughts continued, but they felt as if they were being drawn up from his intuitions. Orion, three Magi with frankincense, myrrh, and gold. The kesil and kimah, Solomon's Temple, the Essenes... Virgo, Gothic Glass, why France?

Carefully he folded the article and tucked it into his backpack and made his way to the plane for the flight back to New York.

CHAPTER 26
Maya - Lake Garda

Maya used the reflections in the windows of the small Malcesine shops to continually check and see if there was anyone following her. If they were not being monitored before, they certainly would be by now. Before leaving for Europe, she had Layla buy them all new burner phones. None were to be activated until a specific day at a specific time.

With fifteen minutes to go before the agreed-upon call time, she ducked into the Olseria Bacala on the Piazza Delle Erbe ostensibly to browse the eclectic collection of old Americana. In reality, it offered her secluded privacy to relive every moment, sensation, and feeling still lingering from the night before. She had shared herself with Robert, unleashing any inhibitions she might have felt. And he had done the same.

She had hoped for an encore this morning, but he had to leave early. When she woke the second time, there was a fresh rose on the pillow beside her. Letting herself get lost in the haze of last night's passion, she was interrupted by the chirping of her phone.

She had programmed it with their new numbers. It was JW, and his call was quickly followed by Rex.

"Buongiorno," she answered linking them all together. She stepped outside the shop and crossed the cobblestone plaza. There was a yellow two-story building on the opposite side with an exterior staircase adorned with hanging flower baskets. From there she could keep an eye on the entire square.

Her heartbeat quickened as she thought of the ramifications of her actions and their possible heightened danger. What came to mind was a truth she learned long ago. *'The difference between bravery and stupidity is success.'* And right now, she desperately needed to get the full download from Rex. Anything short of total success would be deemed failure.

"Maya," came JW's breathless announcement. "I stumbled across someone who may know how to make the Manna!"

She could almost hear his heartbeat from across the Atlantic, but due to the hornets' nest she had kicked over and her fear that her actions could have personal and dangerous ramifications for all of them, she stifled her curiosity about what JW may have found to first address possible security concerns.

"That is great news, lets discuss it after we know where we stand with the Hand." This was her cue to Rex.

"I assume the Israelis know of the bombs?" he asked, taking heed of her pause.

"Yes. Robert assured me this was taken care of."

"Good. I have scanned most of Lord Balforth's data, but I do not think he is part of anything to do with the plague."

"You're saying the Hidden Hand has nothing to do with this?" Her nostrils flared in disbelief. Her words were probably a little sharper than necessary.

"No, I am not saying that. I am saying I do not think that Balforth himself is involved. Which means there are others, even higher ups."

"Oh…" she said in a softer tone. *How high up does this group go?* She wondered. She was breathing in short sharp gulps as she willed her heart to slow.

"Layla is creating a chart and we are piecing together some of the names. But in truth, it is less of a top-down org chart and more like a spider's web. We have yet to identity the black widow. They are very compartmentalized."

"And the Rothchilds?" she asked. This was a name that conveyed all kinds of conspiracies. But from what she had read in Tobias's brief, it pointed to them as the head of the octopus.

"So far, tangential at best. Layla and I have ferreted out some of the digital traffic that is running through the cutout at the Icelandic server farm. One thing that has appeared more than once is the name Apollo. Layla did a little checking.

"Like all the Olympian gods, Apollo was an immortal and powerful god. He had many special powers including the ability to bring illness and disease…" He hesitated before making the connection for them, "as in plague."

Damn… the information was both satisfying and terrifying. Satisfying in that they had found a tenuous link that might allow them to stop whatever was being planned. But terrifying that they had the power and resources to execute something so horrific.

"Okay… keep digging," she said, trying to quickly process the information while thinking about the team's next steps.

"Rex, before you go," JW interrupted. "I'm heading to France tomorrow, but we need to retrieve the vase. Can you organize that?"

"Sure, I'll take care of it."

Maya's heart constricted with the time limitations and the immense pressure of everything unfolding so quickly. She wasn't yet sure of her next move.. "Call Robert if you need anything and be extra careful."

"I will. Anything else?"

"Nope, that's it for now."

"Okay. Arriv-a-der-chay for now."

She let a smile curl at the corners of her mouth. Texas twang meets bad Italian.

"France?" she asked after Rex had hung up.

"Yep. Remember Nascha's recommendation to seek out the man named Drune Melchizedik…" He proceeded to unfold his encounter with Maria Vasquez, which led to the article about Ghost Gold, which circled back to Drune Melchizedik, the one who met with Nascha over twenty years ago.

"Talk about divine intervention." Her voice carried a hint of awe. "Drune appears to have all the attributes of one who has mastered the Manna. So he has either figured out how to make it or has uncovered a good stash of it."

"Maybe…" he replied with a reminder. "Like Professor Hamid said, it could just have accumulated in his system until he could activate it at will."

"What else was in the article?"

"Actually, a lot," he said. "Let me read the last few paragraphs of the interview. According to the article, Drune believed that the Manna is oft mentioned by Jesus in the New Testament."

"The New Testament? Like what?" she queried for specifics.

"Here is one of many passages. *'When you have prepared the proper food and have on your proper garments.'* What is the proper food? It's the food of the angels, the food of the gods, the Manna, the 'What is it?'

"I believe the garment he is referring to is one Meissner field, the key to superconductivity, the code many well-funded labs are trying to crack."

He further explained technical aspects of the article concluding with a passage that resonated with Maya.

"... so when you have your perfect superconducting body, you're not of this space-time. You are a light being, and your mind is one with other people's minds. You literally know their thoughts, and they know your thoughts. You and they are literally of one mind, one heart, and this is science."

It resonated with her due to the telepathy she had shared with Rex when they remote viewed together. "And this has something to do with France?"

"I'm getting to that," he said, seeking patience. "It's about the glass."

"The white powder of gold fuses to form gold glass. It's a transparent glass, just like window glass. In Revelation, it says, *'The streets of the New Jerusalem will be paved with gold liken unto glass.'*

"The cathedrals were built by the Templars. They employed all types of new technologies, like Key Stones to hold up the incredible arches, flying buttresses to allow grand halls with high interior roofs, and they had mastered the art of infusing glass with color and spectrum that to this day cannot be replicated. I believe the same gold glass mentioned in Revelation will be found at the Cathedral in Auch."

Maya's heart quickened as the thrill of the hunt washed over her.

"Ok. I'll meet you in Paris, text me your details once you have them."

CHAPTER 27
JW - Paris, France

JW had arrived at Charles De Gaulle International Airport. He had crisscrossed the city and indiscriminately changed taxis a half dozen times before meeting Maya at Le Bourget. He wanted to lose anyone who may have been trying to track their moves.

"How was your flight?" Maya asked as Robert's jet, which they were aboard, cleared takeoff from Le Bourget Aéroport de Paris.

"Uneventful," he explained with a single word. Across from her, he found himself once again admiring how beautiful she'd become. But there was something else, he could not put his finger on it. There was an aura about her. He had seen it growing since their trip to the canyon, but now it was fully matured.

When he asked about her travels, she had informed him that she was not listed on the manifest when the jet departed Lake Garda and that it was unlikely the enemy was even aware she had left the lake region.

The jet banked high and away from the airport. From the port window JW could see the Eiffel Tower sparkle in the mid-morning sun. They were heading south to the cathedral Maria had mentioned.

Auch was not part of the northern churches the Templars had built. But after his conversation with Ms. Vasquez, it garnered significant interest. With a simple search, he found that Fulcanelli talked at length about this Templar creation above all the rest.

Maya pulled two Perrier waters from the galley and JW felt the shift to business. "Did you bring the article?" she asked.

He fished it from his backpack and handed it to her. As she scanned the story, JW began a running commentary that wove together his reasons and rationales of their next destination. They were all tied in with Fulcanelli, gold glass and the processes for making the Sacred Manna.

"Fulcanelli emphasized the role of science in the end times," he reminded her. "The more I read of his works, the more I can appreciate a passage from his book *The Mysteries of the Great Cross of Hendaye.*

· *'Welcome to the world's greatest mystery. It has everything—clues and ciphers, red herrings, and consciously enigmatic jokes. There are villains, victims, and heroes littering the plot lines, along with ancient books, inscrutable monuments, and strange figures that flit along through the ages as if they had a purchase agreement on eternity.*

"The key to everything is wrapped up in this paragraph. What this implies, is that users of the Sacred Manna seem to defy death and are not constrained by time. It implies that there are monuments that have answers as well as books that may lie in plain sight.

"In his *Le Mystere des Cathedrales*, he reveals clues by discussing a master glazier named Arnaud de Moles and a series of stained-glass windows depicting the Tree of Jesse."

JW went on to explain the similarities within the sapphirine vase they had found with the unknown process the Knights Templars had used to encode Hermetical Wisdom within their stained-glass windows.

He wrapped up his conversation by extrapolating parts of his ayahuasca visions, his research, and a good dose of intuitive guessing. He could see that Maya was trying to get her head around his logic.

"So Drune's recitation about the process obviously leaves out a large chunk, if he even discovered it at all," she said. "According to your loosely defined catalog of ingredients, we need gold, platinum, and..." she paused here. "And frankincense and myrrh.

"Then the source of power involves astral energies supposedly channeled from obelisks, which are directed to the blue crystal vase where the proper recipe and mixture are baked into our bread of light?"

JW nodded his head. "Hey," he smiled. "If the Creator wants this to be discovered, then it will be. If we are wrong, then it won't."

He watched as she paused in this reflection. He knew six months ago she would have scoffed at it. Today, she shook her head with a *what will be, will be*, nod.

The pilot advised they would be landing soon. JW's excitement at what might lie ahead quickened his pulse. He nervously tapped his foot on the floor as he stared out the window.

In the looming distance, he could see the Pyrenees Mountains that separated Andalusia from France as the plane lined up for its descent.

♦ ≋ ℳ ≋ ℋ ♎ ♎ ℳ ■ ≋ ♋ ■ ♎

Maya - Auch, France

The cab from the airport dropped them off on the right bank of the Gers River. As a further precaution they mixed with the tourists along the Claude-Desbons promenade that paced the spacious riverbank, blending in until they reached the cathedral.

Above, the skies were a pale blue and the smell of fresh cut grass mingled with the aroma of fragrant countryside. Nearby, Maya could smell fresh baked bread as JW talked about their destination.

"According to the article, it says that in the Bible that someone will plant the golden tree of life, which in Hebrew is the ORME tree. After Maria Vasquez cryptically mentioned Auch, I did some research. The Cathedral here is particularly famous for Templar-stained glass windows that feature The Tree of Jesse which by another name, is called the ORME Tree."

Orbitally rearranged molecular elements? Orme Tree? Maya once again realized that luck and coincidence were secular concepts that religious people called blessings and providence.

"More specifically," JW continued. "In Revelation it says, *'Blessed be the man who shall overcome for he shall be given the hidden manna, the white stone of the purest kind upon which will be written a new name. He will not be the same person.'*

"The white powder of gold fuses to form gold glass. It's a transparent glass, just like window glass. And in Revelation, it says, *'The streets of the New Jerusalem will be paved with gold of the purest light, as transparent as glass, and the foundations of New Jerusalem will be made with gold liken unto glass.'* I believe here we can see some of this gold glass, the basis of the New Jerusalem."

He paused, a weight to his punctuation mark. "Auch, glass, Manna—the way to leave this worldly realm."

Maya inhaled a short gasp. The feeling that they were getting closer to unraveling the secret caused such an adrenaline rush, it roared in her ears.

Because the promenade ascended from the river, as they approached the front of Auch Cathedral, the edifice seemed small in comparison to other Templar creations such as Notre Dame, Chartres, or Reims.

It was fronted by two rectangular towers, each with three stacking layers like a wedding cake. It was built from a white stone and sat upon a four-sided first floor with three arches defining the front, and an entrance in the middle.

Maya had been in many of the Gothic cathedrals over the years. This one, though a great specimen of Templar construction, certainly did not appear to overwhelm. At least not until they entered through the ancient doors hanging from iron hinges.

Covering her mouth with one hand, she looked up at the ceiling three stories above. It was held suspended by high-flying buttresses supported by columned arches running down both sides of the nave.

She turned to JW, to see if he was as enthralled. He was staring at the huge stained-glass window behind the altar at the far end of a long deep aisle. It was the intended focal point of the entire church.

Still, the windows dominated the room, and she counted the colossal glass structures. There was a total of twenty-four windows, divided twelve down each side of the basilica. These were so brilliant and radiated such a depth of color, it was hard not to stand transfixed and get lost in the intricate details as sunlight poured into the cathedral.

The interior was lit by a dozen hanging chandeliers, but they were muted by the effervescent light flowing from the Templar's gold-fired glass. As the design intended, like train tracks they guided one's eyes towards the large mural above the altar. There were frescos of the apostles looking down at the intricate stained-glass Tree of Life, the ORME Tree.

There were very few people in the cathedral. The hush was distinct, and it felt sacrilegious to let one's voice ring out, so they spoke in whispers.

"The Tree of Jesse originates in a passage in the biblical Book of Isaiah, which describes metaphorically the descent of the Messiah, and is accepted by Christians as referring to Jesus," he explained in a hushed voice.

"Look at those kneeling in worship." Maya pointed to a specific pane. "They are offering up loaves of bread, the same as those that are offered to Hathor. And the glow around the Messiah…" The craftsman's effect of using sunlight to create a halo effect upon the Son of God was magical.

JW stepped back for a wider view. The twenty-four other windows were driving a story from back to front. The ORME Tree was the culmination point of what seemed two divergent paths.

As Maya glanced at JW, she began to feel a tingling sensation and her heart raced a little faster. The early scenes depicted shades of Egypt, as if maybe Moses and the Exodus. But deep in the image, other innocuous images. A small horned hat, Hathor? And a lotus blossom. Symbol after symbol, invisible to the uninformed, the depictions had specific clarity and meaning.

Each progressed towards the ORME Tree and the offering up of the Sacred Manna. They progressed from the departing of Egypt, through the Sinai, the smelting of gold and the power of the obelisks and ended at the destruction of the Temple of Solomon.

"The history of the lost secret," JW whispered in amazement.

"Yes," she said with a nod. "But look here on the left side. On the right, everything follows the known path outlined in the Old Testament, but on the left, once they leave Egypt, it departs from any known Biblical lineage."

Maya had a keen awareness that this was important.

"And see what the woman is carrying. A small blue vase," she pointed. "The same as the one we found in Arizona. And the same as the one Petrie found in 1904."

Maya's fingers twitched while her mind scrambled to fit meaning into the left side of the nave.

"Who's the woman?" The windows depicted a royal entourage heading to a land of forests and mountains that were dusted in snow.

"The bowl," JW said. "We know it's important. But the snow…"

Behind them, the door closed with a heavy thud. Maya saw that the room was completely empty except for two men. Dressed in black denim jeans and tee shirts, they stood blocking the exit.

CHAPTER 28
Layla - New York City

Layla answered the call on the second ring, it was Rex.

"You have a problem," he said worriedly. "I'm standing at the park looking down Eighty-Sixth Street. There are unmarked cars on both the corner of CPW and Columbus, and it looks as if there are a few sidewalk spotters trying to blend in. You need to get out of there."

"-Are you sure?" His blunt insistence throttled up her anxiety.

"You need to leave. Now!" Rex said, nearly shouting into the phone.

"Alright, alright," she said as a million thoughts raced in her head. Layla wasted no time mobilizing. After giving rapid instructions to Tavis, they scoured the apartment and gathered up their folders, computers, phones, and anything else they would need or want to keep from their adversaries. Fear pounded at her chest as anxiety-glistened sweat coated her face.

"Follow me," Tavis told her. Grabbing one of the bulging backpacks, he motioned towards the rear of the building.

The balcony?

"I'll go first," he said and climbed to the other side of the railing.

Layla looked down. All the balconies were structurally tied together, the columns anchored to the ground. She quickly followed.

It was not quite noon. Grey skies and cloud cover threw off a grayish light and a light drizzle covered the alleyway. They were in a rectangular yard hemmed in on all sides by adjacent buildings.

"There has to be a fire exit somewhere in this courtyard," she whispered frantically.

"There," Tavis pointed. It was an old steel door with a panic bar.

Layla took the lead towards their only means of escape. She stayed in the shadows. Time seemed to slow as adrenaline heightened all of her senses. The cold of the rain, the padding sound of their footsteps on wet concrete. Hinting smells of old garbage.

Keeping one eye on the objective and one eye on the apartment above, Layla saw movement in front of one of the windows. Someone appeared on the balcony. It was a man on a radio.

Tavis stepped past her and pushed hard on the rusted bar. After a meek struggle, they were relieved to see the door open to the street.

They hastened up to Columbus Avenue and flagged a cab. It pulled out into traffic with a hundred others just like it. Craning to see if anybody was following, Layla spotted a black Tahoe barreling around the block.

♦ ≈ ℳ ≈ ⋈ ♎ ♎ ℳ ■ ≈ ♋ ■ ♎

Maya - Auch Cathedral

"What do we do?" Maya whispered. She had not made direct eye contact with them, acting unaware of their presence.

"It's a trap," he warned in a low voice. "They are trying to flush us out. Make us run for another exit. Something off the main avenue, away from the crowds. They'll likely have others waiting."

Maya began running through her options. Biting her lip at the uncertainty, she fought to remain focused, willing herself to keep the situation under control. She knew that the hornets' nest she had kicked open was growing and that under no circumstances could she let these goons capture them.

"If they have guns and are prepared to use them, then our options are limited," he answered.

"And if not..."

"Fight or flight?"

She looked at the two men. They were both fit and muscled. She was not sure if JW could take them both on. Maya had taken a number of self-defense courses over the years, mostly for the cardio, but now...

"Look—at the end of the Nave, see the candelabras on each side of the aisle?" JW suggested, implying fight as their best option.

She nodded in understanding.

"On three," he said. "One, two, three..."

Maya took off as fast as she could. The two men wasted precious seconds in indecision. As one man fumbled for something under his shirt, Maya closed the gap and in one swift motion, grabbed the top of the pole supporting the candles and wrenched its base up into a full arc and hammered down on the arm of the man whose hand was on the butt of his pistol. As he collapsed in pain, Maya saw that JW had blasted the other man with a solid jab to the temple.

In an instant, both men were down. And just like that, silence returned to the room bathed in the soft shimmer of the ethereal light of the stained glass.

"Let's go," Maya said, her adrenaline now pumping her full of the primeval fluid of survival.

She pushed open the doors into a sunlit afternoon. Tourists were strolling through the square. She looked left, then right, and chose left. "This area is famous for their Pousterles," she told him.

He gave her an odd look.

"They are long alleyways that meander through the city," she explained. "This way."

She crossed the road and ducked into a narrow alley, maybe six feet wide. There were stout wooden doors on either side of a landing that topped a long narrow set of stairs that went down the hill. There were stone walls on both sides creating a descending alleyway, with a rail anchored to their right.

Where sunlight could penetrate, ivy grew along one wall. The corridor continued down and away as it curved out of sight. From the landing, the Pousterle looked over the city revealing just how high the cathedral was elevated.

"Follow me, she said and took off down the Pousterle, taking two steps at a time.

After descending what felt like an unending series of stairs and landings, Maya entered a plaza full of fruit and vegetable stalls. Yellow and white umbrellas were abundant, protecting the fresh harvest from the sun. Pine-slatted crates stacked with lettuce, peppers, tomatoes as well as cantaloupe, asparagus and a plethora of other goods glistened in the light.

As JW sidled up next to her, the aroma of fresh basil, garlic, mustard, and fresh banquets of bread surrounded them. The square was hemmed in by three and four-story buildings, fed by narrow streets except for on one side, which had a broad avenue.

"I don't think we can go back to the airport, they will be waiting," JW said between labored breaths.

"Over there," Maya pointed, breathing in short sharp gasps. There was a blue and white tour bus with a colorful graphic on the side. It read *'Tour d'Armagnac and the Musée des Jacobins.'*

"Let's hitch a ride. It will get us out of town, and we can regroup from there."

When the busload of chatty tourists circled the square and made for the main point of egress, Maya saw a man enter the plaza from the Pousterle. From his posture, he was not there to shop, his eyes were searching, but he looked unsure.

Fortunately, indecision led to a less critical observation and tourist buses were so common, it was simply background that was easily ignored.

It was an older bus and had booth seats, not individual ones like most U.S. tour buses. Maya let her weight sink into the green plasticized padding, willing her heart to slow as her adrenaline ran out steam.

Tuning out the French and American voices that surrounded them, Maya stared out the window in thought.

How did they know? How are they tracking us? It can't be the burners.

After a few minutes of quiet, they exited the city where she saw from afar the grandeur and immensity of the Auch Cathedral. As suspected, it was the most elevated point in the town. On either side of the road were fields and fields of yellow sunflowers dappled by sunlit skies. All the while, Auch grew further behind until eventually they passed into rolling hills that were abundant with white cattle grazing in fields with splashes of purple lavender between wooded hillocks.

Momentarily safe, her thoughts drifted back to the cathedral.

"Can I look at the pictures in your phone?" She knew there was a reason fate had directed her here. And the reason she expected was fired within those stained-glass windows.

"From Exodus to Jesus," she said softly. What intrigued her was the other story. For half of the twenty-four stained windows deviated from known Biblical lore to something else altogether. There was a subplot hidden in plain view, a story about the Sacred Manna, and all the elements to recreate it. And there was no mistaking the blue vase.

Who's the girl, and where are the snow-tipped forests?

♦ ≈ ᶆ ≈ Ӿ ♎ ♎ ᶆ ■ ≈ ♋ ■ ♎

They sat quietly, preferring not to discuss anything while in earshot of others. The tourist guide started with her presentation. The speakers crackled in French and then she followed up in passable English. She introduced herself as Lilly Claire and her pleasant accent was perfectly suited for the role.

"Auch is the oldest village in France, its origins going as far back as the thirteenth century BC. Some say it was founded by Meritaten, one of Pharaoh Akhenaten's nine children."

'Akhenaten!' The comment hit Maya with a jolt. He was the last of the pharaohs to have known the process for making the Sacred Manna. Before being overthrown by the priests of Heliopolis, his reign was called *'The House of Gold.'*

The guide now had her unwavering attention.

"Most of you have heard of Tutankhamen, but what many don't know is that he had eight siblings. And that his father Pharaoh Akhenaten, and his mother Nefertiti, were the founders of monotheism. Some scholars such as Sigmund Freud believe Moses and Akhenaten were one and the same. Meritaten is said to have resided here after crossing the Mediterranean when her family was forced to flee Egypt because of their one-God heresy. As a matter of fact, Akhenaten's rule is now known in the annals of Egyptian history as *'The Heretic King.'*

"Auch is one of the oldest civilized settlements in Europe…"

"Is Meritaten buried here?" JW asked.

"No, of course not," the woman said with a smile. "Legend has it she continued north and may even be at the root of Gaelic culture." Then with a soft chuckle she added. "Many scholars believe that the Scottish people are part of the early Gaelic culture that evolved from the Celts and are the basis of the myth of a lost tribe of Israel.

"Perhaps this is a blend of old stories about Moses, Akhenaten, and their identical lost tribes. There is evidence that Moses also had a sister, Miriam. And of course, scholars suggest she too may have migrated north away from the path of her brother, but… these are all stories."

Lilly Claire quickly changed topics and went back to Auch during the two great wars and then onto the region at large. Armagnac and its famous distilled spirits…

As the topics changed, Maya reconsidered the mural of the snow-dusted trees. The House of Gold. Meritaten, Scotland or Ireland. Goosebumps of excitement broke out along her arm. She looked skyward with a smile.

Thank you.

CHAPTER 29
Layla - Café de Paris, NYC

After switching cabs twice, then cutting through Central Park on foot, Layla and Tavis made their way to their old meeting place, Café de Paris. Father Book was already seated.

The grey sky had given up its ominousness bent, and the occasional ray of sunlight fought to take a peek. The threat of rain had moved on.

Before Layla could reply, Book placed a finger to his lips. "Let us enjoy the entrecote, then I will show you to your new lodgings."

Layla had no stomach to eat, but she had asked a favor of Book and accepted his timetable. Nonetheless, she continued to scan the streets, letting worry and paranoia reign. Ninety minutes later they were in lower Manhattan in an elevator going up to the fifth floor of a building east of the Village.

"This place is anonymous," Father Book explained as he showed them the compact two-bedroom unit. "It has many ingress and egress points, and most importantly, we have many of our brethren also living in this building who will be watching over you."

Layla assumed brethren meant, Sons of Jared.

"May I call Rex from here?" The knot in her gut would not go away.

"If you believe your phones are secure."

Layla pondered the possibilities, the burners' exposure, and made the call. Rex answered on the first ring and Layla quickly updated him. He replied with the address of his friend's apartment where he would be staying.

Layla let out a long slow breath, slowing her heart as she tried to unwind. All the while she had been flitting from subject to subject, giving Father Book a chaotic compendium of the last forty-eight hours.

She pulled the backpack that contained one of the files she wanted to share and a stack of folders spilled to the floor.

"Dammit," she said, annoyance fueled by pent-up anxiety. Immediately she looked to see if Father Book took offense. His expression suggested he had not heard her.

"I'll get it," Tavis said with a smile. He touched her hand. "Let me, please."

Father Book was particularly interested in the hierarchy of the Hidden Hand, the additions of Lord Balforth, the communication cutouts and the blank spots Layla had marked as *'Watchers?'*

"There seems to be a head atop this octopus, or better yet at the center of the spider's web," she told him. "We have reviewed a number of communications that mention the initials TM. And the strong emotion attached to the initials is apparent."

"Rex also caught a mention of a name, The Maestro. But we have not confirmed whether this is TM or something else altogether."

As Tavis gathered up the spilled contents, Layla noted one of them had caught his eye. And cast a questioning gaze.

"This photo. What is it?" he asked. He had a twinge of eagerness in his voice.

"It's the vase they found in Arizona. Why?"

"I saw something like this when I worked for Allister Stewart back in Scotland."

Layla's breath hitched at the statement. She knew there were at least two vases. The one from Egypt that Sir Williams Flinders Petrie mentioned in his diary and the one they had extracted from Wynn Lambert's cave. She was pretty sure the latter was still buried in Arizona. *A third one?*

"Are you sure? Where did you see it?" There was a growing buzz in her ears, it was a mixture of excitement and the increased flow of blood. Before any of the others had grasped hold of the realization that their quest had supernatural guidance, Layla had seen it and therefore, nothing was too farfetched. Coincidence was becoming commonplace.

"One day Allister asked if I wanted to meet the Lord," Tavis chuckled. "Yes, I told him, but not yet. It was a joke of course. He had meant Lord Perth.

"So, he took me up to Perth Castle where I met the Lord. He was a young man, single, and I believe the last of the heirs. The castle was old. I mean really, really old. The most recent wing was a chapel that had been added around 1300 AD.

"I remember it had beautiful stained-glass windows. But the dominant feature at the back of the nave was a sapphire blue vase about the size of a child's soccer ball. When magnified by the up-lighting he had put in place, it cast whispers from God himself. It was one of the most magical things I have ever seen."

"Where did it come from?" Father Book asked.

"I actually asked the same question; I was so enthralled. It's why I remember it so well. Lord Perth explained that it has been in his family for more than a millennium and that it was brought to Scotland by Queen Scota, the legendary founder of those lands."

"Scota?" Layla asked.

"A mythical Queen from ancient Egypt," Father Book explained. "Some claim she was a daughter of Moses. Others claim she was a daughter of Akhenaten..."

"When was this? Do you think it is still there? Were there other items or things related to Egypt or this Queen?" Layla was trying to fit the pieces together.

"It was over ten years ago," Tavis explained, his tone implying that he could not recall many of the details. "I know that the lord had contemplated selling his holdings, but as far as I know, he still owns the castle. And I am quite sure Allister Stewart still resides in the same estate manager's cottage that is his to use until he passes. It is just off the River Tay near Campsie Falls."

"I need to get ahold of Maya and JW. They need to go check this out. Can you reach this Mr. Stewart and see if he could arrange an introduction to Lord Perth?"

CHAPTER 30
Maya – Toulouse, France

The driver pulled up to the private gate of the Toulouse Blagnac Airport. Maya had called Robert and he had reassigned their jet stationed in Agen, to the La Garenne Aerodrome near Auch. He had the pilot file a flight plan for Lake Garda while making an unscheduled stop here.

The airport was a large modern commercialized center with so much traffic one extra jet would go unnoticed. At the restricted entrance there was a handsome young security guard in black pants and a crisp green shirt with epaulets.

Maya was worried he was going to ask for identification. This opened a floodgate of paranoid conjectures. He would log their names, it would go in a data base, the Hidden Hand would find it, and their anonymity would be blown.

Still, Maya followed Robert's explicit instructions.

"Good day, Sir," she said through her open window, moist beads of sweat gathering at the nape of her neck. "I am a guest of Mr. Robert Vaherees. That is his jet sitting over there on the tarmac." She tilted her head towards the idling aircraft.

The man took a clipboard, examined the list, examined her and her large companion. He seemed unsure, which ratcheted up Maya's worry. He opened the long arm of the security barrier and they passed.

"Phewww," she exhaled on a long breath.

Once they were airborne, ostensibly towards Lake Garda, Maya made her way to the cockpit and spoke to the pilot. After initial pleasantries she made a request.

"I would like to make a change of destination."

"Yes, ma'am. Where would you like to go?"

"Edinburgh."

"No problem, Ms. Harrington."

"One other thing," Maya asked. "Do you have phone communications on the jet?"

"The galley phone is hooked up to the satellite network, it should work just fine."

"Thank you."

"Edinburgh, it is." She told JW, as she returned to her seat.

She retrieved a number from her cell and punched it in to the receiver nestled on the burlwood table.

"Who are you calling?" JW asked.

"Gary McKay," she said with a smile.

He was the guide they had used up in the Orkney Islands when they were investigating the works of Alexander Thom and the discoveries that linked her Master Builders to the builders of Stonehenge.

Gary picked up on the second ring. After a few minutes of small talk, some banter back and forth, she hastily updated Gary on their quest to find the Master Builders, which allowed her to segue into why she had called.

She stayed away from the idea of Manna but explained why they were heading to Scotland. She combined what they had learned from the tour guide and what Layla had relayed from Tavis.

"If you could dig through the legends of Moses, Akhenaten, the lost tribe of Israel, Moses's sister, Queen Scota, and Meritaten and meet us in Perth, perhaps together we can visit this castle and unravel a mystery of the ages."

She wrapped up the call by giving him the burner number and offered up some hefty compensation for his time, and then wished him good hunting.

"Aye, the incredible Mr. McKay…" JW said in bad brogue.

Maya knew he had developed a quick bond with the man and had a fondness for his wry wit. She smiled and sat back, falling deep into her seat. Closing her eyes, she let the soft wash of jet drone lull her to sleep.

◆ 〜𝕞 〜⩛ ⚋⚋𝕞 ■ 〜 ⚲ ■ ⚋

Maya - Perth, Scotland

The midsummer sun stayed high over Scotland, and though it was already nine o'clock at night, it could have been late afternoon. They checked into a small bed and breakfast, where they got a single room with twin beds. They had green and red tartan covers and matching drapes.

"I'm famished," JW said.

"Me too. At this point, I'd eat haggis."

They made their way down the road to the Salutation Hotel and entered its pub from the street side. It was classic Scotland. Inside was a rectangular pergola with stools on two sides that framed the bartender's station. There was a door into a kitchen and a mirrored back wall with whiskeys and a few other lesser used spirits. Predominant were the beer taps.

They found a table by the window and a lovely lass in a plaid skirt came over with menus.

"We'll have two pints of the Fyne," JW said, ordering a local beer.

Maya locked onto the free Wi-Fi service of the hotel. She was going through the terms of service agreement when a message came in.

"Gary just emailed. He will not be able to make it until late tomorrow."

"It is what it is," JW nodded. "Maybe we can go and find Nessie."

He was kidding but Maya thought a break would be good. Since they had the time, she played along. "I'll bring the camera."

After a meal of local salmon, a few pints and a couple of drams of Aberfeldy, they were ready to call it a night. Once back at the inn, JW wasted no time falling into a deep sleep.

Maya looked at him and cracked a smile. She was usually the one who was a bit more enthusiastic with the act of imbibing. But not tonight. Tonight, she'd kept her mind clear. She wanted to do a little exploring via the spirit highway.

♦ ᰔᰔ ᰔᰔ ᰔ ᰔᰔ ■ ᰔᰔ ■ ᰔ

To mask JW's light snoring, Maya popped in some wax earplugs and got comfortable by the window. The fresh air caressed the back of her nape.

She found herself thinking about Robert and dropped into that theta state where the sensation of the spirit coming free from the body was unexplainable. It was a sensory rush akin to pleasure that washed over her as she now hovered over the room.

She visualized Robert and suddenly she was there, watching him talk into a phone while seated in the luxurious cream-colored banquette of his private jet. His jacket was off, and his shirt was opened at the collar.

Just seeing him again gave her a tingling sensation.

Behind him was an incredibly beautiful flight attendant attired in an elegantly trimmed uniform. The little green monster inside of her reared its ugly head and she found herself back at the house.

He wasn't paying her any attention, she rationalized, but the petty thoughts of jealousy had snapped her back into her physicality. Now wide awake and irritated, she opened her laptop and began researching Perth Castle, the surrounding village of Guildtown and any links, no matter how thin, to an ancient woman from Egypt. It might have been Miriam, Meritaten, Queen Scota or any other. But what popped up first was the castle's legacy, its historical association with the Knights Templar, and a raft of legends and myths fit for a novel.

CHAPTER 31
Rex - Upper East Side, NYC

Rex had temporarily moved into a friend's apartment on the East Side. At least until his pal returned from the Hamptons. A lot of people had fled the city for the summer.

He had just hung up with Layla. She had shared Tavis's recollections of the blue vase in Perth's castle. This revelation initiated Rex's use of his ability to roam to their own buried artifact.

It was a quiet Sunday and the street noise from Park Avenue was abated by diminished weekend traffic. It wouldn't have really mattered. Rex was so advanced in his craft, he easily tuned out minor distractions.

He settled into a comfy position and quickly slipped into the theta state required for remote viewing. His intentions were to check the side canyon area surrounding the buried vase. In the time it took for the thought to manifest, he was there.

Excellent. He viewed the soft sanded bank, relieved that the river had receded back to its normal level.

I wonder what happened to the horses.

Had they survived, his thoughts would have seized their aura, but he remained where he was and thus, he had a momentary pang of sorrow for the loss of their equestrian colleagues. It had cost Robert a pretty penny.

He saw the mark Maya had made on the wall and his thoughts manifested an image of the blue crystal. Then he was within it, once again marveling at the fired symbols and hieroglyphs contained deep within each facet.

It's safe. He let his consciousness return to the apartment, relieved it was undisturbed.

As part of his habitual process, he took his journey notebook and entered comments from the trip. With growing impatience, he called the one person he knew who could cut its retrieval time to almost nothing.

"Hello, Robert," Rex said. His boss preferred the familiarity of first names.

There was some initial banter and where Rex tried to answer as many of Robert's questions as he could. He could hear a tinge of worry in the man's voice.

"How's Maya? I haven't heard from her since she arrived in Scotland."

"She's in Perth waiting on a research colleague," Rex explained. "Once he arrives, they are going to Stobhall Castle where she believes there is additional information that could lead to cracking the formula for making the Manna."

There was silence at the other end. So Rex got to the real reason for his call.

"Speaking on the subject of the Manna. I know you are aware that we discovered a crystal bowl at the cave in Arizona and that we had to stow it…"

"What do you need?" Robert asked, anticipating the nature of the question. "I'm assuming you are going to retrieve it."

"Yes, that is correct. I need a helicopter and a pilot to meet me in Flagstaff, Arizona day after tomorrow. Someone who will do as instructed. No questions asked. Someone who will not be overly concerned if we break a few trespassing laws."

"Let me see what I can do," Robert advised. "I'll call you back in a few hours."

♦ ≈ ℳ ≈ H ♎ ♎ ℳ ■ ≈ ♋ ■ ♎

Rex - Flagstaff, Arizona

Rex stepped from the cool terminal at Flagstaff Pulliam Airport and inhaled the fresh August air. It hovered at a pleasant 75 degrees. Typically, this was the wettest month of the year, but for the third year on, it was dry. Precipitation was well below average. He reckoned they could use some rain.

Robert had given him the name of a retired Navy Seal who he explained ran special ops for various branches of the government as a freelancer. He also said he had access to a stealth bird awaiting Rex's call. No questions would be asked. Rex assumed he had been well paid for his silence.

Rex had reached out to the contact and given him the details of their objective as well as a list of criteria to be addressed. He reviewed their conversation.

"I am going to drop from the hovering craft, grab my prize and then you will pull me back up.

"All in all, a total of maybe three hours from start to finish if all goes well."

He pulled the rented Tahoe out onto Highway 17 and headed south for ten miles. The man who identified himself as Mike Shannon had given him coordinates and his GPS said right turn, nine hundred feet.

It was a dirt road, and the Tahoe left a rooster tail of dust behind him as he climbed the gravel path. At the top there was a makeshift parking lot and two hundred yards below was a dried-out bowl of dirt and rock where he saw a Sikorsky UH60 Black Hawk. A man was sitting in the open gunner's door and waved Rex down.

He had read about these new sophisticated choppers, but he had never seen one in person. It was a silent, radar-evasive stealth vehicle with strange panel angles and an enclosed rotor blade.

As he got closer, he could see the man was configuring a harness and winch system. Exactly as he had requested.

"Mike Shannon?" Rex asked, extending a hand to the man whose legs dangled from the opening.

"Sure as shit," he smiled and gave him a firm shake. "I checked you out. Whitmore said that you were an asshole. That was good enough for me."

Rex caught the man's grin. "Takes one to know one." Colonel Whitmore was the leader of Robert's security force who had helped them out in Guatemala and Cairo.

"How do you know that son of a bitch anyway?"

"It's a long and sordid tale," Rex offered noncommittally. "How did you know to call him?"

"Vaherees suggested it. Said it was for my comfort, but I think he wanted to chisel me down on price." He gave another toothy grin, and Rex suspected there was probably a kernel of truth to all of it. "He also had me pick this up."

Shannon swiveled, grabbed a cube-shaped box, and handed it to him.

Once again, Rex saw that Robert was two steps ahead. It was a foam core fitted case, like those used to transport sensitive equipment.

"Perfect." He wondered if Mike had an inkling of what he was retrieving. Then he realized Robert would have kept it on a need-to-know basis. And Mike was a pro who survived by living the mercenary creed: If you don't need to know, don't ask.

◆♒♏♒⧓♎♎♏■♒☉■♎

Grand Canyon

The helicopter was different from any Rex had ever flown in. It was so quiet that noise abatement headphones were not required. And boy, was it fast.

Rex flashed back to his last tour in Afghanistan. Specifically, his mind spooled through that fateful helicopter ride that almost brought his life to an end.

Someone had fired a surface-to-air missile that struck the rotor blade, and they crashed killing three and severely wounding him and two others. It was the catalyst that had caused him to leave the army. It had also instilled in him a sense of vulnerability.

No one should have walked away from that. And with enemies all around, none of us should have survived.

The helicopter dropped over the lip of the canyon just above the river. Rex watched as the silent craft dragged a wake across the waters.

"We are getting close," Rex advised, recognizing the familiar buttes and peaks. His pulse quickened at the prospect of executing his mission. It was something ingrained in him when he was in the military. Plan-execute-adapt-complete.

Shannon reared the nose up and stopped on the proverbial dime. From there they ascended straight up like an elevator.

When they crested the rim, Rex was relieved all they could see on the horizon were rock, buttes, and canyon. No calvary waiting to ambush them, nothing but mother nature for miles on end. Within minutes they were hovering over the beach.

Rex took a camping spade and a mesh net basket and climbed into the harness.

"When you get to the bottom," Shannon reminded him, "simply unsnap from the pull line and let it dangle. I will drop additional slack when you are ready to hook yourself back up. Once you have secured your prize and are confident you are properly hitched, tug the line three times and hang on."

Rex had done this a hundred times; it was part of his training. But looking down, he had a moment of hesitation as the faces of his comrades from Afghanistan flashed before him.

Rex sat with his legs dangling over the edge. His heartbeat elevated and his breath grew shorter. He could feel the rotor wash as his body slid out into space. Slowly he dropped in a controlled descent.

When his feet touched the beach, he realized he had been holding his breath the entire way down. Releasing the harness, he surveyed Maya's mark on the wall and began a methodical and efficient process.

He worked the area in a wide arc, making sure each blade penetration did not risk damaging the vase. After a few minutes, sweat glistened his forehead. Pressing his lips together, he relaxed the corded muscles in his neck. He was so close. He knew that this vase was somehow linked to their success. Failure was not an option.

He spotted the blue cloth. Using his hands, he carefully worked the edges, removing each rock and pebble, one at a time, using maximum care and precision until it was free.

He opened the wrapped towel exposing the object of his mission. He let out a long slow exhale—exculpating all the tension and worry that had been building.

Thank God.

He placed the vase in the net and tugged three times. As he cleared the Black Hawk's doors, he found Mike standing with an outstretched arm and he had a moment of panic.

Who's flying the chopper?

With adrenaline filling his blood stream, he handed Shannon the net webbing, glad to see he treated it with kid gloves. Then Mike helped him into the helicopter, closed the door, and returned to his seat. Rex assumed that for him, it was just another day at the office.

But Rex's heart was racing a marathon. He took in long deep breaths and then exhaled slowly. Once his pulse regained a semblance of normal, he pulled a jeweler's cloth out of his bag and began a soft, but thorough cleaning of the vase.

With shafts of sunlight pouring in through the chopper window, the facets of the crystals refracted a translucent haze of color. The vase was constructed of eight petals like that of a lotus blossom, each fused as one piece and fluted at the top like a flower in full bloom.

He continued to carefully wipe away remnant particles of sand when his fingers slid over an unnatural rib.

"Shit," he muttered. One of petals had a hair line crack that ran from the top left to the bottom right.

He assumed the pounding of the water topside have caused the sediment encrustation to settle and place an undue pressure on the artifact.

Now what? What is Maya going to think?

Suddenly, he had a headache. He focused on the mission. Adapt was the one thing that kept coming up. Things rarely went without a hitch. He continued to execute and carefully fit the item into the foam core container. He gave it a little extra nudge to make sure it nestled below the top of the lid.

I don't know what Maya thinks this vase will do, but now that it's broken...

CHAPTER 32
Maya - Loch Ness, Scotland

After finishing a traditional breakfast of scrambled eggs and sausage, along with baked beans, baked tomatoes, and mushrooms, Maya and JW took a taxi to Duncan Fraser's Autorama at the edge of town.

Low on cash and needing transportation, Maya had reached out to Robert and he had come through again. There was a vehicle waiting for them.

"Mr. Fraser?" Maya asked, flashing a broad smile.

"Aye, you must be Miss Harrington," the manager said with a leer. "Mr. Vaherees told me to expect you bright and early, and here you are."

She ignored his stare. He had all the trappings of the used car salesman that he was. Robert had shared with her that he had let himself get fleeced so there would be no questions asked. But he had not elaborated.

"This way," Duncan said, beckoning them to follow.

Rounding the corner of a rusted metal building, Maya saw a young man wiping down a red Mini Cooper convertible and she smiled.

Ahhh.

The car's hood was emblazoned with the British Union Jack. And Fraser damn well knew no one in Scotland would ever buy a car bearing a British flag. Well, no one but them.

But Robert's assessment was spot on. Duncan required almost no paperwork, just a signature. *Acceptance as is, on behalf of the Globelon Corporation.*

After the docs were finalized, he made a big show that he was giving them a tank full of gas and had added a decent spare that was stowed in the boot.

"You took me, Lassie," he said with a wide satisfied grin. As if they were driving off with such a bargain.

"Ya be a giant amongst men, Mr. Fraser," she said with an exaggerated curtsy.

They put the top down, comforted that it still worked. The day was going to be in the seventies. JW got in and she assumed he wanted her to drive. Then she remembered, when driving in the UK, left is right, and right is wrong. She crossed to the passenger side.

Loch Ness was about a two-hour drive to the northeast, but the scenery was spectacular. They had to be in Edinburgh, south of Perth, at seven o'clock to pick up Gary McKay, but the day was theirs.

"Did you know that Loch Ness is one of the most unique geological formations in the world?" she asked him. "It runs for sixty miles along the Great Glen Fault between Fort William in the Southwest to Inverness in the Northeast, effectively cutting off the famous Highlands from the rest of the country.

"Here is what makes it rare. The Loch was formed when a large chunk of Nova Scotia broke off and in geological time, raced across the Atlantic and crashed into the European continent. So the west side of the Loch is Nova Scotia granite, and the east is mostly European Moines. The bottom is littered with miles of shattered rock from the collision that dates back to Mid-Devonian times. About four hundred million years ago, give or take a week or two."

"So that's how Nessie got trapped," JW grinned. "Couldn't get out of the way of a runaway continent." They laughed.

"What were you searching so late into the night that put you to sleep?"

As the wind whipped about wisps of her long thick hair, she let the breeze carry away tension, worry, and fear.

"Since I am going to need to repeat all of this when we pick up Gary McKay, I'll simply leave it at this. Stobhall Castle. Lord Perth's abode in Guildtown, has a deep, and long attachment to the Knights Templar. We can discuss it in full after we pick up Gary."

"Aye, lassie," he said with smile. "Then let's enjoy the countryside."

Maya spied an old arched railroad trestle in the distance, a train was crossing framed by the scenic Highlands beyond. With crystal waters flowing below, it was quintessential Scotland.

180

They passed remnants of ancient castles and the towers of rehabilitated ones that were being snapped up by the newly rich. This caused her mind to drift back to the castle in Guildtown, the Knights Templar, and the links it may have to Sacred Manna.

The castle was constructed in the early twelfth century but was lost to the English until Robert the Bruce's recapture in 1312. During this period of occupation, Lord Perth and his two sons joined the Crusades and were part of the expeditionary force that made a great, but unknown discovery underneath the Temple Mount where legend has it, lay the remains of Solomon's Temple.

They crested a hillock and below was the infamous loch. The water was as still as a mirror, reflecting the azure sky with its white puffy clouds. Within the glacial bowl, the winds of the Highlands did not stir a ripple.

Driving along the shoreline, they passed Urquhart Castle that sat on a peninsula jutting out into the Loch. Maya recalled Urquhart was once rumored as a possible storehouse of the lost riches of the Templars.

Could Scotland really be the place that the secrets of the Sacred Manna were hidden? Is this what the Templars found in the remains of Kings Solomon's temple?

They continued down the road until they entered the gravel driveway of the Loch Ness Lodge. Here Maya spied a large plaster and wood replica of Nessie cresting the waters beyond the willow trees. A must-see for tourists, also known as a selfie center.

Across the street was the infamous location where the famous photo of Nessie was taken. Maya walked to the shoreline and dipped her hand into the water.

"Damn, that's cold," she said in a light voice. "Can't imagine Nessie could be a mammal."

"Probably not," JW agreed, playing along with her. After spending some time walking the shoreline, they returned to their car and meandered along the sixty miles of the eastern shore until reaching Inverness. Here they stopped to refuel both their bodies and their car. With the temperature dropping, they put up the top and headed east to the seaside town of Aberdeen and then followed the coastal route south towards Edinburgh Airport.

Once they arrived in Dundee, they continued past Glenrothes, St. Andrews and Kirkaldy until crossing the Firth of Forth, to arrive at their destination just as Gary's flight was landing.

♦ ∞ ♏ ∞ ♓ ♎ ♎ ♏ ■ ∞ ♋ ■ ♎

Maya - Guildtown

Maya smiled as Gary folded himself into the rear seat of the Mini Cooper. She recalled when she had met him in the Orkney Islands. Layla had hired him, and he showed up at the small airport dressed in bright yellow wellies, an oversized pea coat and an accent that screamed Scotland. At six-foot-three, he was tall but thin. Incredibly smart, but unassuming. She had liked him the minute they met.

They traveled the six miles to the Anglers Inn at Guildtown. It was past eight o'clock when they checked in. With August averaging seventeen hours of daylight, the sky was still in early twilight. They agreed to meet in the pub, which was a long rectangularly windowed edifice attached at the front of the building and was perilously close to the edge of the main road.

When Maya entered, JW and Gary were already deep into their second pints.

"Taking a nap?" JW asked.

"I wish," she smiled. "I was on the phone with Tavis. Seems he was able to get ahold of Allister Stewart, but unfortunately, he is not around. He's in Florida visiting family."

She saw the frown forming on JW's face and concluded. "As a favor, Allister spoke to Lord Perth who said he welcomes our arrival, tomorrow at 9:30. A local gent, Mr. Sandy Thom, will come by in the morning to drive us there."

Gary's eyes flashed with... recognition? "Yes," she confirmed. "A distant relative of Alexander Thom's."

Before falling asleep in her chair, she had sent some cursory research to Layla about the castle and the Knights Templar. On top of what she had already learned, the material just received from the other side of the pond was proving quite tasty. She marveled at how often Layla had found obscure information from hidden little corners of the internet.

But it begged the question, how much about Sacred Manna and the truth of their quest should she share with Gary McKay?

After careful consideration, she decided to start with the castle and then work from there. As she launched into what she knew of the Templars and Lord Perth's connection, she embellished some of the stories of lost gold and riches galore until she got to the part about the expansion of the castle in 1345.

"Layla took the information she had gotten from Tavis and dug into that. I'll give you the facts first and then the rumors."

Her inward smile belied her love for solving mysteries and who didn't love the Knights Templar, ancient castles, lost treasures? And add to this, Sacred Manna? It would make a helluva book, she thought.

"In 1345, Lord Perth was flush with money, owned most of the lands in the Tay River basin, and added a new wing to the castle. It was a church. Actually, it was more like a miniature Gothic Cathedral with steeples, interior archways with columns and keystones locking in each of the arches.

"There is a complex water clock that still keeps precise time, shows the movements of all the planets, calculates eclipses, and phases of the moon. And most impressive is that it articulates where in the Precession of the Equinoxes our solar systems reside at any given time. It is as accurate as the Mayan Calendar and was a marvel of engineering at the time. To be truthful, it is highly unlikely it could be duplicated today."

Gary's eyes twinkled under a crooked smile which tickled Maya's curiosity.

What did he uncover?

"You said rumors," Gary reminded.

"Yes. Though there are no plans that could be found anywhere on the internet, Layla was able to tease out an arcane fact about the clock's construction over seven hundred years ago. The clock is fed by an underground spring whose waters turn the mechanism and then find their way down to the River Tay via a subterranean aqueduct.

"There have been whispers across the centuries that somewhere within these tunnels are walled-up rooms that are bursting with treasure. Some claim that the Ark of the Covenant may be there, while others claim it is the resting place of the Holy Grail."

With satisfaction, she looked at Gary. "So that's what I got. How about you?" She had not gone into what they were looking for or why, but the idea of hidden treasure was a good deflection for the moment.

"I think we need another round of Tennent's," JW advised going to the bar.

"You know, this feels like we are in that movie, *National Treasure*," Gary said with a tinge of excitement. "What I have located is far beyond the simple spectra of coincidence. And truthfully, I am shocked historians have ignored this.

"Though the Egyptians were master record keepers, there is no mention anywhere of Moses and the story of the Exodus. But there are historical recordings of Akhenaten and his migration out of Egypt.

"The historical period of Moses and Akhenaten and their respective lives align to within fifty years of both Exodus events. And both had roughly the same number of followers and both took the same proposed route through the Sinai.

"Furthermore, both insisted on monotheism which was the root of their troubles with the priests. And the one commonality between Moses and Akhenaten that cannot be easily dismissed is Rameses. He was instrumental in both stories. One as a Pharaoh who drove Moses out, and one as acting advisor, the pseudo power while Akhenaten's son Tutankhamen came of age."

As Gary continued with the parallel paths taken by both Miriam, Moses's sister, and Meritaten, Akhenaten's sister—Maya quietly considered the trail of Manna.

The Cave of Hathor in Sinai was the high priest's laboratory, away from the centers of power. Moses stopped there for the Ten Commandments during the Exodus. Historians believed the place fell out of use after the collapse of Akhenaten's ruling House of Gold.

Did Moses use the Manna to go through the veil into the presence of God? Is this how he brought back the tablets containing the ten commandments?

Then Moses ends up in what is now Israel. And with the destruction of the Temple of Solomon, the secret is deemed lost forever. This, she recalled, was visualized in the twelve panes of glass on the right side of the nave in Auch.

"Without belaboring the point of these two women's travels to Europe, the reasons why for each," Gary continued. "I'll let you read it for yourself later."

He tapped the file with a forefinger. "Suffice it to say, they both ended up in France and from there, made their way through the Pyrenees into Portugal and eventually found their way to the British Isles. How they did this, where they got the money to buy a fleet... I'm still digging."

"Auch?" JW looked to Maya, who gave him a wink.

The story ran through two more rounds of beer. The myths surrounding the two entities soon became bound tighter and tighter. From the Gaelic culture of Ireland and the similarities into the ancient Celt language and Royal Court writings of old, there were so many crossovers, only a truly biased scholar would deny the possibility.

As intriguing as it was, Maya had not slept much the night before and let out a yawn. It was getting late and Sandy Thom was picking them up at 9:00 A.M.

"There were many stories that came out as tales from surviving Templars, that Queen Scota, the legendary founder of Scotland is buried in a royal chamber somewhere in Scotland. With others even speculating, it was somewhere in the Tay River valley. Stories, I might remind you," Gary said.

"One last thing," he went on. "In my research I noted that Perth's castle is currently for sale."

Maya felt a heightened sense that her childhood idea that there was a hidden thread woven throughout all of history was dangling in front of her again. She felt breathless at the converging factors. She had not mentioned the blue vase to Gary or that this may have been a repository to solving the greatest mystery of all time. But each fact painted the picture they were on the right path.

CHAPTER 33
Maya - Perth Castle

They were well into their second cup of coffee when the desk clerk entered the pub now acting as the breakfast station. He was followed by a fiftyish-looking man with a ruddy complexion, dressed in a black polo shirt, blue jeans, and sneakers.

Maya assumed this was their man and rose to greet him.

"Sandy Thom?" she asked with a smile.

"Yes, mum."

She nodded to the hotel employee who gave her a smile and returned to the lobby. Introductions were made, Gary signed the bill, and off they were to Sandy's car.

"Thank you for doing this," Maya said, genuinely appreciative.

"Anything for Allister."

Maya noted his already ruddy complexion went just a wee bit redder.

They pulled onto the main road. Gary was sitting behind Sandy. He asked a slurry of questions about what he knew of his great uncle, Alexander.

"Not a whole lot, to be honest," Sandy admitted. "I know he wrote a bunch of math stuff and that he thinks that Stonehenge was created by aliens or something like that."

Maya saw Gary's shoulders slump, clearly disappointed.

"Tell us about the castle," Maya said. Sandy misunderstood the question, assuming they were still speaking about his great uncle.

"Aye, Xander came here many times. Seems he had an infatuation with the place. He was a welcomed visitor of the lord in those days, though we never understood why. He would simply say to those who asked, we have a mutual friend in Sir William Flinders Petrie..."

"Petrie?" she expelled on a rushed breath. He was the archeologist who was considered one of the fathers of modern Egyptology. But more importantly, he was the one who had discovered the cave in the Sinai Peninsula where they had found the only known remaining cache of Manna known to exist. That it had been stolen by her kidnappers caused a pang of regret.

Maya's father had guided her to David Hudson, who was Petrie's great nephew. He had filled in all the gaps on the power and attributes of this ancient powder.

Her mind drifted to her father, wondering if she would ever see him again. She stared out at the rolling clouds. The sky was overcast, the sun teasing here and there. Passing through fields full of sheep and assorted crops, the road started its rise and soon in the distance off to their left was the River Tay. Sandy slowed the car and turned in the direction of the river.

"The castle's just up the road."

Maya let her wandering go and focused on their objective. There were still so many unknowns. *Are we on the right path to figuring out the secret process for making the Manna? Did the windows in Auch point to this castle?*

They passed through an open gate that had seen better days. After climbing three switchbacks lined on both sides with thick woods, they entered a gravel courtyard. There was a set of old stone buildings whose slate roofs were covered with centuries of moss lichens. In the distance was a panoramic view of the River Tay and surrounding valley.

"Breathtaking," she said, getting out of the car. She noted a middle-aged man exit the primary building and approach them. He was dressed in a cut cloth suit minus the tie.

"Lord," Sandy respectfully acknowledged him.

"Mr. Thom," he replied. "I assume these are Allister's American friends?"

Sandy nodded as Maya stepped forth to greet him.

"Lord Perth, it is a pleasure to meet you. Thank you for allowing us to visit."

He shook her hand with a smile, "Please, call me William. Allow me to take you on a tour of the castle. Let's start with the gardens, shall we?"

They had not specified their objective in visiting, so Lord Perth took them on his version of a guided tour. Clearly this was not his first time. He started in the gardens that were on the river side of the property, which was filled with ten- and twelve-foot topiaries that varied in design.

He pointed down towards the shoreline and they saw a rack of stacked kayaks. "Our Olympic kayaking team practices here," he explained, noting Maya's observation.

"Right now, the water is running too fast. Down below at Campsie Falls we have lost a few athletes over the years." Then, as if thinking out loud, he hinged on a moment of regret and mumbled, mostly to himself. "Tucking into the right side would have spared them…"

Maya sensed the sadness in his voice and forlorn nature of his comment that people recently died on the river?

Shaking free of the thought, he asked. "Is there something specific you would like to see?"

"Two things actually," Maya said. "We understand the chapel was added on later and contains examples of the Templars' exquisite glass in your windows."

With a pause before her second point, she took her phone and opened it to a picture of the vase from the Grand Canyon.

"We understand that you have a similar vase…" She showed him the picture and noted the surprise that registered on his face.

"May I ask where you got this?" He failed at masking his surprise.

"We have located a cave in the Colorado River basin that by all evidence, shows proof that early settlers may have come from Egypt during the end of the Pharaonic era."

As he weighed her words, his body language projected intrigue, and she dared ask the same. "May I ask how you came across your artifact?"

"Sir William Flinders Petrie gave it to my grandfather years ago," he told her. "I was never told why. It was a family secret that died three generations past." Then his face lit up. "Do you know its secret?"

"Petrie?" JW mouthed. The recent assumption of three vases was back down to two.

Maya was conflicted. Her anticipation had heightened thinking perhaps the Ancient Ones were more widespread and prolific than they could know. Now that hope was dented.

"Come," William decided. "Let's go take a look."

Maya followed William down a well-worn corridor that was lined with suits of armor, swords, javelins, and other devices of battle. Between the historically arrayed knights, hung old tapestries of tartan design. Eventually they passed into a room that had to be the library.

"Everyone who comes here wants to see the water clock," he said with a hint of pride. "I thought I would get that out of the way first."

The room was a two-story library overflowing with ancient books, portfolios of papers, and old maps. Banistered stairs ran up two sides to a second-floor landing with more shelves brimming with more books.

Maya stopped to take it all in. Every detail. Next to her was a small table beside a leather chair with two books. She noted one about Nelson Mandela opened to a title page filled with musings of what could have been if Mandela had not died in prison. The other was *The Bernstein Bears*, one of her childhood favorites.

"My cook's daughter," he explained, following her gaze. "She loves it when I read to her." Maya recalled *'He is the last of the Perth's. There are no heirs.'*

But that thought was short-lived. On the far wall, running from the floor, past the second-floor landing and all the way to the roof, was a clock that had so many moving pieces, it was hard to remain focused on any specific point.

Without considering that she might be trespassing on convention, she asked a question related to her research. In part she was curious about the water clock that dominated the library, and in part she wondered about the tales of the Knights Templar and lost treasure.

"I understand this is powered by an underground spring. How do you get there?"

This was such a commonly known element within his family, he took no offense at her question. He walked over to one of the bookshelves and pushed at its edge. It was a spring latch.

The room appeared to be seamless shelving broken into four-foot sections delineated by moldings. The pressure released a latch and the section swung inwards to reveal a dank landing set atop a descending staircase.

The invisibility in plain sight surprised her. She marveled at the craftmanship from centuries past.

"No one has ever asked about this before," he said with a smile. "It's quite damp and musty, but you're welcome to take a look."

She wavered; it was the vase she really wanted to see. "Maybe after we look at your urn," she smiled, appreciative he was being so open.

They returned to the hallway and exited through a side door that opened to a graveled lot fronting the chapel. It was a miniature of Gothic design with the odd exception that it had matching silos that rose up along both sides in the rear.

She stopped to look at this odd design. Everything about this chapel incorporated classic Templar Gothic design—except those two protrusions. *What are they?*

It was built of the same lichened stone and covered by the same steeped roofs as the main building. Though slightly out of context to known designs, it was regal and whispered of ancient secrets.

The entrance was framed by a pair of stout oak doors that were at least nine feet high. Maya's attention was caught by the design incorporated into the doors. It was a circle of spaced medieval nails with the doorknob centered like a point.

The symbol for Manna. An unexpected adrenaline rush caused her to bite down on her growing smile.

William saw her studying the design. "For hundreds of years our family crest was a circle with a point in the middle. That is until around 1820 when we changed it to a double-headed dragon with a single set of wings. More formidable," he said with a grin.

"I believe that is when the fabled Loch Ness Monster made her first appearance, though it would be another hundred years before that infamous photo was taken." His tone was one of fancy, as if he didn't believe a word of it, but it was local lore, so he embraced it.

"Come," he said. She followed him, with JW and Gary right behind her. Like Auch, the place was rife with stained glass and awash in color. And sitting at the very rear, behind the altar beyond the nave, was the vase.

Maya inadvertently sucked in a large gulp of air. She was speechless. *It's exactly the same as the one we found in Arizona.*

This led to a series of mental questions. *Who made these? For what reason?* They were all cut exactly the same and as she examined the item closer, saw that within the glass were the same symbols, glyphs, and the stars of Orion's Belt.

Lit from below, its facets twinkled as it threw out sparks of light that danced like fireflies on a moonless night.

♦ ≈ ♏ ≈ ♓ ♎ ♎ ♏ ■ ≈ ♋ ■ ♎

Oleg - Guildtown

Less than forty minutes earlier, five men had gathered in Kinross. It was a little over twenty miles from Guildtown. They knew Alex Harrington's daughter was on her way to Stobhall and they had been given very explicit orders to take her, but to be sure that in no way was she harmed.

Oleg, the leader who was Ukrainian, was getting tired of this cause-no-harm bullshit. The Brotherhood had never cared about collateral damage in the past. It made the job that much more difficult. But he knew the cost of disobedience, a price he was not willing to pay.

"The bitch doesn't know how lucky she is," he muttered under his breath. He preferred to hurt them up front, then dangle medical treatment as a carrot to those who cooperated.

Passing through Guildtown, the van with markings of a local plumbing business followed the innocuous sedan.

"We are three clicks out," Oleg said into the radio. All wore earbuds and all carried silenced weapons—a major offense if caught here in Scotland.

"Don't forget, they want that blue bowl smashed into a million pieces."

♦ ≈ ♏ ≈ ♓ ♎ ♎ ♏ ■ ≈ ♋ ■ ♎

JW - Perth Castle

JW held back as their host led Maya past the altar to the blue vase. He was clearly enamored by her enthusiasm. Sandy, on the other hand, grabbed a seat before Jesus hanging on the cross, apparently taking the opportunity to catch up on his prayers. And Gary... he seemed still focused on the ancient marvel of engineering, asked to return to the library to study the clock.

Maya and William continued talking, so JW busied himself by studying the church. He wondered about the silo-shaped section outside the confines of the nave. It did not match any other Templar design and Maya had said this place was associated with their fraternal order.

Rising from the floor was a stone obelisk that reached up and out through the roof. He had not seen its tip from the graveled lot. On the other side of the cathedral, he saw a matching pillar. But that was not all.

Inlaid into the floor was a path made of a different material from the slate used predominantly throughout the room. And this alternate material connected both obelisks to the altar, which was also made of the same material.

It's granite. The obelisks, the floor and the altar are all connected by Nova Scotian granite? A conduit for astral energies?

Suddenly, the crystalline vase, the obelisks, and the windows of Auch converged into a thought. *They made Manna here.* JW's heart skipped a beat.

From his research into astral energies and obelisks, he knew that scientists said that for them to be effective in transferring energy, they could not have the metaphysical current broken by any alternative substance.

He moved back towards the entrance to take in the entirety of the design. Since they began this quest, his intuition had grown stronger and could no longer be ignored. His grandfather had said he was becoming attuned to the Akasha—and he needed to pay attention.

Once again, it vied to be heard. It rang so loud that he expected that at any moment the voice he had experienced in Guatemala would start pouring out of him.

The windows are the key. Pay attention to the windows.

He systematically reviewed each pane.

The process. Like Auch, these windows are alluding to the ancient secret for making Manna. Each of the windows cast hints at a replication process. One window showed the three wisemen on bended knee offering gifts to a young woman. *Scota? Miriam? Meritaten?*

The next image depicted this same woman standing behind the altar with the blue vase sitting at the ready. Next to the crystal were the three offerings. Gold, frankincense, and myrrh. The last element had been worked into an oil which she was applying to the inside of the bowl.

A catalyst?

He no longer saw quiet Sandy sitting in the pew or Lord Perth and Maya deep in discussion. The blood pounding through his veins now gushed though him until his sole focus was on the clues around him. His dream journey had depicted these ancient wise men and that they were bound to the constellation of Orion.

The next window was a collage of many frames, each imaging aspects of adding elements to the bowl. Gold, frankincense, something that could have been platinum.

In the final window, it showed the cathedral at night and a brilliant white light poured in through the chapel's windows. He recalled the mesa where Maya had pointed to the infused symbols in the vase—Orion. *We are close!*

◆≈ℳ≈⼂⩄⩄ℳ■≈☌■⩄

Gary McKay

Gary appreciated Lord Perth allowing him to peruse his library. He found himself eventually climbing the exquisite, railed stairs to the second floor, studying various titles, spanning many languages that covered a thousand years. History, legend, politics of the time.

There were tall clear panes of glass that separated sections of shelving. From one of these panes, Gary spied movement below.

There were four men dressed in dark clothing and one carried a pistol. He needed to warn them…

CHAPTER 34

Gary - Trouble

Gary raced down the stairs and flew across the lot before the men had made their way to the back. Pushing open the stout doors, in a harried voice he called out a warning. "We have company. Four men, and they're armed."

Maya did not hesitate and took immediate action. "William, where does that staircase end up?"

"Ah—ah—ah at the river," he stammered, stunned.

"Come, quickly," she directed, steering William towards the library.

They made it back safely and closed the tunnel door without being seen. William found the light switch and the illumination was meager at best. But it was enough. The deeper they progressed down the ancient passageway, the thicker the air became with must. Dampness permeated all things and somewhere farther down they could hear water.

"Take a moment to catch your breath," Maya said, trying to figure out what to do next. She noted that the frightened owner of Stobhall had regained his composure and now had adopted a haughty bearing.

"What is going on here?" Lord Perth demanded. "Are you people criminals? Should I be worried?"

Sandy had sidled up next to the lord and suddenly there were two factions confronting one another.

"I don't have time to explain," Maya said. "You do not need to worry about us. But those people up there are criminals. And they have been trying to abduct me for over a month. I don't know how they found us here, but they are dangerous men." She saw his steely resolve soften.

"Well, we can't hide in here forever," he relented. "Mr. Thom and I will remain here and the three of you continue down until you come to the exit by the river."

Maya was relieved he was not going to be an added burden. It was the logical option.

"Thank you," she said. "For everything."

"Certainly."

Leaving their host behind, Maya led her colleagues through the tunnel, which maintained a downward slope. They passed the spring that powered the water clock but there was no time stop.

Ahead Maya saw the door, but unlike any she had seen before. It was a faux rock plug that had a handle on the inside. JW turned the makeshift knob and there was an audible click. It popped open on a spring hinge.

Maya saw the rack of kayaks down by the river. "Are you guys up for a water getaway?" she pointed.

"Whatever," Gary expressed in exasperation.

They followed a trail that entered a copse of tall pines heading towards the single-man hulls.

'Pffft, pffft. Pffft, pffft…' A hail of bullets kicked up the soil behind them. Maya ducked deeper into the boughs and turned to see two men rushing down the embankment.

"Quick, into the boats. Now!"

Maya was experienced with kayaks and was worried about JW's size. These were racing hulls, not pleasure boats. Sleek and agile, but tipsy and temperamental.

Gary helped shove the big fella out into the river and quickly followed. Another round of bullets sprayed through the branches. Their aim was blocked by foliage and limbs, but that advantage was rapidly disappearing as they closed the gap.

She weighed tossing the four other boats into the river, but another rain of bullets killed that idea. Maya threw her hull into the water and paddled out into the current, trying to place as much distance between them as her strength would allow.

♦〰〰〰〰〰〰〰〰■〰〰■〰

Back at the castle, the two remaining men continued their hunt. They entered the private chapel and saw the blue bowl. Their orders were explicit—destroy it.

"Wait by the door," Oleg told his henchman.

He strutted down the aisle, uncaring of the sanctuary's history or the beauty of the room. He stepped around the altar and grasping the barrel of his Smith & Wesson M&P22 Compact, slammed it down onto the fragile glass. It exploded into a thousand pieces. He weighed hitting it a second time but considered his precious weapon.

"Let's go," he barked. Outside was a fifth man who had been unseen.

"Stay with the car but get it the fuck out of here and wait for my call. Come with me," Oleg ordered.

"Let's get them while they are on the river."

Within minutes, there were now seven inexperienced kayakers on a river deemed too dangerous for experts to be training upon this time of year.

CHAPTER 35
Rex - The Great Mystery

Rex sat in his friend's Upper East Side apartment. He had an uneasy feeling that would not go away. The more he dwelt on it, the more he attributed it to the broken bowl.

It was time for a thorough assessment, to see if he could repair the artifact. He laid out some paper and carefully removed the vase, putting the empty container on the floor.

With great disappointment, his worst fear became clear. One of the petals had come free, no longer fused with the others. And were the images of Orion had been fired, grains of sand spilled out and onto the brown wrapping.

It reminded him of ancient Tibetan sand paintings, where each grain of sand was placed with care, but in this case, each had been placed to form art within the structure of the glass.

"It's Manna," he said in recognition. "Holy shit, the grains of sand are actually grains of Manna."

He had lusted for months trying to replicate the journey he had taken in Egypt augmented by a small dose of the Manna. He had combined his remote viewing talents with trace amounts of some recovered powder and set his intentions on finding Alex Harrington, Maya's father, his mentor.

His spirit had ended up in an alternative dimension, a place known in mythology as the Garden of Eden. Unfortunately, during a long discussion with Alex and an older man named Enoch, he had been ripped back into his physicality when two Cairo narcotics officers had burst into their hotel room and arrested both him and JW.

Unlike Alex, who had succeeded in transporting his entire physicality to another dimension, he had been limited due to the fact he did not have with him the key ingredient that allowed the Sacred

Manna to be elevated from a consciousness enhancer to a physical matter transporter. The extract of the blue lily. Something Maya had procured and lost.

He knew it was prudent to take a moment, willing his heart to slow. Right now, he simply needed questions answered, not a physical quantum jump to another dimension.

Find Alex? And find a path to make more Manna.

◆〰ℳ〰⅓⚍⚍ℳ■〰☺■⚍

The throaty sound of the black Tahoe strained at its leash waiting for the light to change. Heading north on Park Avenue, the four men were dressed in business chic and wearing aviator glasses. They had been given their orders. *Kill the target, destroy the artifact.*

For them, killing was just another task to be carried out without question.

"Circle around once, then we'll go around a second time and the three of us will get out on the corner of Lexington. You keep moving and await our call."

They understood the plan. Timing was a matter of traffic. And today it sucked as usual.

◆〰ℳ〰⅓⚍⚍ℳ■〰☺■⚍

Rex took out his journal and made note of the time, date, and his belief that some of the sacred powder was fired inside the ancient glass. He completed the basic entry by memorializing his intent.

His excitement was an obstacle to a successful launch. He willfully slowed his breathing while prepping for the journey. He set his journal atop the pile of mail on the counter and took a bottle of water from the fridge. He scooped some grains of powder into it and got into a comfortable position with his back against the couch. Excited at the prospect of reuniting with his mentor, he ran through a checklist of questions, and then set his intent.

Find Alex Harrington.

He drank half the bottle and began his process. Successfully closing the final pinhole of thought, his spirit floated up and out of his material husk. The sensation was very different from what he now deemed an ordinary voyage. Normally he would hover over his presence before being drawn towards his intended target. This time he found himself on the shores of an expansive river. The soft sandy beach was edged by cultivated fields on one side and sweeping waters on the other. Behind him the river raged as it jetted from narrow canyon walls. In front, the waters settled into the widening alluvial plain that flowed down and away towards distant mountains.

It was the same as the first time he had experienced crossing the dimensional veil. He did not stop to consider what or why, experience telling him that would be the kiss of death for a successful trip. He wanted to see Alex.

He followed the beach and noted the experiential differences from when he remote viewed without a dash of the sacred powder. In the typical theta state there was no touch, taste, feeling or smell—but here...

The sun felt warm on his face and the air was fragrant with the smell of a million flowers. So much so that the scent softened his taste buds and caused him to salivate. He was experiencing all the feelings of a physical body, but without one, something quite different from the mere transition out of the theta state. This powder somehow activated the senses of the physicality.

Peering ahead, far down the beach he saw an unfamiliar man who was waving to him. His breath quickened—again another experience he never had when viewing. He ignored this and picked up his pace.

Hurrying now, he was overwhelmed with a sudden sensation of falling, followed by dizziness and confusion, as if he had tumbled into a well.

The stranger reached out to help him up and Rex saw his face wore an expression of great sorrow.

"What happened?" he asked, wondering why this man was so distraught.

"They killed you," the man replied.

"What do you mean 'they killed me?' I don't understand."

"You are dead."

Rex sank to his knees as a river of denial washed over him. *Dead? How? Why? It can't be true—he must be wrong...*

◆♒︎♏︎♒︎⯈⯑⯑♏︎■♒︎♋︎■⯑

Rex returned to the apartment to find his body lying face down in a pool of blood. His legs were crossed in an unnatural pose and his skull had a hole in the front and a chunk missing from the back. Brain matter was splattered against the couch and wall.

He flinched and turned away. A sudden overpowering wave of nausea overwhelmed him. With that came a flood of anxiety and so many questions, deep-seated worries of the afterlife. Worries about Heaven, hell and... well everything.

Am I a ghost? Why am I still interacting with the living? Is this normal—is this how it's always been? Now what? Where's the tunnel and the white light? Is my out-of-body spirit affecting everything?

He worried that maybe he had ended up in a cosmic limbo. A Catholic's version of purgatory. He needed answers and willed himself back to the beach. The stranger was there, waiting.

"How did you know?" Rex asked.

The man opened his hands with a gesture that said, "I just did."

"Who are you?"

"My name is Drune." With a crooked smile, he turned and started back down the beach. "Come—they are waiting."

They? Is Alex or Enoch one of 'they?' Trying to match Drune's pace, he began asking a stream of questions.

"Are you dead too?"

"Me? Of course not."

"Then how did you get here?"

Drune stopped. With a kindness in his voice that was laced with a hint of impatience, he replied. "You know how I got here. It's the same way Alex got here. It's the same way all who leave the earthly plain alive get here. Now come, we have work to do."

"Work?"

Do dead people work? What can I do? One part of him was relieved—he wasn't going to hell. Another part, actually most parts—were total confusion.

As they walked down the beach, birds squawked overhead in a sky that was as blue as anything he had ever seen. His thoughts returned to the living. Things left undone. Hopes, aspirations, concern that he had abandoned his friends, and this led to another hundred questions about Maya and her quest.

CHAPTER 36
Maya - The River Tay

Maya's command of the kayak, coupled with her athleticism, allowed her to catch up to the other two. They stayed in a loose formation, but due to JW's inordinate size, his weight displacement was slowing them down. And that was becoming a problem.

A quick look over her shoulder confirmed the worst. Behind them came two waves of hunters. The two original guys were now closing the gap and two others had jumped into the fray.

"Shit," she muttered, as she raced through the options.

Meanwhile, the pull of the water was picking up and control was becoming more difficult. The flow was accelerating, and she had no doubt that by the time they got to the falls, it would escalate even further.

She formed a plan. Daring, risky, and reckless but one of the few options on the table. She pulled alongside JW's kayak and waved Gary over.

"Campsie Falls is close. I can feel it... William said tight and right is the only safe route."

The bulges of their eyes revealed their discomfort, but in unison they nodded. Maya glanced back upriver. They were closing in...

"Let's go."

She took the lead but never allowed herself to become separated from JW. As expected, the closer they got to the falls, the faster the water roared. Based on William's comments, she assumed the rapids would be dangerous. Ahead the water swirled and turned like a washing machine creating a sucking whirlpool on the right. Whereas to the left, it appeared to smooth out.

Lord Perth – I hope you are right! Because nobody in their right mind would choose that swirling maelstrom. But she gave in to fate, hoping one more time it would lead her in the right direction.

"Left then right," she hollered above the din. She tried to hold back and fought the pull of the current, willing JW and Gary to go ahead. She could feel their pursuers gaining, fortunately their hunters needed to use both hands so could not pull out their guns.

"Come on, come on," she urged. So far, they had the upper hand, so far fate was cooperating… and then it wasn't.

She saw JW's paddle get caught on a rock and ripped from his hands. "Damn it," she screamed. "Gary, move it—now."

She turned her bow towards JW, who was drifting off towards William's dead pool. Her heart raced, she strained her paddle, heaving against the waters. She pushed every ounce of strength to reach him.

Maya closed quickly and managed to get her kayak between him and the shore. She grabbed the edge of his scull and turned him away from the silent waters, reduced to only paddling on one side. The others were closing in fast.

She could see the smirks on their faces. She pushed, willed, heaved, and swore, all the while edging them closer and closer and closer to the turmoil and torrent of what by all appearances was the most dangerous part of the river.

She didn't have time to think, or to fear, or second guess herself. It was a race of seconds. Live or die. Drown or survive.

"Let that bastard think his prey is going to be another casualty of the River Tay," Maya swore under her breath.

Maya had one eye on Gary and saw him shoot through the falls and slip into the shallows of the far side. She aimed both kayaks towards the whirlpool and just like Gary before them, skimmed rapidly over the roiling water towards the other side.

She turned to see her pursuers were in a quandary. That fleeting hesitation sealed their fates. With a sucking sound, the boats were being dragged under.

"Oh my God," she said, bringing her hand to her mouth. First one, then another began to sink below the quiet waters, until the last thing she saw was the brown foam covering the spot they had just been in.

Maya jumped into the shallow waters of the far shore and was pulling JW's hull onto the beach as she spied the last man going under.

She had led her adversaries to a knowing death, but this time, the only emotion she felt was thankful—that her friends were safe.

♦〰♏〰♓♎♎♏■〰☉■♎

Maya - Stobhall

They made the trek back to Perth's castle. Wet, bedraggled, and physically exhausted. Maya weighed the secret entrance versus the steep slope and chose the latter. Cresting the hill, Maya caught the sight of a local constable's car, but he had apparently finished and was exiting under the archway. She also noticed that Sandy's car was no longer there. Was Lord Perth?

She was relieved at the sight of the police, even if they were leaving.

"I assume there are no bad guys left," she said to JW. He nodded.

Walking through the topiary gardens they exited into the lot separating the main building from the chapel. Maya needed to see the crystalline bowl, see that it was safe.

"William. Are you in here?" she called out from the foyer of the chapel. Her words fell silent on her sinking heart. The bowl had been smashed to smithereens. She winced. With heavy feet, she trod down the aisle.

Maya consoled herself with the idea that Rex was retrieving the other vase, but for some reason, that thought felt empty and hollow. She needed to update Robert.

Reaching into her pocket, she was glad she had not soaked her phone. She had no idea how reliable these burners were.

Burners? How does the Hand always seem to know where we are?

"Shit, it's not us, it's Robert," she said in a sudden realization. Of course. After Lake Garda... why did I miss this? Why did he miss this? That had to be it. They were listening in on his calls.

She thought through her discussions with Robert and the events that followed. Each time she had exposed where she was and what her plans were. They had been tracked.

Damn it! They now have all our numbers...

"We need to lose the phones. Robert's been compromised and so have we."

207

"Give me your phone," he told her. "I'm gonna take the last kayak and send it down river. It will misdirect anyone who may still be tracking us."

"Right. Here," she said offering up her phone. "Wait..." she snatched it back. Just for a minute."

She opened the camera and took photos of all the windows, then made a video and uploaded it to the cloud. Once done she handed it back to him.

Maya saw that Gary looked shell-shocked. Probably thinking he would be happy if he could just slip away and go back to his islands in the north. She couldn't blame him. That sounded pretty good right about now.

"Come on, Gary," Maya encouraged. "Let's go see if we can find Lord Perth."

CHAPTER 37
Rex - The Garden of Paradise

Rex arrived to see two men sitting on a bench, deep in conversation. Above them were branches protruding from a beautifully flowering tree. In the distance gurgled a soft stream that meandered through lush gardens. He recognized the two men. Enoch and Alex Harrington.

Rex was glad to see Maya's father again. The familiarity eased his anxiety and allayed some of his fears. He trusted Alex and his presence offered a cocoon of normalcy.

He wanted to reach out, to feel another human being and assure himself this was all real and not some elaborate dream. But whereas the others had a dense solid physicality, he realized his body was more like a holographic projection. An astral aura of shifting light waves.

He had a million questions. His mentor's presence eased his worry somewhat and he felt safe. But he had no idea what to expect next.

"I am sorry this happened to you, Rex," Alex said by way of hello. "But death spares no one and most never see it coming."

Enoch stood and moved to another bench where he was joined by Drune. Alex patted the seat for Rex to come and sit next to him.

"There will come a time when we will all stand before the righteous one and will need to explain ourselves," Alex said, his tone that of a father to a son.

"Fortunately, in His great wisdom and knowing the end from the beginning, He created the vault in the upper Heavens for those children of His who through faith, were willing to take the first step."

Rex had made a theological commitment back in that cavern in Guatemala but had never really considered a day of reckoning. Until now.

"Don't worry, my friend, I see you have taken that step and your faith glows like a beacon. But for so many, they remain in darkness. This is what Satan desires. He believes that by distraction, division, and by amplifying the human desires of self, he will keep many from ever discovering the light of true and eternal hope.

"He is trying to turn as many of God's children as he can, against Him. Or just as effective, keep them distracted from even considering the aspects of God, salvation, and what lay beyond the veil of their four dimensions.

"Satan's greatest trick has been to convince the world that he does not exist. But sadly, he does. And he is using God's fallen angels, as well as unsuspecting men and women to fulfill his aim of ruling the world."

Like a light that shines on darkness, Rex understood the importance of the quest he had been a part of. Or that he had been a part of. More humans were gathered today than at any time in history, and Satan wanted them. All of them. Rex felt a sadness that he could no longer help. A deep ache that grew as he considered man's fate.

"He wants to be the undisputed King and Lord. But the harsher truth is, he wants to exterminate so many people that only a few hundred million souls will be left to serve him. This is what we are up against. Since God gave breath into the first soul here in this garden, this is what Maya and the others have been destined to prevent."

"Maya explained to me that she had learned in Gobekli Tepe that Earth was a game board and man the object of collection," Rex said in a soft utterance. "That mankind was created to be part of a contest. He who collects the most souls wins."

It was Enoch who replied.

"She is closer to the truth than most theologians have ever understood. But calling it a game? For man it is eternity. For the angels of Heaven, it is a teaching moment.

"The fallen one believed he should sit higher than God and should shine brighter than all the rest. He will learn a lesson in humility. Our Lord knows all things and therefore He knows how this will play out. We are all instruments of His will," he said. And with a new sense of gravitas, he alluded to what would come next.

"Your role is far from over."

Rex thought of the nuclear bombs and his team's success in neutralizing the threat.

"Yes. Great. I want to help. We need to stop the Hand from releasing the plague." His spirit gained a little fortitude with a renewed lease on… Well, certainly not a new lease on life.

"Yes," Enoch said with doubt. "But there is a much greater threat facing mankind. A threat which He who knows all contemplated at the onset of time.

"There is a rogue planet hurtling towards Earth. What was once called Nibiru, is now referred to as DeeDee. It is the final event the enemy is counting on. All he is doing is a smokescreen, a distraction…"

CHAPTER 38

Maya - Perth Castle

Maya searched the property and concluded the place was deserted. JW had sent their phones floating downriver as a decoy, and Gary removed the battery from his own.

"It makes no sense. Where did he go?" Maya's worst scenarios filled her head.

"Maybe they left with the constable," JW suggested.

"Perhaps…" This lacked conviction. Her fear was that Lord Perth and Sandy Thom had been taken.

"I wonder if he has anything to eat," Gary suggested.

Maya scrunched her face, but he remained unabashed.

"I know, but I'm starved."

"You guys go check. I need a few minutes to think." She knew Gary was not aware of her out-of-body talent. For now, it would be too much to explain and she didn't have the time.

The two men left in search of a kitchen. Maya sat quietly in one of the pews and started the process of thought elimination. It was a struggle. So much had her roiled. Leading to so many questions.

In, out. In, out, focus—breath… she was on her fourth attempt when finally, the metaphorical zipper opened to let her mind run free.

Clearing her physicality an unexpected shock nearly crashed her back into her resting body. Rex was there waiting in all his ephemeral glory. He said something to her. The words did not stick but she knew something dreadful had happened.

"They killed me," he said a second time. "I am dead."

"What do you mean you are dead?" She asked, thinking he was pulling her leg or something. "Are you working too hard?" The question was hollow.

He was speaking in that telepathic parlance she had become familiar with from their trips to the cave in Arizona

"No. I mean I am dead, like physically dead. They killed me, and they destroyed the vase."

"The vase?" This was the catalyst that galvanized her attention. She realized he was serious.

"Shit—how? Rex, I'm so sorry." Suddenly Maya was flooded with a tide of competing emotions and fought to keep it at bay or risk coming out of her trance. Still - her friend having been killed filled her with sorrow and also fear. The Hidden Hand was no longer playing around. As this wave crested, a different thought came, which brought dejection and defeat.

The vase. It was the only one we had left. Now the Hand has destroyed both of them.

Seeing her friend watching as she pushed through the turmoil within, she let her pragmatic instincts take over. "How? I mean if you are dead, how are you here?"

She was a long-time atheist who only recently saw the world differently. She had not formulated any fixed concepts of an afterlife, so this was not her conflict. It was simply a need to know, to understand—to grasp and grapple.

"I was remote viewing when they arrived. The bowl was broken, and I saw powder leak out of one of the petals. The stars that were fired in the glass are made of Manna. I added some to my remote viewing and in an instant, I was back on the beach of the sacred river. While I was there, they must have come in. They shot me in the head."

This revelation came in like a third wave and washed her in anger, then sorrow, and then she had a sudden realization. "Did you see my father? Was he there?" It was a straw—a grasp at something to change the downward spiral of her emotions.

"Yes," Rex assured. "Along with Enoch and another man who calls himself Drune."

JW's man in the article?

"Now my eyes are open, I can see things much clearer."

Even though he was a spirit, Maya could feel his sense of pride. Not hubris, but more like he had found peace. A feeling of fitting in. As if he were unexpectedly a key player on a winning team.

214

"And?" she asked.

"We must stop them. You must stop them. You are the Lioness of prophesy. You were the one who was chosen so long ago. When your father accepted this reality, he enlisted the help of many."

"Is Robert part of this?"

Since that night with him, she had put away all thoughts that he was aligned with her enemies. What she had not expected were the new thoughts. *Did my father recruit him? Why did Rex go to him?*

"Robert, Father Book, and to some degree myself. We were all recruited one way or another by your father."

So, my father planned out everything. How did he know? This of course only added the to the growing mysteries about her enigmatic father. Things she had never seen before.

"What am I supposed to do? How do I stop them?"

Rex said nothing and she saw that he was grappling with an answer. Does he know how to stop the coming plague? Does Enoch have his own brand of watchers? Can they give me intelligence? Can Rex be like a cosmic secret agent? All these thoughts passed through her mind as she tried to discern what Rex was thinking. She let her hopes rise.

"The plague is still a threat, Maya—but that is not what we must focus on. There is something much worse. The destroyer is coming to crush civilization and kill billions and billions of people. It literally is a calamity of biblical proportions. It is the wormwood of Revelation."

In an instant, the images from Wynn Lambert's drawings and his written word popped into her thoughts and with them, a shudder.

She realized it was the Sumerian tale of a rogue planet that returned every four thousand years to wreak havoc and destruction.

"DeeDee?" she said, the very words sparking terror at the what ifs. "How am I supposed to stop a planet hurling through space?"

"By amplifying the power of the Manna," he answered with great certainty. "You must learn the secret process and use the Manna to fire God's sacred grid. This is what the Master Builders created before the turning of the poles.

"God knew Satan's final play would be to count on what he deemed his celestial conclusion. His final ace. God wanted him to think this. But one of the reasons God created the Sacred Manna was so that Enoch and his sages could cross the veil to initiate and implement the path of God's great design."

He paused as she considered his comments.

"I was told to relay this to you. I know nothing more than that."

She stared towards the altar in worry. This bowl was crushed; they were both gone.

"How?" The question was a holistic summary of all that was engulfing her. The overwhelming feeling of inadequacy, loss, and grief.

But there was something else. There was a growing sense of responsibility and a hardening resolve, all creating the mortar that was fortifying her faith. It grew inside of her, reminding her she was not alone. This feeling was drawn of spirit that came to strengthen her and convict her.

"Destiny will reveal a way," he reminded her. "It is meant to be."

'There is a way, you just need to use your intelligence to find it.' All these things ran through her head when Rex made a final comment that led her to smile.

"Just call out my name and I'll be there."

She thought through the number of times Rex had referred to an old song to make his point. She was glad he had not lost his since of style even though technically, he was dead.

"Stay close," she told him. "We got a rough ride ahead."

"Goodbye for now, Maya." And then he was gone.

She drew back into her body and sat quietly digesting everything. She felt a sense of calm laced with sorrow. She was sorry Rex was killed, but she saw a glimpse of an afterlife and it strengthened her resolve.

"You okay?" JW asked walking into the chapel.

She gave him an odd look.

"What is it?" he asked.

"Wait," she whispered. She turned to Gary who had followed JW into the nave and taken a seat in a nearby pew. He was polishing off the remains of a sandwich.

"Mr. McKay," she said in a tone that bore a note of seriousness. "I need to confess something. Something I will fully explain in time. We have not been candid with you."

He stopped chewing.

"I need to explain a few things to JW that you are going to overhear. And I am absolutely sure you are going to think I have lost my marbles. But I promise you, I haven't...

"Give me some time and a little latitude and I will reveal everything that has happened and what we are really after."

JW's expression showed surprise. But Gary's begged an explanation. "Please."

"You guys certainly are not boring," he capitulated with a shrug, returning to his sandwich.

Fixing her eyes on JW, the serious expression on her face took a grim twist. There was no easy way to say this, but it had to be said. She swallowed the lump in her throat and got it out.

"Rex is dead. They murdered him and smashed the other vase. He was remote viewing and outside of his body when they showed up and shot him. I just spoke to him."

She saw the bug-eyed expression in Gary's eyes as JW digested the loss of a friend and colleague.

"He met with my father, Enoch, and your buddy Drune. I was told that the greatest threat the world is facing is 'The Destroyer.'"

"Shit—Tavis warned us about this in Egypt, but we had forgotten all about it." JW said, dropping into the pew in front of her. And we are supposed to do... what?" His face registered doubt and his shoulders sagged in defeat.

Maya understood his dejection. The vases were smashed, the enemy seemed to be in control, and they were in deep over their heads being tasked with saving the world. She bucked up and leaned into Rex's comment that destiny was on their side—and by extension, the power of Heaven.

"Rex was cryptic. But he mentioned the Manna and the global grid."

"Did he mention where we could get more Manna?" JW's voice leveled in a tone of frustration shading towards anger. His eyes darted to the remnants of blue glass.

She saw where he was looking, but knew that the 'Powers,' would not leave them hanging. She just needed to figure it out. Continuing in a calm confident voice, she strode past the altar. She was grateful the glass had been broken into large pieces and not been pulverized to powder. She could see trace amounts of loose grains. Rex said it was Manna.

Choosing to see the glass half full, a thought tugged to be heard. It would not go away, so she massaged it into making sense.

"There is another vase here in the castle." This was proclaimed with utter conviction.

"Why would you think that?"

"These windows show the sacred bowl being here," she pointed, now adopting the familiarly of her pragmatic self. "But they were installed over seven hundred years ago. So if Petrie delivered his vase here, that was only about a hundred years ago." So there had to have been a different vase.

"I am going to go find it."

CHAPTER 39
JW – Perth Castle

"Gary, do you know what remote viewing is?" JW asked once Maya had dropped into the theta state and was gone.

"Can she hear us?" He was either ignoring him or not comprehending the question. So JW asked again.

"I don't think so."

JW proceeded to lay out a foundational background about what RV was, how the government had incorporated it and how Maya's father had taken it to a level unseen by anyone before him.

"And this is why people are looking for him, for her father?"

"In part, but there is a lot more and trust me when I tell you, you're gonna want to reject it lock, stock, and barrel. But I swear on our lives, what I am going to tell you is true. It is the real reason we are here today."

By the time JW had explained to him a summary about the Sacred Manna, Guatemala, Iraq, Gobekli Tepe up to and including her disappearance in Egypt and her reappearance in New York, Gary's face hung heavy in doubt.

"You know, I like you guys," he said with hesitation in his voice. "But really? And what's this about her talking to a dead man? Does she do ghosts too?"

JW did not know how long Maya would be under and could see Gary was at a tipping point. He did not want to be the one that scared him off but at the same time he had only given him the preamble. It was now time to lay out the full story. Chapter and verse.

"Maya was chosen by God at the dawn of time to be where we are today. Her father has passed to an alternative dimension and is in Eden with the Biblical Patriarch Enoch. There are at least two ancient prophesies that refer to her as the Lion, the one who will arrive at the end of days.

"We believe we are now in that place."

What he did not articulate was a thought that had been percolating for some time. The influences of astral energies could be fanning the subconsciousness of man and that this was all ordained from the onset. He continued his explanation returning to the hope of their calling.

"Maya has already stopped a nuclear war from starting."

"Nuclear war?"

"Yes. And if you saw the calamity in the Canary Islands, then you should know that was a trial run undertaken by the same people who are after us. Who placed the nukes." JW unraveled the entire saga. He noted the Canary Islands had registered a hit.

"She said a ghost mentioned the Destroyer," Gary mumbled nervously. "Has she always dealt with ghosts? Do they give her prophesies and shit like that?"

JW was set to explain when Maya's eyes flew open, and she jumped to her feet.

"Are you okay? What happened? Did you find what you were looking for?" JW asked, concern tinged his question.

"Yes, yes, yes I did," she said appearing almost giddy. She was trembling in a nervous but excited kind of way. "We need to see Robert right away."

CHAPTER 40
Maya - Sandifjord, Norway

In the end it was FedEx that came to the rescue. Maya knew they could not trust their phones, which were now gone anyway. They were sure Robert's phone was being monitored, and they needed to get his attention. So they sent an anonymous overnight package and prayed he got it in time.

They had returned to Perth, and between the cash she had left and Gary's debit card, they were able to hole up in a B&B until the proposed pick-up time they had expressed to Robert was upon them.

When they arrived at New Scone, the small airport three miles north of Perth, Maya let out a deep sigh of relief. She saw the now-familiar jet. Their plan had worked. She stepped inside and recognized the two pilots from before and exchanged a few pleasantries.

"Three of you?" asked Captain Magnusson. He was polite and respectful.

"That is correct."

"Yes, ma'am," the pilot said. "There is a slight change of plans. I was told to inform you that we will not be heading to London. We are going to go to Norway."

"Norway?"

Yes ma'am. Mr. Vaherees said he would fill you in when you arrive. He will be there waiting when you arrive."

Her heartbeat gave a slight flutter and a warm feeling suffused her at the thought of seeing him again.

Less than three hours later they had landed at Skien Airport in Geiteryggen and were met by a chauffeur who drove them to the coastal town of Sandifjord. It turned out to be a busy seaside port that reminded her of the coast of Maine.

They continued past the city center to an area that smelled of old money. Here large opulent estates sat upon bluffs that looked down the fjord from which the town was named.

When they pulled through the open gates, they climbed a long sweeping driveway that was protected on all sides by stately evergreens. As they made the final turn, a dignified mansion appeared and standing on the front step was Robert.

◆ ≈ ♍ ≈ ♓ ♎ ♎ ♍ ■ ≈ ♋ ■ ♎

"How was your flight?" Robert asked, welcoming the arrivals.

Maya introduced Gary. She was not sure what she was going to do with him. But for now, she had to keep him out of harm's way.

"Come," Robert suggested. "Let's get you guys settled and then we can have drinks before dinner." A servant appeared and took the two men through the grand foyer and up the sweeping stairs to the floor above.

"So," Robert asked Maya once the others had gone. "What is so important that you had to see me face to face?"

"Well for one thing…" She pulled his head down to her open lips, hoping he still felt the same way. His lips met hers and for a brief moment, Maya relaxed.

"I must say, Ms. Harrington, you do make quite an entrance."

She took his hand and led him over to the corner where she spied two seats and set out to explain what she had uncovered. After unfolding a tale so fantastical, so tantalizing, and answering every question he could think of, he asked the million-dollar question.

"So, what do you propose we do?"

"My understanding is that Stobhall is for sale. You must buy it. I am sure it will be the best investment you ever make. No matter how much he is asking. Offer a premium for a quick sale and be sure to write the contract in such a way that it includes everything, all the grounds, the estate, throw in mineral rights, any ancient ruins, or remnants of history, et cetera," she told him.

He smiled as she explained how to write the contract.

"Once you have closed on the sale and he is gone, you need to have Colonel Whitmore station a complement of men that you trust, who will not only keep our enemies at bay, but be sure that nothing that transpires there is ever whispered beyond the gates of your new castle."

"Alright," he surrendered. "I'll get my lawyers on it immediately. Let me show you to your room and then I will make a few calls.

"By the way," he assured. "No one knows of this place and I took heed of your letter. All the phones are direct to satellite and fully encrypted. If you need to make any calls, they cannot be monitored or traced… by anyone."

♦ ︎⌇♏︎ ⌇Ж⚏⚏♏︎ ■⌇ᨓ■⚏

She spoke to Layla. There was little joy that could be found in the conversation except for the single bright spot. That since he was out astral roaming at the time of his death, this somehow left Rex's spirit still connected to the earthly plain.

Maya had a heavy heart, and her throat felt scratchy. But Rex had a final wish, and Layla was the one burdened to fulfill it.

"Rex would like you to go to the apartment where he was staying. Collect the broken glass and powder, find his journal on the counter and secure the half-empty water bottle, which still has some of the Sacred Manna dissolved in it."

She gave her the address and the hiding spot Rex mentioned where a key could be found.

"Make sure you wear gloves and leave no fingerprints. Once you are safe, make an anonymous call to the Police Department." Then Maya had her final lament. "I'm sorry I am not there with you."

Even though the call was encrypted and reached out halfway around the world, Maya could sense the fear that permeated Layla's thoughts.

CHAPTER 41

Maya - Stobhall, Guildtown Scotland

It had taken a few more days of preparation before the logistics of getting everyone to Scotland could be worked out.

As it turned out, Lord Perth and Sandy Thom had survived unscathed and Robert had concluded his purchase of the castle a week ago, and already Colonel Whitmore had sentries in place who continued to update the security of the property.

But now that they were all finally here, Maya and Layla rode in one vehicle, Robert was with the colonel, and the three men rode in another car as well as their guards. There was a total of five black Range Rovers whose built-in lethality was expertly camouflaged for local consumption. These would remain the property of Stobhall for the immediate future.

At this point, only Maya, Robert, and Whitmore knew what she had seen in her remote viewing quest. She opted not share it with anyone else until she was actually able to show them. Words would never be enough and besides, she wanted to see the expressions on their faces. She knew this was a huge step towards their objective.

As the caravan passed through Guildtown, Layla asked. "So? Tell me. What have you found?" Her face bore a pleading smile.

Maya put an enthusiastic hand on her friend's knee and lowered her voice to a whisper. "Patience is a virtue." And she laughed, happy all her friends save Rex, were safe and gathered.

The remaining drive was a blur of Scottish countryside. When they got to the main gate, it had been changed. It now housed a security station. It appeared benign, but Maya knew better.

Driving up the tree-lined road, Maya saw men with dogs and felt the blanketing presence of protection. She knew that there were encampments down by the river and that the place had been turned into a fortress.

Maya wondered if Rex was watching. She looked up and winked—letting him know he was still part of the team.

"Welcome to Stobhall," the colonel said, the first to exit the vehicles. Two men appeared and gave the colonel a smart salute.

What Maya came to appreciate was that Robert had released all of Lord Perth's staff with three years of salary and the colonel had brought in his own people. The cooks, valets, and cleaners—all were prior special forces. Apparently, Robert had told the colonel they would be here on a long-term lucrative contract and had made a very desirable offer to everyone.

"Shall we?" The colonel asked with a sweep of his hands. Whispering into Maya's ear, he assured her, "Everything you asked for is waiting."

♦≈♏≈⌘♎♎♏ ■≈♋■♎

Entering the library, Maya noticed the book on Mandela and *The Bernstein Bears* were still there. Of course, she had asked Robert to make sure 'everything' was included.

Her intuition made her pause and stare at the books. For a brief moment Maya wondered, *what would he have happened had Mandela ever gotten out of prison?* But the thought passed. It was time for the great reveal.

She had played this out in her head over a hundred times but that did not arrest her rising heartbeat, or the gathering beads of sweat as she licked her lips in anticipation. *This is going to change the world,* she thought.

Maya noted Tavis and Layla gaping at the ancient water clock. When they had had their fill, she pressed the special bookshelf and the hinge latch opened to reveal the hidden staircase. Yet one more wonder to inspire awe. But Maya knew this was nothing compared to what was coming.

"Come along," she smiled. Maya descended the staircase with the others following her. Everything she saw on her dream journey told her she was about to discover the mother of all archeological finds. But her thoughts skirted the idea of fame or fortune, she was myopically focused on her mission—to find or make more Manna and fulfill her destiny.

Hope, worry, anticipation, these thoughts all competed for dominance as she halted the group at the midpoint landing.

Beside the walkway a natural spring bubbled up—the water source that for more than a half-dozen centuries powered the sundry of cogs and wheels that dictated the movements of the water clock in the library above. And sitting on the landing was a brand-new sledgehammer.

Maya took it and felt its weight. Her breath grew shallow as she flexed her muscles along the heft of the ax. She found herself bouncing on her toes as she licked her lips in anticipation.

All eyes were on her and the shuffles grew hushed when she stepped over the rope railing onto rocks that were slippery from years of moisture. Steadying herself beside the mechanism that ran from the floor to the ceiling, she looked up to the roof of the cavern. Then with a final glance at her audience, she warned them.

"Stand back. A little farther." She drew back the eight-pound hammer and slammed it into the vertical rod. Again, and then a third time. The clang echoed off the damp rocks sending loud reverberations down the tunnel. On the fourth whack, the pole buckled and fell away. Without the support of the shaft, a hole opened in the roof and hundreds of gallons of water splashed down and around them. It was fast and furious but abated quickly.

"The clock," Gary yelled in horror. Anguish splayed over his face.

"It's fine," Maya assured him. "Really, this is all a ruse. A deception. I promise, it is still working fine."

Gary had one hand clasped over his month, eyes on the wreckage when two of Whitmore's men approached with a long extension ladder. Colonel Whitmore handed Maya a flashlight.

"Ladies first."

Halfway up, she stopped to observe the room below. She had to see their expressions. It was a moment she knew that would remain with them for the rest of their lives.

The gathering was divided into two camps. Those whom she had told what she had seen on her vision quest and those she had not. She noted that they had unintentionally gathered in two pods along those defining lines and mused at the power of the subconscious mind.

When she was halfway through the hole, she could hear the hushed shuffle below. She half expected that she could hear the palpitation of their hearts, as her own was now racing. Maya aimed the flashlight and did a three sixty before pulling herself up off the floor. Standing tall, the flashlight cast a beam whose narrow cone revealed one ancient wonder after another. The room was beyond huge.

"Un-fricken' real," she whistled under her breath. She had seen this in the muted vision of her dream quest. But here, in all its glory, she had found what has been hidden for over eight hundred years. The answer to one of history's greatest mysteries.

"Colonel, start sending them up."

◆≈♏︎≈♓︎♎︎♎︎♏︎■≈♋︎■♎︎

The chamber was carved of solid stone, likely from a subterranean river that dried up eons ago. It could easily house a high school gymnasium with room to spare. Having previously reviewed this no less than a dozen times, she knew that this was simply one of many rooms. There were others that were hidden in shadows.

One by one, their heads crested the lip of the floor. And one by one, speechless amazement and awe overcame them.

With their additional light pushing at the edge of centuries' old darkness, Maya grinned with excitement as she watched her friends and colleagues try and take in what they were seeing. The magnificence continued to unfold in the roving beams of light. Her proclamation was giddy with excitement.

"Ladies and gentlemen, may I present to you the tomb of Queen Scota. The body of Meritaten, the daughter of Pharaoh Akhenaten, the last ruler of the House of Gold."

Dominating the room was a large stone sarcophagus crusted in priceless gems and surrounded by chests heaped with gold. Sitting securely on top of the tomb was the last known crystal blue bowl on Earth. The vessel held the hope of the world.

She approached it and let her hands caress the curved glass. Her nerves tingled in elation, a sense of triumph washed over her and for the briefest of moments, she became oblivious to everything around her. With a faraway look she pondered destiny.

Is this the Holy Grail? The key to success?

"Let's have a look, shall we, colonel?" Robert whispered in excitement.

Their movements brought her back to the moment where she noted that Tavis and Layla seemed transfixed by all the gold. It had to be worth billions if one simply melted it down. As ancient artifacts, priceless did not come close to describing its value. It was like being a parent, watching children overwhelmed on Christmas morning.

While their colleagues ventured farther into the depth of what might have been the world's greatest treasure, Maya returned her attention to the tomb.

"JW," she asked as he sidled up next to her. "Do you see what I see?"

"I see it," he said smiling triumphantly. Inlaid jewels within the sarcophagus forming a perfect circle with a large diamond dot in the center.

"The sign of Manna," she said, transfixed by the magnitude of their discovery.

Interlocking pictograms heralded scenes that alluded to their holy grail. In a tone of reverence, Maya felt as if she was floating, as if finding this essence of hope had removed all of their burdens.

"The lost secret of the ancient ones," she said softly, as she exhaled deeply for the first time since they entered the tomb..

◆ ♒ ♏ ♒ ♓ ♎ ♎ ♏ ■ ♒ ♋ ■ ♎

Within a week they had a huge generator placed outside of the library. There was now a constant source of power running into the chamber. The entire space had been illuminated. There was a total of twelve rooms within the hidden sanctuary.

There was the main room that they had entered through the floor. This was the grand hall that contained the sarcophagus as well as other riches. But it was the opening in the very back, which was framed by a traditional Gothic arch topped by a solid gold keystone; that led to the greatest of discoveries and opened one's mind to yet more mystery.

Beyond this archway were eleven more rooms. Five on each side with a large hallway separating them. And each room contained its own bevy of priceless artifacts of wealth and historical importance. Some rooms acted as a treasury, loaded with precious metals, golden pieces of intricate art and chest after chest after chest of precious gems. Another room was stacked with a king's fortune of raw ingots of gold, platinum, palladium, and other metals that would need to be tested. Additionally, there were containers full of frankincense and myrrh as well as other unidentified florae.

Maya was sure that this room contained the base ingredients for making the sacred bread of light. This chamber was maybe fifty feet wide by fifty feet long. Though housing unimaginable wealth, what struck her were the walls.

They were adorned with scenes so vibrant in color that they jumped out at her. Scenes that showed the high priestess making the Sacred Manna.

The process, she whispered. Time and again she would return to these images in hopes of unraveling the secret.

Another room had stone tablets of ancient Egyptian hieroglyphs interspersed with symbols similar to an ancient Gaelic. They were comparable to the runes left behind by the Druids, and it was clear that they contained the linguistic roots of the British Isles. One tablet caught her eye. It contained similar symbology as the sheet she had stuffed into her boot in Georgia, now uploaded into their digital archives.

That was another unknown that would need to be unraveled. But what drew the biggest mystery was that aside from the expected treasures and the storehouse of Manna-based ingredients, there were other treasures that spanned centuries, across dozens of civilizations, like a time capsule of historical wealth all gathered up in a single place.

Chinese, Nubian, Indo-American, Vedic, Slavic, and Mongolian, like someone scoured the world for lost fortunes and then deposited everything here. It was an enigma wrapped in a conundrum, cloaked in mystery.

Robert had made a decision, this discovery belonged to the world. The bulk of what they uncovered would be turned over to archeologists, albeit maybe not for a year or two. And that only the gold and platinum ingots would be culled out to cover the costs and bonuses he intended to distribute.

The generosity of the proposed dividends to all the players and soldiers now camped at Stobhall, was in part to assure temptation amongst the soldiers would be dampened, if not outright extinguished. He announced this over a celebratory dinner which led to back slapping, and mile wide smiles.

The compound now included a complement of fifty of Whitmore's most trusted and capable men and women. Each day they continued to improve the facility's security physically, electronically, and digitally.

They even went so far as to buy a nearby farm and install a retired military family. The husband became a regular at the local pub with an ear to the ground and the wife volunteered at the local library, doing the same. Gossip of interest or nosey inquiries were all collected and passed along to the colonel.

Cameras were placed in the chamber and monitors were set up in a converted master control room. Entrance was off limits except to a very narrow list. Most had only their imagination to consult about what had been found in what was now affectionally called "the chamber."

The story was refined to simplicity—an ancient Egyptian sarcophagus. But they knew there was more and often whispered in professional speculation amongst themselves.

Still, to Maya's great disappointment, there was no Manna. None. She had searched every container in every room and even opened the sarcophagus. But there was none—it was nowhere to be found.

◆〰〽〰〶〓〓〽 ■〰𖣘■〓

Maya walked Robert to the door. He was going to meet with a different set of lawyers. Salvage experts and antiquity specialists, to be sure that what they found was theirs to do with as they determined and preempt every avenue that governmental thieves would try to use to cull for themselves, or for their constituents.

"Be careful," she reminded him.

"I will. I promise. Colonel Whitmore is providing me a security detail."

"Good." She gave him a kiss and he got in one of the Tahoe's and was gone.

That was hours ago. That evening she encouraged her team to let their hair down. The feeling of total security was a welcome respite from the last few months of paranoia and the constant wear and tear of always being on guard.

Layla was tucked deep into Tavis on one couch. Gary, who Maya suspected was going to become a permanent fixture, was on another. And JW sat in a wing-backed chair across from her.

Maya considered the people who had become a fixture in her life. Including the soldiers who were either on duty or upstairs. The castle had been zoned into areas designated as soldiers' personal spaces, Maya, and her team's personal spaces, and the communal areas. She liked the arrangement. It was efficient, methodical, and was a comfortable accommodation that served them all.

Looking back to her friends who were all settled in with a drink, she cast a gaze at JW and asked a question that was an entrée into something that had been tugging at her for the last few days.

"So, which came first, the chicken or the egg?"

"Creation versus evolution, that is the true nature of the question," he quipped, defining the intellectual element contained within the famous question.

"That's not what I meant," she clarified. "What do you think was here first? The treasure or Queen Scota's tomb? Let's look at the facts.

"During the Crusades, the Knights Templar found something under the Dome of the Rock in Jerusalem which led to an overnight accumulation of great wealth and power. That was the place where Solomon's Temple was rumored to have been buried. We know Solomon was one of the last of those that knew how to make Manna. He called it the bread of the presence.

"We know that Enoch and Fulcanelli are both supposed to have been able to move in and out of time, which we have wrapped around the myths of the Philosopher's Stone. Our white mystery powder.

"But my father..." she paused. "Remember early on he was using his time travel capabilities to seek out, anticipate, and capture the secrets of the Hidden Hand? Going so far as to record some of their secret meetings even before audible recording was technically feasible."

"What are you suggesting?"

"The Templars were at their peak in the mid-1300s when they were betrayed. Yet their riches were never found. And the source of their instant wealth was never discovered. Meanwhile, at the same time the chapel at Stobhall was being constructed. By all accounts we have uncovered the lost treasure of the Templars," she suggested.

"And...?" he asked again.

"What if the Templars uncovered a large cache of Manna during the Crusades? Remember that Lord Perth and his two sons were part of this early gentry. After the discovery, a few adepts learned how to use the powder to move through time.

"Imagine throughout history all the legends handed down from around the world of lost treasures. Think about it. The library at Alexandria, the lost gold of the Incas. The Golden City of the Sahara. I was doing research and there are over thirty different legends of lost treasures that predate the fourteenth century.

"What if they used their time travel resources to find these before they were lost? They followed the trail forward until pinpointing truth from fiction and marked location from misdirection. Then they excavated and added the discovery to their treasury?"

"It would explain how they amassed a collection with such a wide span of time and geography," Gary said, setting his scotch on the table.

"Correct," Maya beamed as if he were a star pupil. "It would also explain how they were able to move everything before they were betrayed."

"Meaning..." Gary appeared perplexed.

"Meaning they went back in time after that fateful Friday the thirteenth, and before it happened, they secretly moved everything."

"Wow," Layla said. "I guess I've never really considered the rules and restraints of time travel. Of cause and effect, and how that shit works."

Maya continued. "So, let's go back to the original question. Was Queen Scota's tomb already here and is this why they chose this spot?

Or did they use the same techniques and move her here along with all the other lost riches?"

The room went silent.

"If she was moved, then is everything we need to create the Manna from scratch available? The ingredients, the recipe? Has it all been articulated to be readily replicated?"

JW offered some encouragement.

"There is no doubt the chapel was built as a spot to make the Manna. With the obelisks, the altar, the connecting stone, and the stained glass. It's all here. Might I suggest we ask Rex to help us, maybe see if your dad has an answer?"

Her eyes grew wide in realization. *We have a conduit to the other side...*

One more tool destiny has laid into their arsenal. "Good idea."

♦♒♏♒♓♎♎♏■♒♋■♎

With some down time, Maya decided to reach out and see how Austin's recovery was proceeding. She had let more time elapse than originally intended before she made the call. Her heart tightened with each ring. She was not sure if she should come right out and tell Austin about Robert or say nothing at all. These thoughts were unresolved when halfway across the world; her call was answered on its fourth ring.

"Hello."

"Hey, Austin?" She noted the deep resonance of his voice.

"Maya, are you okay?" This reinforced the young boy she still remembered. Always considerate and caring about others.

"I just wanted to hear your voice," she deflected.

She suspected his phones were being monitored, though Robert had assured her their encryption could not be traced back to them. So she kept her answers as benign as possible.

"How's the therapy going?"

"Getting stronger every day. And smarter," he chuckled. "Mom got me a new laptop. The things you can find on the internet..." There was a pause. "I suppose you still can't tell me where you are or when I will see you next." Austin's tone acknowledged this was the right strategy at the moment. "But I'm glad you called. Last week somebody came by looking for you."

Maya's heart thudded into a lump that caught in her throat. *Is Austin in danger?*

"Looking for me?" It's all she could get out.

"Yeah. He knocked and asked to see me and gave me a message for you."

"A message?"

"Yeah. He said that you do not have all the pieces yet. But he knows where you can get what's missing. He was vague but asked that I tell you that he would be staying with Maria next week, I believe that would be starting tomorrow and for the next three days."

"Maria? Tomorrow? Who was it? What did he want?" Immediately her mind raced through the question of why, and who. Her nerves tightened at the thought of the Lamberts in danger. Were they being used as bait? Fear raised her blood pressure, which amplified the pounding in her ears.

"He said his name was Drune."

Drune? This brought her heightened concern back down to ground level. She now understood.

We need to make arrangements to travel back to Phoenix ASAP.

But her worry about Austin's phones being monitored made her deflect her intent.

"I'll have to try and figure out who that is," Maya said, and the conversation returned to the safety of banter...

CHAPTER 42

Maya - The Dream Journey

Drune Melchizedik. Shit—talk about divine guidance... A warm glow infused her like a tonic that turned fear into confidence.

How could he know what we have found or need?

I need to talk to Rex.

She settled into the lotus position and followed her process. It was becoming second nature. Within moments, she was greeted by her friend.

"Hello, Maya."

She recalled Rex once stating he had never used his talents to play peeping Tom. Still, he always seemed to be there when she went looking for him.

"Hey, Rex. How are you doing?"

"Adjusting," he said with an expression that implied this whole situation was still weirding him out. Then he anticipated her question with an answer.

"I understand you are going to try and recreate the Manna. And you wonder if you have everything you need to replicate the process."

He did not wait for her to answer.

"You are still missing some of the knowledge. But Drune knows where to find it. He has set out to connect with you. It was at the request of Enoch."

"Enoch?" For some reason she had assumed her father was guiding her. *He's involved in all this?*

"The dangers are growing, Maya. The enemy is getting agitated. He smells your success and knows it is a direct threat to his end game. Be careful—all of you."

237

CHAPTER 43
Havasupai Reservation

Having left the cool climes of Scotland, Maya found herself in the oven called Phoenix. The sweat on her brow reinforced the heat. There was a pall over downtown as the scorching dry wind caught up loose particles of sand and flung them across the valley.

Robert had provided them with new credit cards and identification, which allowed them to move around in obscurity. They rented a car and were now on the street where Maria's house was located.

As they approached, Maya noted the house was old, made in the adobe style architecture of the 1950s. She knocked on the door, and a woman whom she assumed was Maria answered with a grin. Her face was lit with excitement, like a child on Christmas morning.

"The wayward travelers," she greeted them happily. "Come in, you must be Maya."

"Hello," Maya replied.

Maya and JW entered. In the back of the room was a man sitting in the shadows. Tall, thin, and of an indeterminate age. Somewhere between forty and seventy, Maya could not tell.

He had an odd glow about him, almost as if he shimmered. She squinted and imagined she saw waves like a heat mirage. Her first thought harkened back to early descriptions of the Watchers.

The Shining Ones. Manna travelers?

"Greetings, Maya," he said rising to offer his hand. "I am Drune Melchizedik."

She let out a slow breath. The man Nascha had said could help them. The man from the article and the man to whom Enoch had guided them. The relief she felt at finally meeting him gave her a sense of comfort.

His grip was firm but soft. She felt a current pass between them at his touch.

My imagination? Her hand tingled.

Introductions were made and seats taken. Maria exited the room to gather refreshments.

"I am glad your friend was able to reach you." Drune said. He had an unusual twinkle in his eye.

Maya had read early on about remote viewing. The government was paranoid that remote viewers could plant biomorphic suggestions into the ear of an unknowing recipient.

Had he suggested she call Austin?

She dismissed this without concern. Her destiny was no longer a call—it was a mandate. One she was determined to fulfill.

There was something about this man. She could not put her finger on it, but his tone and demeanor were... Maya searched for the right word. *Playful.* Like this was all a game. She also got the feeling he could read her thoughts.

"His recovery is proving that he is more man than boy," he offered without being prompted. "Imagine being in another world for fourteen years..."

This remark stung. Was he intentionally poking at her emotional rollercoaster?

"Austin mentioned that you have a message from my father," she said, deciding there was no malice in his comment.

"Yes. That is correct. He said that you are the light of his life and that he is so proud of your courage and dedication. He knows you want for him to return, even if only in a dream journey. But he needs you to understand—the risks are too great." He stopped to emphasize a point.

"The enemy is after him. Even in the dream world, the adversary is lurking, waiting, hiding..."

His comments brought home every fear and worry at the reality of her father's circumstances. Though there was no longer open trepidation at the idea of following her destiny and completing her quest, uncertainty always lingered. He had simply reinforced what she already knew. And it was the reason they were here.

If I am to ever see my father again, I need to go to him. I must learn how to make more Manna.

Drune continued. "Part of your protection from these unfathomable forces is the fact that the evil one does not know to what extent your father has gathered evidence. Could it set them back a year, a decade, a century, longer? They would love nothing more than to take him out."

"Since you know about Stobhall, and apparently Enoch has filled you in on our quest, can you tell me what are we missing? What we need to make Manna?"

He smiled and Maya thought she saw that glimmer again.

"You must learn how to draw the power of Orion down through the kimah and the kesil," he told her, adopting a more serious tone. "This is the heat and the cold that creates the spark of life that turns the ORME powder into the bread of the presence—the light of sha-nan-na. And...

"You must understand how the grid of your Master Builders was built explicitly for the Lioness to come and activate it. It has remained dormant for centuries."

Grazing her fingers along her lip, she noted his eyes radiated truth, an honest statement of fact. She felt as if something that had been waiting for an eternity was about to be revealed. She inherently knew the doors of destiny were almost open. Hers, his, theirs.

Maya felt an overwhelming sensation that the entire cosmos was holding its breath, waiting for her to make a choice, a decision. Time stopped. It could have been a second or it could have been a day. She spoke.

"What do we need to do?"

These six simple words released the stasis. Time flowed again, the sun danced again, and the motes picked up where they had left off.

"We need to go back to the cave," he explained.

This was not the answer she expected. The fact the enemy had beaten them to the punch was a disheartening truth.

"The enemy has cleaned it out."

"I understand you are well aware of the cave that Michael Fottrell and Tim Carruthers discovered. The one that Kincaid and his team closed down after looting. But what they never uncovered were the secret rooms ancient Egyptians packed with their wisdom just waiting for the chosen one. This is where I have been destined to lead you."

♦ ♒ ♏ ♒ ♓ ♎ ♎ ♏ ■ ♒ ♋ ■ ♎

Maya, JW and Drune drove along Route 66 until they arrived at the Havasupai Indian reservation on the south rim of the Grand Canyon.

"The people are connected to the water that runs through the canyon," Drune explained. "Havasupai means people of the blue green waters. Their reservation contains more than a million acres and controls close to a hundred miles of the river. They have been on this land for over 800 years."

As they proceeded down the dusty road, Maya saw twin spires of red rock. They were very distinct and dominated the horizon.

"They are the Wigleeva," Drune explained. "Legend has it that these are ancient watchers who protect the tribe."

She said nothing while staring out at the red painted landscape, but her mind reeled at the varied tapestry of her quest. Secret societies, shadowy enemies, lost wisdom, Knights Templar, a fortune in treasure and now, ancient Egyptians in America.

When they arrived, the community was a collection of adobe buildings with corrugated roofs ensconced within a horseshoe valley of tall red cliffs.

The bluffs were adorned with green swaths of pine, and in the cleft was a distant waterfall that poured from the side of the mountain.

"Greetings," the elder chieftain said as he embraced Drune. They began to speak in a language unfamiliar to Maya. JW translated for her as the two men engaged in a lengthy discussion, leading her to assume it was a dialect of his own tribe.

"It seems that the chieftain is the guardian of the sacred cave and that to let in white men, that would be you," he chuckled. "Is strictly forbidden."

"Ha ha," she laughed, quite insincerely. The comment was meant as humor, but it prickled her.

Drune was giving the chief an impassioned explanation. Maya could see the body language of the tribal elder stiffen, and then he turned his gaze on to her and she dared not whither under his scrutiny.

"Drune has explained for my benefit that the great mosaic created for the chosen one was built for you. That you are the lion." As the chief continued to study her, it was clear in his body language he had doubts.

"Humph," the elder grunted as he circled her. As if he was examining a prized mare, he looked over every part of her body. She half expected him to pull back her lips and check her teeth.

She held steady. Shoulders back and eyes fixed on a spot in the distance. No flinching, no backing down. *What will be will be.*

Acceptance relaxed her and the confidence of knowing she was where she should be emboldened her.

He leveled a gaze at her that she felt penetrate to her soul.

"I cannot stand against the tide of the Creator," he said in perfect English. "We will provide you horses and guide you to the mountain of yesterday. From there my old friend Drune will lead you.

"But first, we will feast. And afterwards, we perform the purification ceremony. Tonight, under the cold breath of a billion stars, your aura will be cleansed, and you will be made ready. At sunrise you will start the journey to fulfill the will of the Creator."

Maya did not realize she had been holding her breath. She let out a long slow exhale, not sure what to expect next.

♦ ≈ ᶬ ≈ ⱈ ♎ ♎ ᶬ ■ ≈ ♋ ■ ♎

Maya woke to the most beautiful sunrise she could remember. She recalled snippets of the ceremony and once again, had to reassess her skepticism about ancient customs and ceremonies and the power of words, chants, and dance.

Last night she had slept a deep trouble-free slumber. Her mind was clear, her conscience free of worry and her spirit glowed with a new surge of power and purpose.

She was brimming with anticipation. Enoch had sent this man to her service and he had told her that her questions would be answered today. Her spirit was light, ready, and all her senses were heightened with the thought of destiny being revealed.

JW emerged and together they made their way to breakfast. It was not the traditional fare of tortillas, beans, and meat, but instead from the bounty of God's harvest. Assorted fruits, dripping honeycomb, and freshly baked bread still hot from the oven.

When it was time to leave, the entire village turned out. The attention was directed at her and she felt both proud and embarrassed. She did not like being the center of attention.

This was a momentous day. The chief was adorned in colorful traditional wear. He had a red, blue, and white feathered headdress that fell down to the middle of his back. He wore flowing blue robes over buckskin pants and calf-covered boots.

In one hand he held a scepter. As they mounted their painted ponies, he used it like a baton to give them a blessing in a language she could not understand, but knew it was an incantation of protection from evil spirits.

Thinking of Rex and then their experiences in the cavern in Guatemala, she did not dismiss his ritual. The reality of demons and evil was unsettling, but it was also a reality she was beginning to accept. In fact, it gave her a modicum of comfort.

Escorted by two aged braves, they started down the path towards the towering escarpment. Along the way, there were mud-fired homes that were far older than those with the corrugated roofs. Standing in the doorways were woman of indeterminate age who were dressed in the colorfully dyed garments of their tribe. As an archeologist, Maya knew the quiet elders made up the backbone of the tribe. She assumed it was no different amongst the Havasupai people.

They passed the last hovel, which earmarked the edge of the village and proceeded to make the long trek to the lake of the falling waters. When they arrived, the sun was high. They dismounted and let their horses drink.

"Here is where we must leave you," a guide told her.

"Thank you, friends," Drune said with a bow of respect. They nodded, turned, and receded from view.

"Shall we?" Drune suggested to Maya and JW as they mounted their steeds.

After an hour of carefully picking their way between the walls of converging bluffs and navigating the loose stone, they reached a point where the horses could go no farther.

"We need to leave them. Instinct will draw them back to the lake. We will go and fetch them when we return."

Maya surveyed the trail. It would be downhill and mostly shaded on the way back. They took backpacks that had food, water, flashlights, and a few other assorted items. It was enough to last until they returned to collect the horses. Maya had a fleeting thought of the mares they had lost in the canyon and a wave of sadness washed over her.

Trekking towards their destination, Maya peppered Drune with questions. "How long have you been using the Manna?"

"Maybe twenty years, give or take," he explained.

Longer than my father. This excited her.

"Where did you get it?"

"From my friend, the Chief of the Havasupai."

"Does he have more?" Her heart now beat a little faster. *Perhaps this is why we are here. To get some more Manna.* She never considered that an old tribe of the American west could be part of this lost secret of the ancient ones. Her pulse raced with hope and anticipation.

"I do not know."

"Do you have more?" Her voice had a tone of pleading.

"No. I no longer need it."

Maya recalled the professor in the Cave of Hathor explaining that one's body built up a reservoir after a significant amount of consumption.

"So you could simply pop into the cave we are heading towards and skip all the fanfare?"

"What would be the fun in that?" he said widening his arms to embrace the entire panorama. "Look around you. This is God's country. Unsullied by the world of today. And..." he paused to add, "You would not appreciate the extent they have gone through to keep this place hidden." He continued to smile with that mischievous grin as he circled the conversation back to the mundane.

The terrain was steep and there was a lot of loose rock and talus from broken rubble. It was clear that unless one had a reason, no one would ever climb this wash. They painstakingly picked their way. After her previous experience, one of her worries was the possibility of setting off a rockslide.

Maya would periodically glance up the long sloping incline. Each time, all she could see was rock, wall, rock, and more rock.

"How much farther?" she asked. Now understanding why a hidden cave could remain hidden for so many centuries. Instead of discouragement, it added to the credibility of what she had manifested would be discovered.

Drune stopped and took a deep breath. Maya saw him turn to check on JW, who had fallen behind and was dragging up the rear.

"Let's give the big fella a chance to catch up," Drune suggested. With heavy breath he took a seat on an adjacent boulder. Taking out his canteen, he downed a gulp of water. Maya did the same.

When JW arrived, his shirt was damp with sweat. After he had had a chance to catch his breath, Drune asked.

"You got your wind back?"

JW exhaled with a long deep breath. Wiped his brow and looked up the long steep slope ahead.

"I guess," came his half-hearted reply.

"Good, we're here."

With a chuckle, Drune got off the rock he was sitting on and worked his way to the other side. There was a narrow space that fronted the sheer wall of red rock. And hidden in shadows was a thick patch of vines. Drune pushed the weave to one side, revealing an opening.

CHAPTER 44
Maya - The Sacred Cave

Maya cast her flashlight beam into the hollow. It was less than inviting. Sharp stones hung from the roof and it was so confined they would need to be severely hunched over or crawl.

Probing with her flashlight, she could see the tunnel grew smaller and narrower.. Not even worthy of a bear's hibernation hole. Hopefully, it was perception versus reality.

"Follow me," Drune said.

She licked her lips, eager to see what was so worthy of protecting.

Squatting, he began moving forward. He was almost as tall as JW but had nowhere near his bulk. The deeper they went, the tighter it became and the anticipation Maya felt changed to apprehension. After a few minutes, Drune paused. He turned slightly, looked back at them with that mischievous smile, and vanished.

Maya blinked once, then a second time. Her heart went racing. She could hear JW behind her. His breathing now came in short shallow rasps.

After a few more paces, Drune appeared on their left. He was standing inside a tunnel whose roof was at least a dozen feet above his head.

Thank God, she whispered under her breath. She had built up an image that this place was going to be some grand enshrinement. She had started to worry that maybe her expectations had been misplaced.

Maya stepped from the tight crawl space and stood to her full height. Her back was knotted from the squat walk. She found herself in a time-worn passageway.

"Welcome," he said with open arms.

"Damn," JW said with relief, standing, stretching, and letting out a long, deep exhale.

Maya noted the smattering of hieroglyphs, clearly Egyptian in origin. The floor was smooth, evidencing man had used this space for centuries. But it felt empty, a relic from long ago.

"Come," Drune beckoned. They proceeded down what was best described as a tunnel. Maya wondered how many soles had padded along this path. Or rather, how many souls.

"We're about a mile from what is called the Citadel," Drune explained. They were engulfed in a very deep darkness, only the three shafts of yellow light and the echo of voice off stone evidenced their surroundings.

As they drew closer to what Drune described as the hub, the center wheel of the giant complex, Maya's curiosity replaced apprehension, and anticipation quickened her pulse. She had a tingling sensation, like she was awash in carbonation. Her skin had a pleasurable crawl that simply added to her heightened awareness.

"How big is this place? Have much have you explored?"

"These tunnels go on for miles," he said. But his voice hinted of something more.

"But..." She suspected he had been here hundreds of times. Both physically and on vison quests.

"I have taken many dream journeys down these ancient corridors," he conceded. "The walls are replete with scenes of the life of the ancients. The deeper you progress, the more ancient the depiction. If you explore far enough...

"I am talking about miles into the Earth. The paintings detail the crossing of the ocean and the exodus from Egypt and then...

"They reveal the prophesy of the Lion."

The lion. My name since being a child. The ancient prophesies. How can this all be tied together? How far and wide has this plan stretched? She was in awe at it all.

After nearly an hour of walking, she could hear the changed timbre of their voices. They were approaching a larger space.

Is this it? She wondered. She was hoping against hope that all her questions would be answered.

Even within the blackness, she sensed the enormity of the room they had entered. This was the Citadel. The splay of lights lashed into the inky depth but were feeble against the primordial darkness.

Drune lit a lantern sitting on a stone bench. Watching as it pushed back the dark, a gathering dawn revealed multiple benches set in a wide half circle, and each had a lantern waiting to be fired.

Once Drune had completed the task, Maya noted that the room was painted in some type of bioluminescent undercoat and as the luminosity grew, the room had a twilight feel to it.

Soon the darkness dissolved, and Maya saw each opening to the twelve caverns Drune had mentioned. They were black holes draped in deep shadows. And equally spaced around the room—like numbers on a clock face. But it was the ceiling that grabbed her. Constructed as a perfect dome. It stood over forty feet above them and was painted in a perfect replica of a one-dimensional face of Mother Earth. At the center was the Great Pyramid of Giza. From this central point, all one hundred and forty-four sacred sites Maya had delineated in her thesis fanned out, like spokes of a wheel.

"My grid," she said in a hushed tone. "The Master Builders. The sites. They're all there. It's beautiful," she marveled as the glow continued to increase in the room.

Her thoughts drifted to intuition, destiny, subliminal suggestion, the road they had traveled. Her father and the book *Path of the Poles* he had given to her that opened her mind to the idea the world had shifted.

And that if the cavern in Guatemala was correct that it was members from Pharaoh Akhenaten's people that came to North America, then this ancient site here was constructed over three thousand years before the concept that entered her head flourished and finished as her doctoral thesis.

This is the reason. This is my destiny—but what is it?

Below the edge of the Earth sat a belt of stars, maybe ten feet top to bottom. It surrounded the entire cavern. And underneath the stars, directly above each of the twelve passageways, were detailed images. Distinct, but different. And beneath each of the twelve images stood a lion ostensibly reaching above its head and holding the portrayed illustrations aloft.

In a moment, the room grew from a twilight to bright noon.

"This has never happened before," Drune said with a hush. "At least not when I have been here."

Maya's breath quickened. With so many unexpected events that had stunned her over the last six months, she should have become immune. But she felt awed.

Something's happening.

Floating in and amongst the dark band of stars, icons began to appear on the dome. The roof came alive with depth like a television screen. The twelve stations now felt like the face of a clock. An image of the blue bowl manifested itself at the one o'clock position. *It appeared from nowhere.* The thought was peppered with nervous anticipation.

She dropped to one of the benches. She felt an overload of stimulation—all of her senses were pushed to saturation. She didn't want to miss a thing—she knew it was all important. Any doubt or apprehension she may have harbored was now gone. Only wonder remained.

It started to crackle. Coming alive, she involuntarily shuddered. It was a type of lighting that jumped out of the bowl into the two o'clock position. Then three, then four, five, six, where the obelisks stood. Above, the constellation of Orion glowed, and the illusion of an ephemeral translucent light tube poured down onto the two pillars.

Instinctively, she understood. The twin columns drew the yin and yang powers of the kimah and the kesil.

Seven o'clock, eight, nine, ten, eleven, the growing power of the light energy culminated at the twelve o'clock position. The sacred sites exploded into color, then as one, all twelve stations shot light into the sacred grid. Twelve stations of twelve. All one hundred and forty-four sites were now set aflame radiating the most wonderful translucent luminosity.

"It's just like Guatemala," she exclaimed. Her wide grin accentuated the sparkle in her eyes. She felt the onset rush of adrenaline amp her excitement. There were no words, just awe.

Light from the Pleiadean stars of Orion poured more and more beams of ephemeral light into the mouth of the shaft of the Great Pyramid of Giza. This fueled the one hundred and forty-four sacred sites to dance with and around, the pyramid.

"JW, are you recording this?" she whispered, prompting him to reach for his phone. Standing, she watched all of the various elements come to life and form an intricate dance.

Like strings on a May Pole. Round and round the images floated and fluttered. Each rotation was building to a crescendo, generating more and more kinetic energy. When it reached its boiling point, there was a giant flash that spread out in slow motion. One wave after another pulsed until they dwindled to mere ripples of light. And then, just as suddenly, it ended.

In the muted sound of silence, with only black spots remaining in Maya's eyes, everything returned to its static position, except that was not quite correct. There was a tube of dim light that seemed to flow long and deep into the ceiling like a hologram boring through solid rock.

It opened a wormhole, like a retreating view of what by all appearances were people throughout history. It was a long corridor and as it materialized, it also drew closer and closer to her. This caused her to take a step back.

As the umbilicus came into focus, she saw ancient and wizened people. Her gaze landed on eight people, sexless. Maya inherently knew these were the ancient sages who were talking to her. Their voices were clear and their message unmistakable.

She glanced over at her two companions. From their body language, they were oblivious. *Can't they see what I am seeing?* But she did not have time for emotion, to stop and question. There was too much happening at once. Things came, and then left. She absorbed everything. Her eidetic memory captured the totality of what the eight entities were telling her. This felt like it went on for an eternity and as the process was revealed, she marveled at the clues she had seen over the last year.

Of course—it makes so much sense.

Eventually they faded into the empty space until the tube of light was gone.

The message explained by the ancient ones was now seared into her soul. She did not need a camera and she did not need to decipher what had happened. It was clear what they needed to do and how to do it. And it was not going to be easy. But they now had a path.

CHAPTER 45

Maya - Perth, Scotland

The flight began its descent into Perth. Maya was still replaying the events of the last forty-eight hours. On one hand the scientist in her found it difficult to conceive that accurate prophesy could exist, but she could not dismiss what her eyes had seen or deny the path she was on.

"Your aura," Drune had explained when they were walking back to collect the horses. "The Citadel recognized you as the Lion, the one the Ancients foretold would arrive when it was time."

With reverence, he added. "And it is time. And you are she and thus, I present myself to you as your humble servant." He bowed and his tone and demeanor shifted, as if she was royalty.

This reverence bothered her. All her life she had lived an invisible existence, keeping a low profile, and sharing little. Now, suddenly people were shining a spotlight on her. It was like glare in her eyes. People viewed her differently, as if she had all the answers and would solve all their problems. She wasn't sure how she felt, but she knew she didn't like the spotlight.

"Why didn't Kincaid and his men destroy this?" Maya had asked on the ride back to the village.

"They never knew it was here. They simply found the tip of the spear. A wall had been erected centuries before to prevent anyone not allowed by the ancients from ever entering. This is why the chief took so long in studying you. He was reading your aura along with his spirit guide. It was the latter that gave him the green light for us to proceed."

The thought that the chief had read her aura and deemed it positive helped dampen some the spotlight irritation that was getting under her skin.

When they passed through the Havasupai village, something had changed. She could feel it. People dipped their heads as she passed.

Not in fear, but in respect. It was the first hint that people saw her in a different light.

Before getting in their car, the chief had come and whispered in her ear. Strangely it was in a language she had never heard before. *An ancient version of his native tongue?* And yet she did not miss a word. This interpretation all happened within her brain as if she had found a Rosetta stone that could decipher any language that ever existed.

On the long flight from Phoenix, she shared with JW what the chieftain had told her.

'The long shadow of the destroyer wants to devour good. We cannot tame it, for evil cannot be tamed. You must hide us so it can pass to seek retribution for another day.'

It was clear he was not speaking in metaphor. As her path of what needed to be done grew clear, his statement rang the bell of truth. Every single nerve ending tingled on the twitch of destiny.

"JW," she began. Her eyes conveyed a bond of trust. "Everything we need to make the Manna is at Stobhall. It has been waiting for centuries for this moment.

"We have the ingredients, the tools, and I now understand the power to begin the transformation process." She proceeded to explain their mission at large. The most imminent threat facing mankind. A quest that had been clarified and brought into focus while his eyes stared down the deep umbilicus of history.

How long has this been in the making? She wondered. But she knew, since God painted the canvas of man at the onset of time. This gave her confidence that the guiding hand of providence would be waiting to assist when it was needed.

"Planet DeeDee is closing in on Earth. She is the destroyer. Planet X, Nibiru, it has had many names over the centuries, but when it arrives, chaos thrives. The enemy has calculated this and is looking to strike when humanity is at its lowest point. It is on a path that will come so close to our planet, we will be lucky if even five hundred million people survive."

"You're suggesting there is a way we can redirect its course?" His face did not mask the incredulity of the idea.

She understood. Even with all they had been through, this was a mighty big leap of faith to think mere mortals could move planets.

"The grid," she said as if that was the answer to all the questions. "It is why it was built. We must place a cache of Manna inside each of the one hundred and forty-four sacred sites. This will energize the lay lines of the world and awaken the global grid. Then, when the Pleiades are in just the right alignment, we must fire the cannon that will draw its power from the Creator's astral energies…"

"The cannon?" The puzzlement on his face grew more pronounced.

"The sighting shaft within the Great Pyramid that is aligned with Orion. The ancient ones explained to me how to calculate the optimal alignment and when that day comes, we will have a six-hour window to coordinate a load of the Sacred Manna in its interior with the rest of the globe's sacred locations. This is the real reason the shaft was created."

"And this all ties into the Sumerian Lions Gate prophesies? Then what happens?"

She smiled, struggling not to dismiss her wild assertion. "We fire up the grid and we move Earth into another dimension, one that is on the plains of the blessed and out of harm's way."

♦︎〰︎♏︎〰︎♓︎♎︎♎︎♏︎■︎〰︎♋︎■︎♎︎

Upon returning to Stobhall, Maya realized the world marches on regardless of one's own circumstances. Everything seemed to be just as she had left it. The routines, people's lives—each in their own bubbles. She considered death, and then for some reason, an old joke made her smile.

When you die, you don't know you are dead. It is those around you who suffer the pain. It is the same with being stupid. She laughed aloud.

She watched as the colonel approached. His body language was rigid, and his frown pronounced.

"Welcome back, ma'am," he said, a formality that did not bode well. "We have a problem."

This triggered a dry metallic taste in her mouth.

"As you know, our network is secured with the latest encryption protections and firewalls… Someone has infiltrated our computer system," he said flatly. Before she got out her first question, he added. "We don't know how long they were in there, but as you know we archived photos of every room, artifact, and image. They now have what we have."

"Shit," she muttered under her breath. Her heart fluttered at the reminder that no matter how powerful the hand of destiny, there were mortal enemies hellbent on stopping them. And here they were, rearing their ugly heads. She bit down on her lip, pulled back her shoulders, and vowed to succeed.

"They also have the schematics of our security systems, the names and next of kin of each of our security team and…" There was a long pause. "We believe an attack is imminent."

"Why?" She had not considered someone would dare to brazenly attack their stronghold. *Shit—time is running out. They don't need to succeed; they just need to delay us… that is just as bad!*

"We received notice this morning from the state that tomorrow a cadre of governmental officials will be arriving. When I inquired about why, I was sternly informed that they would be here on official business."

This was not a coincidence and she was suspicious of the timing. The enemy had planned their foray to coincide with Robert's absence.

Her mind raced through the implications, the scenarios and stratagem and these simply reinforced what was intuitively becoming clear, time was not on their side.

"This is what I need…"

◆♒♏♒⚹♎♎♏■♒♋■♎

Within an hour, the chapel had taken on the appearance of a laboratory. The gold, platinum, and palladium bars were brought up from the chamber and placed near the altar along with the frankincense, myrrh, and of course, the blue vase. Maya now referred to the bowl as *'Hope's crystal.'*

The colonel had a cadre of men working outside cladding the tips of both obelisks with thinly pounded gold. Additionally, she had instructed that the generator lines powering the lights in the stairs be diverted to the chapel. She showed the colonel's appointed technicians that on the back side of each obelisk was an iron rod that was recessed in what looked to be a handhold. These were to be clipped with the negative and positive ends of the power lines similar to the way jumper cables clip on to a car battery.

She was concise in her instructions. She emphasized the need to be done and on the road before the government bureaucrats arrived, and probably their assailants right behind them.

Maya had laid out ninety percent of her plans to the colonel and her friends. Already, Whitmore was arranging the logistics of moving men and Manna to one hundred and forty-four separate archeological ruins. Though scattered across the world, the operational theatre needed to be coordinated and their timing very concise.

She spent a few minutes with the colonel, who gave her a synopsis of how they would communicate, who was best for what sites in each country, transportation… redundancy, backup, and such. Maya was glad to have him on her team.

She had been adamant that she would be the one to deliver the payload to the Great Pyramid. And of course, this created its own unique set of problems. She was the prize coveted by every operative of the Hidden Hand.

Tavis was given the task of using his positional software to figure out the astrological timing of the celestial window based on the optimized position of the primary stars in the constellation of Orion. The Pleiades contained the mythical stars of the kimah and the kesil that were the keys to lighting the fuse that would fire the grid.

With threats at every turn, and global logistics weighing upon them, Maya discussed the option of calling in more troops. The addition of more men would add a rippling effect to the knowledge they wanted to keep hidden, but she left the final decision to Colonel Whitmore.

♦ ≈ ♏ ≈ ♓ ♎ ♎ ♏ ■ ≈ ♋ ● ■ ♎

It was well past midnight when the time had come. The number of participants who had traveled upon this long road of destiny, across the pantheon of history, to participate in this moment could not be counted. Those who had gathered the treasures. Those who had built this chapel. The windows in Auch, the entombed body of the last daughter from the Amarna age, and her siblings who went to America to become the proclaimed white Gods of the Indo-American cultures. It all had been laid down centuries before.

Even before Akhenaten and his house of gold had taken the secret of the ancient ones and dispersed along two separate paths, one to Israel, ending with King Solomon and the other to the far side of the world. The prophesies of King Shulgi and the seer of Uruk had foretold of this day.

But they had no time to savor the moment—Maya could feel the presence of evil building. It was like static electricity foreshadowing the coming of a dangerous storm.

Security had been doubled and the guards, dogs, and electronic surveillance were all on high alert. The remaining troops, as well as her team, now sat in the pews watching her with expectation.

She stood behind the altar and had slipped into a focus so intense that those in front of her were no longer in sight. She was locked into another space—a chamber within her mind that was doling out a recipe so ancient, so powerful, and so world-changing—she was humbled to be part of it.

She placed the crystal vase on top of the altar. Its hard-stone surface was roughhewn. From there she took frankincense and myrrh and began the process of kneading it into the bowl. Slowly, carefully yet completely, it was turning from a dry powder into a viscous fluid. She continued the kneading as if she was greasing a baking pan.

The bars of precious metal had been cut roughly into ten-ounce nuggets. When she felt the bowl was ready, she began to put in a ratio of gold, platinum, and palladium. Five to two to one. She then instructed the two soldiers who were readied on either side of the nave to clip the hot wires of the generator that could be heard outside in the distance.

"Everyone ready?"

On her command, they attached the two power lines to the obelisks. She inherently understood that one of the marvels of the Ark of the Covenant was its ability to create a power source. Their generator would have to do the same.

Maya held her breath, anticipation was palpable—all doubts suspended by threads of hope. They waited and waited, but nothing happened.

Why isn't anything happening? Maya was crestfallen. *What have I missed?*

She lifted the bowl, nothing. She stepped from the altar and went first to one obelisk and checked the connection. *Perfect.*

She proceeded to the other side of the nave and saw it too, was perfect. Confounded and disappointed, she started to turn away, when something caught her eye.

The handhold, it's different from the other one.

She removed the electrical clip from inside the obelisk and ran her finger over the metal rod. She scratched the grip with her fingernail. An insulative covering peeled away under her fingers. She smiled.

This was one more safeguard to thwart those who did not belong. She stripped away the thin covering and refastened the wire.

In that moment, she felt a vortex open as ripples ran down both obelisks and filled the nave. The pulsing energy crossed the granite causeway and brought the altar to life. The glass inside the stained windows burst into a neon intensity of white light, their images taking on life, like a hologram dancing in midair. But none of this compared to the essence that grew from out of the bowl.

Like the Aurora Borealis, the space in and around the altar began to brighten and expand. The light now flowed, shimmered, and pulsed. It danced as if freed from a cage, freedom after centuries of entombment.

Maya rushed back to the altar. The physical bars were dissolving into a liquid. She let her intuition guide her and lifted the bowl from the altar. Breaking contact with the astral energies, the liquid changed characteristics and manifested itself into a fine powder. As white and pure as the powder they had found in the Cave of Hathor.

"Behold," she exclaimed like a high priestess, pouring a bread sized loaf onto the altar. "The bread of the presence, Sha-na-na. The Sacred Manna."

The proclamation broke the spell of wonderment and at once, they all started talking.

Maya simply clasped her hands together, looked skyward and mouthed two simple words. "Thank you."

The remainder of the night was a frenetic crusade as they raced against an unknown enemy and a deadline that was self-imposed. As bushel after bushel of Manna was created, two by two, Whitmore's team secured large Ziplock bags and a redundancy provision for each of the sites to which they had been assigned.

Maya had briefed the designated soldiers on their objective, where to place the Sacred Manna and reminded them to be sure it was removed from the plastic bags. It had to be open to the energies of the cosmos and free of encumbrance.

By the time the sun was up, and the day was warming, each team had dispersed. They were headed to the four corners of the world and according to Tavis, their window would open in just under forty-eight hours.

She had given specific instructions to Tavis and Layla, who had also departed and would be waiting at the hotel in Cairo. Maya would catch up with them tomorrow, she needed to be here when the bureaucrats showed up and hoped Robert would arrive sometime in the next few hours.

◆≈♏︎≈⧘♎︎♎︎♏︎■≈♋︎■♎︎

The site commander for the Hidden Hand waited for a reply. It did not take long for word to come down from the top. They didn't have the manpower to follow every team that had departed the castle. Otto, who was watching Stobhall from a distant hillock, assigned men to track five of the teams to see where they were headed.

It was the second part of his orders that caused a curl of malice to make his heart beat a little faster. "Kidnap the girl," he had been instructed.

When asking what to do with her male companion, the command was short and chilling.

"He is expendable. Get the girl to tell us everything we want to know. Then dispose of their bodies."

Otto dialed one of his team who had been placed at the airport north of town.

"She is just pulling in, sir."

"Grab them!"

Within ten minutes, Otto got a call. A mixed bag of success and failure.

"We have the girl and her companion," the underling stated. Then in a lower voice, added the failure. "The other teams we were following... Out of nowhere a dozen Apache helicopters descended and departed with every team. We had no way to follow."

Otto thought about this and decided they would get the info from Ms. Thibodaux.

"Take them to the farmhouse," he instructed. "I will be there shortly." Leaving his second-in-command to watch things at the castle, he took the old truck that blended into the local scenery and hastened to interrogate the girl.

CHAPTER 46
Layla - Guildtown, Scotland

Layla was gagged, cuffed, and tossed into the trunk of an old sedan. Wedged up against Tavis, each bump, pothole, and turn added to their discomfort. But nothing compared to the fear. Layla's faith denuded the impact, she was readily willing to accept death as a liberation. But she worried about the man trussed up beside her.

When the trunk was lifted, the planked roof above their heads revealed that they were inside an old barn. Layla saw the big doors were closed. Her fear amped higher. This was not going to turn out well.

Three men removed her from the car and Layla was lashed to a nearby chair. Her feet were placed into a tub of water. A pair of jumper cables lay close by.

Her breath came in ragged short rasps as tremors grew uncontrollable. With trembling lips, she began to mutter soft prayers, willing her fear back into its cage. Pleading for intervention.

Watching how they treated Tavis ripped and tore at her heart. He was handled much worse. As if the infliction of pain was a sweetener for their captors. His hands were bound by a rope that straddled the rafter high above, and once fastened, a brute of a man with a salacious grin began pulling one end until Tavis's hands were stretched high above his head and his toes extended beyond measure, unable to touch the ground.

Layla's gag was removed but no one said a thing. She couldn't scream. It was psychological torture. The men said nothing, the fear building worst-case scenarios of what was to come.

As the intensity of silence grew, the door of the barn opened, and two men entered. It was clear one was the boss. And Layla knew their time was running out. She fought between glaring in open hostility and worrying for Tavis.

"You can call me Otto," he said, leveling his gaze at Layla. This was followed with him extracting a knife from his pocket and without preamble, he slashed an X across her chest.

Tavis, who was still gagged, screamed and the brute jerked his feet off the ground.

Layla cried out. "Please, please, what do you want...?"

Otto peeled away her clothing. The knife expertly sliced free the shirt and bra without touching the skin until she was naked.

"When I am done, she is yours to do with as you please," he said, offering a prize to his men. Then looking at her companion, he added. "Make him watch, then dispose of their bodies."

With her feet immersed in the water, he took a small pail from behind the chair and scooped up liquid from the metal tub. He poured it over her exposed breasts.

Setting down the pail, he reached for the live jumper cables and clipped them to her flesh. Had it not been for the excruciating pain of the intense jolt of electricity, the biting of the clamps would have been unbearable in their own right.

Layla bit hard into her lip. She did not scream but instead began reciting scripture, albeit rushed and breathy as she tried to block out the torment. "As I walk through the valley of the shadow of death, I fear no evil..."

Bam! Otto turned the voltage dial up and the intensity caused her body to go into an involuntary spasmic convulsion.

The pain was unlike anything she had ever experienced. Her mind fought to go blank, but she used every ounce of stamina to keep from blacking out. To see what they were going to do to Tavis. She willed her prayers to be loud enough to hear. To tell them, "I will not surrender."

"Yea, though I walk through the valley of the shadow of death, I will fear no evil: for thou art with me; thy rod and thy staff they comfort me..."

He repeated the process. Soon a pattern was established. "Where did everyone go?" Question, silence, shock. "What is their plan?" Question, contempt, shock. This went on for hours.

Layla lost track of time. It felt like an eternity. At one point she became cognizant of dawn's light slipping in underneath the barn door. The night had passed—and she knew she was at the end of her tether.

By his change of tone, through the haze of torture Layla could tell the man had developed a grudging respect for her.

"Not many could withstand what you have, my dear. Let's see how your lover boy holds up in your place."

Clinging to the barest thread of life, his comment caused her eyes to grow wide in fear, a different kind of torture. Concern for the one she loved.

"Yes, that's it, isn't it? You simply tell me what I want to know, and we can dispense with the pain, and my men can give you pleasure." His face was as evil as one could imagine. She saw his mirth and lust glow like a demon's heart.

Layla knew this was the end. No one was aware they were missing. No one was looking for them and there would be no cavalry to save them.

Layla focused her priorities and prayed. She prayed for Maya's success, she prayed for humanity, but mostly, she prayed that Tavis had found that place of true faith and that his soul would be saved for all eternity.

♦︎⚏♏︎⚏♓︎♎︎♎︎♏︎■⚏♋︎■♎︎

Robert arrived just as the sun was coming up over the Scottish morning. The fields were laced in dew, the blue tinges of daylight revealing the onset of a perfect day that was to follow. Events were moving quickly, and worries were piling up faster than cars in an interstate accident.

At the sound of courtyard gravel, Maya ran from the building and flung her arms around him as he stepped from the car. Nearly toppling him over, she didn't care who saw.

He met her mouth and for the briefest of moments, all the cares of the world had been sealed out and their passion had provided a cocoon of respite.

After they'd released one another, the colonel made a strategically timed appearance and in crisp concise sentences updated them of their progress.

"So, you cracked the code," Robert said after the colonel was finished. "Perhaps it is time to visit your father…"

She hugged him again and for maybe the first time ever, her science and pragmatism were replaced by faith. Her body was washed over by the belief that she had done what was necessary. But he was right, she should finally go see her father. The crunching of gravel interrupted them. It forewarned of the parade of cars approaching the driveway. One of the colonel's men whispered that it was the government. He further explained that security was at DEFCON 1, maximum alert. The cars entered the courtyard and a formation of Whitmore's men appeared as nine men in suits exited. Robert strode forth to meet them.

Maya watched the arriving men and took stock as their faces drew shadows of concern. As if they were expectant or simply making a prudent assessment of their situation.

No one moved. Maya sensed they were waiting for something, or someone. They had all been versed on the probability that this was going to be the distraction that gave the enemy their opening. She continually scanned as far as she could see.

"Are we waiting for someone?" Robert asked the rotund man whose suit was stretched tight across his ample belly.

There were feet shuffling and throats clearing, but still no one spoke.

"If you are expecting your reinforcements," Robert said in a low, stern voice, "They have been detained."

Unperturbed, the man waddled up to shake Robert's hand. Maya thought he looked a lot like Lord Balforth and had to suppress her disdain. She could sense the hope in his stride, wanting desperately to believe the plan was simply a bit off in the timing, but still in effect. But that dwindling hope was eventually snuffed out. Still, the man had to say something, he needed to justify his reason for being here.

"We are here because it has come to our attention that you have uncovered something of historical import to our country. Something that transcends ownership, title, or boundaries."

Maya noted he puffed his chest in bravado, looking to reestablish the moral high ground.

Robert replied without hesitation. "And how may I ask has this 'something,' you mention, come to your attention? What is the basis of this accusation?"

Robert had boxed him in. Was he going to confess that he got intel from his enemies or that they had hacked their network? Robert let the man squirm as he sought an answer. Until he pulled a sheet from within his pocket and handed it to the puffed-up walrus of a man.

"Read it," Robert demanded.

The man's lips moved, and his eyes scanned down the sheet. His body sagged in defeat. It was a letter from the chief arbiters of justice of the country, dated yesterday. Demanding that any person or official seeking to overturn what is deemed the legal rights of this owner, shall face the consequences and the full wrath of Her Majesty's Government.

Maya had not seen what was written but was clearly satisfied when the official's face grew pallid, and his expression soured.

"I am sorry to have bothered you, sir," the man said meekly as he backed away; giving signal to those who stood behind him. "It appears there has been a mistake."

Maya had not expected what Robert did next. The art of the deal, she smiled.

"Please, when you are up for reelection, come see me. I would be happy to contribute to the campaign of a man who has shown wisdom and practicality." He reached out and the clasping of hands was like a tonic, the defeated bureaucrat had a new bounce in his step, and Robert had the makings of one more ally.

CHAPTER 47
Maya - Crossing the River Styx

Maya needed to confirm the process had worked, and more importantly, she needed to bring her quest towards the end of her original intent.

Find my father.

She entered the library and sat in the reading chair. Seeing *The Bernstein Bears* and *Mandela* on the ottoman, she recalled this was where Lord Perth sat with his cook's daughter.

She had taken a pinch of the Manna and lamented that she had left the vial of Blue Lotus perfume back at the apartment in New York. This was the needed catalyst to lift the powders conversion capabilities from a consciousness-awakening tonic to actually being able to move the physical body across the veil of Earth's dimension, and out on to the Fields of Iaru.

But she did not care. She had longed for this moment since the day her father's diary had arrived. What seemed like a millennia ago was in fact, only six months.

Maya closed her eyes and began the rhythmic breathing, paying strict attention to nothing more than the space between the top of her lip and the bottom of her nose. She set her intentions of being with her father and one by one, she walled off each errant thought that in the past had seemed so frantic to fill the empty vacuum of her mind.

Her spirit came unzipped, and the physical constraints placed on ordinary men gave way to spiritual freedom. Floating free, she viewed her quiet body below. Her breathing was steady. In out, in out, in…

She manifested a thought of her father, the clothes he had been wearing the last time she saw him at Christmas, and in an instant—she found herself deep under waters so crystal clear that the sun shining far above, was begging her to reach up and touch it.

There was no panic, no worry, the waters were temperate, and she had been here before; albeit on an ayahuasca journey. She kicked towards the surface as she considered the biblical chasm in creation that separated the sea above from the sea below. *Could this be that gulf?*

Unlike traditional remote viewing, enhanced with the Manna, loss of intention did not collapse one back into the human shell.

She crested the surface of the placid waters. It was vastly different from the time she had arrived before. Then she had been squirted out of the raging waters upriver. Here the alluvial plain had widened, and the surging currents had gone quiet. Unlike her prior visit, the beach that was off to her right, which before had been deserted, was lined with hundreds and hundreds of people. And standing prominently in front of everyone was her father. His face was wide with a smile and his eyes twinkled like a distant lantern in the storm.

Oh. My. God. Thank you, thank you. Tears streamed down her face, the taste of salt confusing her. All her experiences with remote viewing argued against physical sensation. Still, she did not care. She had hoped and longed for this day since receiving her father's dairy. Her heart pounded with joy.

She glided through the waters with a few simple strokes. As she left the river, her body shimmered. And she was dry.

She was not physical, so the thumping in her chest and giddiness in her smile were simply a manifestation. They were not real, but...

As he approached, her pragmatic mind gave in to accepting her ignorance. Her father wrapped her in an audacious hug which should have simply slid through her like a hand crossing a beam of light. But he didn't. They squeezed, pressed their bodies, and she held on tight as the tears of joy ran unabated down her face.

All the while the crowd, the pantheon of people who lined the beach for as far as she could see down the side of the river continued to roar. Wave after wave as if they were riding the roller coaster of her emotions.

An older man appeared, which triggered the catalyst to let go. She knew who he was, Enoch. She reached out her hand, but he ignored it. Instead, he stepped in close and like a grandfather, embraced her and whispered in her ear.

"The lioness has begun to prowl."

It was a line from the Sumerian Prophesy. Enoch pointed to a man about twenty yards down the river, dressed in an odd array and told her. "He wrote that—he is the one whose prophesy you are destined to fulfill."

She felt infused with a glow. The concept of fate and that she was a queen on the chessboard of destiny had been a continual struggle to accept, though the idea gained momentum with each passing day. The doubt and fear always swam just below the surface. His words washed away any final trace of doubt.

He widened his arms to encompass everyone in view, adding what she had already determined on her own. "These people, they have all heard the call and all willfully fulfilled their role. Now we await you to complete what must be completed. Complete that which the Creator has ordained."

Her father had a grin so wide, she thought it would split his face. Before her, the crowd began to part, and through the huddled masses stepped her friend.

Rex looked at peace, as if he was finally home. She wanted to shake him with excitement, but not wanting to cry, she deflected with humor.

"Even the ghosts are here."

He smiled. A look of pride shone through.

"At some point, we will all become ghosts, even you," he quipped. "But that is only until after the reckoning, the sifting of the wheat from the chaff. Then the resurrected bodies will be delivered to the promised land."

She knew all this and no longer let her science dictate her faith. She now knew more than most, that science and faith were not a dichotomy but ran hand in hand. God's rule was manifested through the physical laws of the universe.

♦♒♏♒♓♎♎♏■♒♋■♎

Maya had no idea how long she was in Eden. It could have been days, weeks, or simply a mere moment. For time did not matter upon the Fields of Iaru, which in western theology would be known as the mystical Garden of Paradise.

She spent time alone with her father, she spent time together with he and Enoch. She learned that the more she knew, the more she did not know. She came to understand the nature of their adversary. The head of the Hidden Hand was not a man, but was the legendary one called 'The Enemy.'

Enoch took her on an intellectual journey down the long hall of history and the places her father had insisted she visit. Stonehenge, Gobekli Tepe, Uruk, and the Orkney Islands. Through his eyes, the logic of it all made sense.

"The Destroyer has been God's instrument throughout time to create radical change and alter the playing board," Enoch explained. "He allowed his opponent to gain a false confidence that he has banked on throughout history. It assured him he would be victorious. Man could not change what was in the Heavens."

She came to accept that her doctoral thesis about the Master Builders, may not have been such an original idea after all. More likely a biomorphic suggestion was planted, and she seized it. But it did not matter. None of it mattered.

With the diminishing flow of the conversation, she knew the time was coming when she needed to return to her physical self. Enoch had her repeat what she needed to do and congratulated her on having such keen insight and recall.

"The Adversary will not go down without throwing everything he has at you," Enoch offered as a final warning. "But you have allies. Understand that when you succeed…"

She noted he did not convey '*if*' you succeed.

"We will not be finished. As your calculations so rightfully concluded, the two eclipses that form the beginning and the end have not changed. This process you are undertaking will simply move us to the next level. But fear not, one step at a time."

This led to a host of questions, but some were not meant to be answered. This was made clear by the fact that when she opened her eyes, Robert was sitting patiently in the chair across from her.

"How long was I gone?" she asked. She felt exhilarated and extremely grateful. Seeing her father again was the fuel she needed to drive her to complete her mission.

"Gone? You were sitting there quietly when I walked into the room just after you sat down."

She stood, stretched, pushed blond strands back from her face and planted a deep passionate kiss onto her man's lips. She was definitely not ready to leave this world. Not yet. She knew what was waiting, it would be there when her time came.

"Come on," she said breaking the embrace. "We have work to do."

CHAPTER 48
Maya – Cairo, Egypt

Maya's nerves were taut. She continually checked, assessed, and reassessed that they were still on target. Their window was very tight. Colonel Whitmore, who had been monitoring the situation, told her that so far there had been only a few minor problems. Two separate teams at two different locations had been stopped and searched by customs, and the powder seized, and the men arrested. Fortunately, the redundancy of his plans paid off—he had required two individuals to travel separately and they were in the process of fulfilling their missions.

She appreciated that Robert's diplomatic connections and the colonel's retired military contemporaries had extracted concessions from the government. Robert had provided photos of Queen Scota's tomb to the highest levels of the Egyptian government and insinuated she would be returned to Egypt at some point in the future. In return, they were granted a window of access to the pyramid complex of Giza.

When the pilot announced they were less than an hour out of Cairo, Maya and Robert showered and dressed. A steward laid out breakfast and coffee on white linen.

Maya checked her watch for the hundredth time. It was set to local time. It was the chronometer from which their six-hour time frame had been established by Tavis. They were now within their window of opportunity and the clock was ticking down.

She fought to quell her anxiety. There was no margin for error. Her fired nerves heightened every sensation. Her brain raced, continually plumbing the depths of worst scenarios.

Looking at the satchel of Manna on the credenza, her thoughts drifted to Layla. She had not checked in and there was a pit in her stomach since she woke. An ache with a face attached.

She lifted the handset and entered Layla's number. There was a pause then the call went to voicemail. She placed a second call to the hotel where the reception desk informed her that they had not checked in yet.

"What is it?" Robert asked.

"It's Layla. I sent them ahead as a precaution and we were going to meet at the hotel, but she has not arrived." There was no denying the concern she had for her friend.

"Look," Robert suggested eyeing out the window. They were on final approach towards Cairo International and off to the right, the sun draped the pyramids in a timeless beauty.

She knew he was just creating a distraction. And it worked. Momentarily, Maya forgot all her worries and let her mind drift through years of speculations as to the whys, who's, how's and when's of these ancient sentinels. Today she was just a little bit closer to the truth.

These have always been part of my destiny.

♦ ∿Ⅲ∿⪥⚏⚏Ⅲ ■∿☺■⚏

"We have four hours remaining," Robert reminded her as they stepped from the jet. The air was hot and dry, waves of heat rose from the tarmac all around them. As they descended the gangway, directly on their heels a C-130 Hercules transport whose unofficial designations barely drew a second look, had landed. Military craft were common and often it was these older types of aerial beasts that were the tools of today's African air freight trade.

With military precision, the plane came to a halt next to their jet and the back end lowered to immediately begin jettisoning sand-colored trucks, SUVs, and armored personnel carriers.

Maya was once again reminded how much juice Robert and the colonel had spilled to get a foreign government to look the other way and to open their most prized possession to the whims of a few Americans.

In what was becoming a habit of thanks, she looked up, acknowledging the celestial forethought and grateful for the people who had been placed in her path.

♦ ≈ ♏ ≈)(♎ ♎ ♏ ■ ≈ ♋ ■ ♎

She tried the hotel again. And again, the same disappointing reply—no one had heard from Tavis or Layla.

"Damn it," she said. Her angry tone showed her fear. She was worried. Very worried, and now the gates of every worst-case scenario were open, letting the hounds of panic and apprehension run free.

Maya noted as they departed from the airport that their caravan stuck out. It would hardly go unnoticed by the locals. Or by spies reporting back to the Hand. This was partly by design, but they were secure in their firepower and by the palms that had been amply greased in the local halls of government.

Their progress from the airport to the pyramid complex was slow, as the streets of Cairo were jammed and there was nothing they could do.

Maya checked her watch, they had less than two hours to place the Manna, or they would miss the window Tavis had calculated when the powers of the kimah and kesil would be maximized as they rained down from Heaven. If they missed this window, they would need to wait another...

We are not going to miss it, she muttered under her breath. She had two aces in her hand. Help from above and her most trusted friend, JW.

She fully expected that they would be stopped, delayed, or worse. It was why she had sent JW out the day before. He was the primary; she was simply the back up. Layla and Tavis were to be an 'if all else fails' redundancy. Again, her mind slipped to of her friend.

She was having second thoughts about everything. Regret for past actions, failure to provide adequate protection, and...self-recrimination for not keeping everything under control. Biting her lower lip, she pressed her palms against her pants.

Returning to JW's role, she had arranged for him to meet with some Bedouins and slip in and out as a wandering Arab. She wondered how he was managing on that poor camel's back.

And as if her judgement that she would somehow be delayed was not to be proven wrong, traffic came to a grinding halt. They could see the pyramids through the slits of building rooftops, but they might as well have been a million miles away. She pulled the Manna closer.

Tick tock, tick tock. There were less than forty-five minutes remaining by the time they got to the gate that protected the only road into the complex. It would be easy to bypass since the fence only extended ten feet either side out into the sand.

What they could not get around, was the alignment of military vehicles with armed 55 caliber machine guns that were now trained on their caravan.

She saw one of the guards continually checking his watch. Maya suddenly felt a chill blow through her.

They know the size and time of our window... How? Where's Layla?

Fear fractured her ability to think clearly, to speak. With her stomach wrapped in knots, she succumbed to prayer.

◆ ≈≈ ℳ ≈≈ ℋ ♎ ♎ ℳ ■ ≈≈ ♋ ■ ♎

JW was soaked in sweat. He did not like cramped spaces. Surrounded by unfathomable tons of ancient block, he struggled to keep his haggard breath even and his mind focused.

He had examined known schematics and there were three shafts that penetrated the Great Pyramid. Two air shafts that opened roughly one third from its peak, and another that was well below the Queen's chamber, not far from the base. This was the main public shaft that led to a descending passage leading down to a subterranean chamber that was bisected by a narrow path to the Grand Gallery. From within the center of this chamber were sighting shafts aligned with the stars in the Belt of Orion. And it was here that he was instructed to place the Manna.

Many still believed this was created as an eternal resting place but could not articulate why no sarcophagus was ever found and no stelae ever referenced any specific Pharaoh. In light of all he knew, this was more likely an ancient power source whose engines were about to be reignited.

For years, the Grand Gallery went undiscovered. Two stone plugs had been engineered to slip in place and keep hidden the empty chamber.

"Damn, it's tight," JW lamented as he paused to mop the sweat from his brow.

He had cleared the narrow third of the ascending tunnel and could finally stand; albeit at an angle, as the shaft angle was an unrelenting forty-five degrees and he still had a way to go.

By the time he reached the King's Chamber at the very heart of the monument, his chronometer told him he had less than thirty minutes. He paused to reflect as he sat and viewed the schematic of the known interior.

There were false passages called thieves' tunnels. There was a Queen's chamber, a false tomb chamber, the Grand Gallery, and King's chamber and from here, were the two air shafts that were sighting shafts.

He checked his compass and found the shaft that was aligned with Orion. Opening his satchel, he paused to give reverence to the Creator. Letting a solemn moment of introspection and thanks pass, he emptied the contents with twenty-two minutes to spare.

Please, oh blessed Creator, watch over our team and guide them to success for your glory.

He reached the outer face of this grand behemoth with two minutes to go before Tavis's calculated lift off. He could see the station gate about one hundred yards away. He noted Maya's correct prediction. She had been waylaid. He smiled at her insight, intelligence, and in awe that he was part of something so cosmic and biblical in nature.

"You are one clever lady," he whispered, and gave her a big wave. From afar he was a mere speck a third the way up this ancient sentinel's sloping side. But he waved like a madman as the window of expectation ticked down. Three, two, one…

CHAPTER 49
The Sanctum of Sanctums

The Maestro was alone. This was his preferred mode. Here time stood without boundaries. Here, deep in the bowels of his sprawling estate, a place that man would consider the pinnacle of achievement, was a location that simply reminded him of all that he had lost. Worldly goods were no match for the things of Heaven.

"God's creation of these free-willed creatures is pathetic," he said with utter contempt. Contempt for them, for God, for the whole shit show.

"Leading them to their chase their own sinful desires is like letting water run downhill.

"God is dead, churches a palaces of pedophilia, and pro-lifers are now decreed Racist and White Supremacist."

He smiled at his handiwork. György Sorensen had been born a Jew but was corrupted into helping to put God's chosen Jews into the camps. He had made a fortune crushing poor countries and creating misery for tens of millions of these locust-like leaches. And now, all his money was fueling the unthinkable.

Abortion is right, life is wrong. Churches are bad, enlightenment is good. Rational thought... He burst out laughing at the notion. People were so easily manipulated. His thoughts harkened to the Gates of Eden, the watchers, his brethren. Those who were captured, and those who he had ruled.

I know I am winning, there have to be more souls that have died without ever accepting that God is real or gives a shit about them, then those myopically focused martyrs.

With almost eight billion souls left to sift, he knew the balance lay here and now. And he fully intended to press his advantage and get rid of them while their eyes were still blind, and their ears were still deaf.

He was well aware of Maya Harrington's role and her efforts to thwart his plans. He had learned what he needed and would wage total warfare against all their efforts.

Sure of his success, he let a mirth-filled smile curl his foul lips. It was quickly interrupted when, without a trace of warning, a large figure appeared before him.

"What do you want?" The Maestro demanded contemptuously to the familiar figure of the Angel Gabriel.

"Are you having fun?"

It was Gabriel's non-concerned nature that always pissed The Maestro off. That lingering hint of a secret that always made him wonder about the score.

"I'm here to remind you of your deal."

"And what deal would that be?" The Maestro asked with nothing but spit and rancor.

As Gabriel set out to remind him of the occasion when he had challenged God over one of his favorite children, The Maestro's face dropped. As the argument he had built that Job only revered God because of his wealth and the abundance the Lord had bestowed upon him was thrown back at him, realization gripped him like a vise.

"Remember, you wagered that if Job was stripped of all of his worldly possessions, his love for God would stop in its tracks," Gabriel said in a neutral voice.

"So what? I lost. Have you come to rub salt into an old would?"

"No, I'm here to finish the contract."

The Maestro racked his memory, and a dawning realization gripped his throat.

"God had only had two rules with you in the Job affair. One, you cannot harm him directly in any manner. And two, if you lose, you may never touch a hair of a specific woman who would be identified in the future."

Gabriel then hammered the final nail. "It is now time to reveal who she is."

The Book of Job detailed God's victory over Satan, but within the sacred cannons of the Bible, there is no mention of a second part of the deal.

"Damn me!"

"Hmmm," Gabriel teased. "I thought you already were? But that's right. Maya Harrington. Harm her or any of those who are close to her, and the whole game is over...And you forfeit."

Satan's seething anger transformed into something else. Suddenly he knew the shelf life of his hope was about to expire.

"You have minutes."

Gabriel said what was clearly painted on his opponent's face. "When they die, you lose."

CHAPTER 50
Maya – Cairo, Egypt

Even from a distance, there was no mistaking the large frame of the man whose body was half out of the pyramid and waving like a mad man. Or as Maya knew, a man who had achieved his goals.

She nudged Robert. Destiny was no longer in their hands. At least not for today. With their hands clasped together, she lifted her arm and watched the chronometer tick down. Five, four, three, two, one...

They exited the car. The sky was clear, blue, and cloudless. The heat bore down on their shoulders and then without any warning, it was dark.

Not night dark, and not a gradual eclipse dark. It was deep space dark. A wind began to blow. It was coming from the direction of the three sentinels. But it wasn't a wind, for the sand lay flat. It was a wave. A pressure. Maya began to hear the faint strains of an eerie sound. Like the doppler effect of a passing train.

A green glow burst from the greatest of the pyramids and grew. And grew and grew. Passing them, engulfing Cairo, Egypt, Africa, and she knew, the world at large. The most pervasive green shimmer man would ever witness. Like a cosmic Aurora Borealis.

Then the celestial tube appeared. It was the same ephemeral tunnel of twinkling light she had witnessed in the caverns of Guatemala. The tube that ran from the shaft of the Great Pyramid up and into the belly of the Orion Star System.

"We did it," she mouthed. Robert pulled her closer. Maya sported a grin that could not be contained. Not sure if she should jump for joy or fall to her knees in awe, she whooped, danced, and it became infectious. Both friend and foe were caught in the astral energy. It reflected hope, peace, and righteousness.

Tears poured down her cheeks. Robert had thrust his fist into the sky.

At this point, even the bribed guards blocking them no longer seemed to care. Many fell to the ground in worship.

Maya lifted her chin and pulled her shoulders back. Proud of her team and thankful of the resources that had been laid along her path. She took stock of the decisions her father had to make, knowing full well the danger he was going to put her in, and she loved him even more for the trust he had bestowed upon her.

As the glimmer of the borealis light returned to the pale blue of Earth, she saw the lone rider approach upon his steed, the mighty camel. She suppressed a grin as he came near. It was JW who was dressed in a traditional disdasha with his head covered by a ghutra.

♦ ∰ ℳ ∰ ⊁ ♎ ♎ ℳ ■ ∰ ♋ ■ ♎

They did not stay in Egypt very long. Maya was worried sick about the fate of her two friends and besides, JW was still declared persona-non-grata here from their previous forays in Cairo.

As the three flew west towards the castle in Scotland, Maya called Layla and Tavis's phones. By now the calls were simply going straight to voicemail and with each call her anxiety ratcheted up further. The colonel had teams scouring any known place she could be, and Robert had alerted Interpol. No one knew anything. Maya's heart was breaking with each passing moment.

Now that their mission was complete, she was preparing to remote view Layla's aura. She knew that if she could not locate it, chances were her friends were dead. Just then, the fuselage phone trilled, and Robert picked it up on the second ring.

He listened, and then handed the receiver to Maya. "It's Colonel Whitmore," he told her.

"Hello, colonel. Congratulations on a brilliantly executed operation. I hope we are successful." She was exhausted, worried, and unsure of what came next.

"We have recovered both Ms. Layla Thibodaux and Mr. Tavis Wiley," he said in a perfunctory report. He set out to explain the particulars, but Maya was so overcome with relief and gratitude, it went in one ear and out the other.

Her joy and elation got an immediate tamping as he explained their poor conditions. He concluded with the doctor's belief that they would both make a full physical recovery.

It did not matter; her world was upright again.

Many changes had come over her in the last two weeks. She understood every word of Arabic that the Egyptian military had spoken. She let down her guard once and for all and accepted that her intuitive possibility was firming into a totally different thing.

Receiving, deciphering, and understanding things she should not know. Things physical laws failed to explain. And one of those things was the inherent knowledge, that though their enemy was still out there, they were licking their wounds and plotting, always plotting.

But for now, the pressure was off. A divine force had intervened and given them all a reprieve. She decided it was time to close another chapter and excused herself.

♦ ♒ ♏ ♒ ♓ ♎ ♎ ♏ ■ ♒ ♋ ■ ♎

"Hello." The voice was deep, the timbre of a fully grown man.

"Austin? It's Maya." She was on the phone within the fuselage bedroom.

"Praise God. I am so proud of you. The world will never know, but we do." There was admiration in his voice.

"How? How do you know what we just we pulled off?"

"I felt it. The wave was like that of a one-roller. Like some of our local earthquakes," he clarified. "But as it passed over the world, through our universe, a part of my brain activated an old movie reel and I watched as everything unfolded."

She wondered about everything. As if he could read her thoughts, he extrapolated them to ease her worry and bring a chapter to a close.

"Everything," he told her. "I am glad you are happy. I am staring at the inscription on the ring you gave me fifteen years ago.

'Neither time nor distance shall come between us.'

They said it at the same time, and she knew he was giving her his blessing. The words bore no jealousy, simply a deep and lasting bond between two friends that would last well beyond the constraints of Earth.

"I saw my dad." Tears of gratitude ran unchecked down her face.

"That's good. And Enoch? How's he?"

"Wise," Maya said, bursting into laughter. Pent-up emotion sought to explode in the joy of talking with each other.

The conversation lasted forever. It was the captain's announcement that they would soon be arriving in Perth that brought the reunion to a temporary end.

"I will come see you soon," she assured him. "There is still so much to tell you."

"I look forward to it. Please give my regards to JW and your new friend. I look forward to meeting him as well."

CHAPTER 51
Maya - Stobhall

Maya rushed from the car and almost collided with Layla who was opening the door to greet her. Wrapping her friend in a giant hug, she was careful of her wounds.

"We're okay. It was a miracle. They just left. They just walked away and left us there," Layla explained as they walked inside. Tavis was standing inside the foyer, one arm in a sling.

Robert and JW greeted her and began to ask a thousand questions until Maya cut them off.

"Give the girl a break, would ya," Maya mildly admonished the men, then gently grabbed Layla by the arm.

"Come, come. I want to hear everything."

They went to the library and Maya fell into the chair that Lord Perth had used for decades. She was exhausted. Both mentally and physically. Her emotions had been on a roller coaster and the events of the last twenty-four hours… well she only hoped they had succeeded.

How will I know? It was a nagging thought that kept seeping into her psyche. As if the universe wanted to give her a sense of affirmation, Maya's eyes were drawn to the book on Mandela. It lay open, but what the chapter screamed, was not his death in prison as before, but his leadership of the African National Conference, and his message of unity, not retribution.

"What the?" Sitting next to this was the book of *The Bernstein Bears*. She noted the title had changed. It was subtle but changed, nonetheless. It was now called *The Berenstain Bears*. She was shocked to see something so familiar changed.

Have we created a new reality?

She was familiar with the new age concept called the Mandela Effect and wondered, *has the world been fundamentally changed?* Will our truth simply become a memory and eventually fade away?

I wonder what else has changed? Maya was desperately hoping the plague that had felt so imminent before, would be reduced to a memory. But her intuition said otherwise. They may have dodged a bullet for the moment, but danger was still out there.

As day turned to dusk and Maya, Layla, and Tavis drained their pent-up emotions by sharing their experiences with one another, the euphoria of the reunited eventually settled into more mundane activities like prepping for dinner. Life drifted back to a semblance of normal.

Maya sought solace out on the terrace. Looking down upon the rushing waters of the River Tay, she considered their new reality.

What has really changed?

Across the world the sun still rose, and the sun still set. Climate change had not abated. People went about their day. Working, loving, hating. Prejudice, arrogance, greed—people had not changed. This was reflected in the continued strife in Hong Kong, Lebanon, Venezuela, France, Catalonia, Bolivia, Chile, and of course her home country, the United States.

With a new clarity, she knew the sad reality that hate did not occur naturally, it was manufactured and amped by the Hidden Hand. With their control of the global media, they pitted one group against another. Left or right, they were two sides of the same coin.

With a deep sigh, she looked beyond the valley out to the horizon where the River Tay dumped into the Firth of Forth. Maya could see storm clouds gathering. It was a metaphor for everything they had accomplished up to this point. But for now, they were far away.

She took heart and simply accepted the wisdom that she could no longer ignore.

"God is large and in charge."

The End

GHOST GOLD

Book II
The Manna Chronicles

PROLOGUE
Discovering the Cave - 1908

PROLOGUE:

Flagstaff Arizona – 1908

The hot, dry air churned the arid earth. Wynn Lambert thought the name of the bar was appropriate. *Dusty's Saloon.* A fine silt coated everything, from the windowsills and liquor bottles to the little piles gathered in the corners.

It was only 10:00 AM, but already it was hot. *Damn hot*, he thought, as he chased away the grit with a second whiskey. Staring into the aged mirror, he was reminded of how old he had become.

Has my life come down to a bar stool at ten in the morning?

He had a wife and a son back in California, but that was from a different life. With hunched shoulders and vacant eyes, his thoughts blurred through the events that had pockmarked his road to ruin.

Lifting his head at the sound of voices, he saw from the mirror's dull reflection, he was no longer alone. Two men in their early thirties had come through the swinging doors. Their faces were seared by the sun and their clothes were covered in trail dust. From their accent, he knew they were easterners.

Bored, curious, and looking to forget, he listened while eyeing them in the reflection. The taller of the two carried a rucksack which he slung over the back of his chair. The other ordered whiskeys.

From their body language, Wynn saw triumph, hope and the optimistic energy of youth. The antithesis of his own life.

"To us," the taller of the two toasted enthusiastically. "Who would have ever thought that we would end up rich beyond our wildest imagination?"

"It certainly was good fortune," said his companion. "If that river raged like normal, we would never have found that place."

"But it begs the question, do we tell anybody about what we found? I mean, who would ever believe what's hidden in that ole' canyon? Can you imagine the history books? The famous explorers Tim Carruthers and Mike Fottrell changed everything historians ever believed about the American Southwest..."

"Yea, yea, yea..." Tim smiled, as he patted the bulging rucksack. "Let someone else have the fame, I prefer fortune."

"Amen brother," Mike agreed and raised his glass in another toast. "To gold."

Wynn's breath hitched. *Gold?*

He had been prospecting these hills for the last five years and had barely scraped by. *The river?*

Because of the prolonged drought, now in its fifth year, Wynn had witnessed the torrent of cascading waters wither to a limp current bordered by sandy shoals.

Eyeing his reflection with renewed vigor, he noted everything about them. The stain-creased cactus tears in their clothes, the dust caked on their jeans, the worn edges of their boots, and the differences in their mannerisms.

Their hats lay on the table. One was a typical brown leather type worn by most people around here. It could hold canteen water if you needed to trough the horses on the trail. The other was a little flashier. White with a band of rattlesnake skin fastened around the brim.

He gazed past the hats to the worn leather rucksack that hung from the back of Tim's chair. Partially blocked by his body, Wynn caught a glimpse beneath the unclasped flap his heart began to pound.

His foot jittered against the floor at the exposed glint of yellow.

They really have found gold!

Sitting a little taller, with his back still to them, he strained to catch their every word.

"Tomorrow we can cash out this stuff, get some additional horses and fresh supplies and then return and gather up as much as we can carry. From there, let's head north to Denver."

Tim nodded and the two men set about getting drunk.

Late that afternoon the heat driven wind was moaning through slats in the old buildings as the two easterners stumbled out of the bar, towards the Weatherford hotel.

Wynn followed discretely from a distance. He found a quiet spot in the shade where he could keep an eye on the hotel. He had formed a loose plan with a renewed sense of optimism. Something that had been missing for a long time. It infused him with a warm glow.

The next morning, Wynn was still on the alert. He had stayed there all night. He saw the two men exit the hotel. Tim carried the satchel over his shoulder. Wynn saw they were heading for the Gold Assayers Pawn Shop on Leroux Street.

Once the men entered, Wynn slipped into a narrow alley between the buildings. Leaning against a splintered wall, he watched through the shop's grimy window. Tim removed a gold statuette from the bag.

What the hell is that?

His heart started racing at the sight of the gold. It had remained completely elusive in the years he had searched. He could not hear the conversation between the men, but it was apparent the item was being weighed and tested for purity.

Once the shopkeeper finished his analysis, his demeanor changed. He pushed strands of thin grey hair off his face, as his body language shifted from excitement to that of mild interest.

Wynn knew this was the man's opening gambit, the *'I'm not sure of its worth, but I will try to help you fellas out,'* schtick. But from his vantage point, the conversation was brief and amicable, and the easterners' nods were vigorous, as if they never bothered to haggle.

Amateurs, Wynn thought with mild disgust. He watched the shopkeeper go to the back of the store and return with a large bundle of bills.

Holy shit, Wynn thought as he calculated the amount being paid by the merchant.

Once they were gone, Wynn entered the shop—hoping to get a better view of the item—but the shopkeeper had already taken it to the back room.

"Mary, call the museum in Denver," the shopkeeper called out. There was a note of triumph in his voice. Then returning, he asked Wynn in a rude tone, "Can I help you?"

♦ ᨓ ᠓ ᨓ ⨯ ♎ ♎ ᠓ ■ ᨓ ♋ ■ ♎

After three days of waiting and watching, Wynn knew the moment they were ready to depart. He had gambled every last dollar on a fresh horse, a map, extra canteens, dried beef, sketch paper, and some charcoal pencils.

Watching their two mounts and four mostly empty pack horses, Tim and Mike set out on a course heading south. They passed the abandoned water tower at the edge of town and skirted the old graveyard. Wynn followed safely from a distance, continually balancing discretion against the possibility of losing them.

After four days of winding through thorny scrub, tumbleweeds and the occasional dust devil, Wynn was running low on water. They had been riding high up on the canyon rim. He had looked below a few times and was shocked at how low the Colorado River had become. In many places, it was nothing more than a winding bed of gravel sluiced by a thin stream.

That night, as darkness approached and the early stars pushed out onto the indigo sky, his quarry finally left the open plateau. They followed a switchback and carefully worked their way down to the edge of the river. Its steep banks were very risky for their six horses and for that matter, Wynn's lone mare. He waited until they had made it to the bottom and rounded a bend before he dared expose himself.

Once he was confident the men had set up camp, he led his horse quietly to the river's edge. The wind-worn rock formations showed evidence of ancient flooding and the shoals bore fresh tracks of thirsty animals who had slipped in under the cover of darkness to drink. He pulled out his map and marked the day's progress. Once again, Wynn was struck by the curious names of the various buttes and peaks listed on the governmental survey of the territory.

The Tower of Set, the Tower of Ra, Horus Temple, Osiris Temple, and The Isis Temple. The map was dated 1883.

Why are the peaks around here all named after Egyptian gods?

Eventually he dozed off, but he never let himself fall into a deep sleep. His instinct to stay vigilant paid off, for he awoke to the sound of activity long before sunrise. Breaking from their typical routine, Tim and Mike were on the move before the sun had risen above the valley's rim.

Between the high walls of Marble Canyon and the shoreline, was a width of tossed stones exposed by the extended drought which allowed easy passage for the horses. They picked their way slowly and carefully, stopping periodically to check their map. By noon, the sun was high and the shadows elusive. Temperatures were rising and heat mirages shimmered off the rocks. Without shadows, it was hard to follow without being seen. Often, Wynn would slip into a side canyon and pray that his quarry had not made a turn.

Stepping over the scattered deadwood as he exited the latest vent, Wynn had lost them. His chest tightened and fear caused a panic. His breathing became labored and for the next few minutes, anxiety had taken hold.

Finally, he saw movement across the river. It was Tim and Mike. They were following an unseen trail high up the side of the cliff.

Letting out a deep breath, he whispered to his pony. "They must have crossed downstream." And with that expectation, he fixed his eye on the landmarks surrounding their trail. Impatient but prudent, he waited before going forth.

To pass the time, he took out his pad and sketched the butte that loomed above him. It was known as the Temple of Horus. With pencil and charcoal, he created a drawing from the point of view of the riverside all the while he let his mind wander.

How did they find this place? Was that statue part of a lost Spanish treasure?

He stowed his drawing along with the others and set out along the water's edge with his chestnut mare.

As he suspected, about a thousand yards down river he spied a sliver of cloth tied to a piece of driftwood. The path's entrance. Crossing the shallow waters, he started to pick his way up the face of the canyon, as impatience began to beat back caution. Navigating an almost invisible trail, he was careful with each step. The dizzying height and sheer wall cloyed to his left and the track was narrowing. It was turning into nothing more than a goat trail. Bessie's hooves sent the scrabble of small stones cascading over the side as he hugged in close to the face of the cliff.

Constantly reassessing his situation, he dismounted and walked on foot. There was a protrusion squeezing the trail and he wanted to surveil what was on the other side before continuing. With the tang of grit coating his tongue, and the sun boring down from above, he wiped his brow and poked his head around the outcropping.

Holy shit! His breath hitched in his throat.

Five hundred yards ahead was a large opening hollowed out of the rock face. And carved into each side of the entrance were large statues of dog-headed men. He became lightheaded as his heart rate surged.

Tim and Mike were nowhere to be seen, but they had left the horses to graze outside. It was an area big enough to hold a small corral, but it was clear the path stopped there. Beyond was a wall that marked the end of the trail.

What in the hell is this place?

And then on a more practical note, Wynn realized that when they left, this was the only way out. Not knowing how long they would be, and outnumbered if caught on the trail, he went back along the path to see if there was a place to hide.

About a quarter mile down the trail, he spotted what looked like a vertical row of notches in the cliff face. To the left he saw the unending colors of the Colorado canyons. Above, he heard the shrill cries of predatory birds bounce off the high walls. He hesitated, torn between curiosity and prudence.

These must lead somewhere.

He dismounted, measured the situation, and curiosity won the moment. Leaving Bessie alone on the path he started to climb the wall face. The climb was brutal. The sweat of exertion created rivulets of grime on his skin and the moisture attracted insects. As flies buzzed his face, he was afraid to look down.

"Last thing I need is for my vertigo to kick in," he mumbled miserably, questioning his sanity. About a hundred feet from the top, he found a respite from the grueling ascent. It was a stone alcove littered with small animal droppings which conjured up a hard-earned warning.

Watch out for rattlesnakes.

He noted the alcove was boxed on three sides with high walls of red hued rocks. They were covered with strange petroglyphs. Over his years corralling through these canyons, he had seen many ancient carvings, but these were different. Older and of a much different style. They looked more like symbols he had seen in a picture book, called hieroglyphs.

His eyes wandered to the other side of the river. The sun was sinking and fired the striations of the high cliffs with every shade and hue of crimson.

What's that?

He sharpened his focus. It looked like another cave and it became clear the place was well hidden. Impossible to see from above or below.

Because of this viewing site, he assumed the two caves had to be related to one another.

If Tim and Mike found treasure in their cave, could there be more in the other one?

The idea filled him with desire. His heart raced all the way back to Bessie. Right where he had left her. Carefully, they made their way to the canyon floor.

Fervently he searched along the river's edge seeking evidence of handholds that would lead to the cave he sighted. One hour passed, then

another. Frustration consumed him, and darkness was approaching. Listening to the sound of the slow-moving water, he dismounted to let Bessie have a drink.

"Go ahead girl, take your time."

He stooped to wash the grime from his face. Next, he filled one of the empty canteens. With the sun dropping below the escarpment, long shadows crept down the rock face. While fastening the top of the canteen, he watched the growing shadow line. There he noticed a mark. Looking up he saw others.

With a spike of fresh adrenaline, he went to investigate.

This is it... I found it. The excitement swelled within. The fluttery feeling in his stomach said go, don't wait. See what is up there. But night was near, and he didn't want to leave Bessie exposed to any predators that might be coming to the water's edge to drink under the cover of darkness. And truth be told—looking up the steep face of the cliff left him a little uneasy.

It can wait until morning.

Wynn continued down river where he found an opening that led to a small ravine off the main waterway. It was flat with a dry sandy bed at the base of a cliff and was well protected.

"Okay, Bessie. We'll camp here tonight. I'll brave the climb tomorrow."

That night he slept a thousand sleeps. Destiny's door was waiting. He was safe, secure, and had the companionship of Bessie, maybe his only friend.

When morning came, he tethered her to a long line, making sure to clear away anything that could cause it to become entangled. He did not know how long he would be, so he left out food. The rope was long enough to reach the water.

"You stay here girl and be quiet. I'll be back as soon as I can."

As she neighed against his shoulder, the one worry that nagged him was her vulnerability to a mountain lion, but it was a risk he had to take.

Exiting the ravine, he looked across the river and was relieved that Tim and Mike were nowhere to be seen. Of course, thinking of them led him to question the same things he had been asking himself over and over.

Who left that treasure they found? What else is in that cave? They said they needed all those pack horses to carry out the next load...

He gazed up at his destination. Nothing but rock outcroppings. With a sack of supplies that irritated his prickled sunburn, he set forth.

Okay. Wynn, you can do this.

As the strain on his muscles grew unbearable, he started to have doubts. "I'm too old for this shit," he muttered, but never dared to look down.

When he was sure he could go no further, he found the ledge. He pulled himself up and over, stopping to catch his breath. His heart was beating double-time—from both the exertion and what lay before him.

The landing area was smaller than the other cave, but it was level and had a manmade feel about it. The framing of the entrance caught his eye.

The opening was perfectly concealed from every direction and he could sense it was ancient. There were intricately laden carvings cut into pillars that had been hewn from the rocks. The cave's entrance had been expertly chiseled, until two huge obelisks remained protruding like sentinels watching over everything.

Wondering what they could see, he turned to view the canyon up and down the river. During normal times, these walls would enclose a raging torrent, unpassable by any means.

Was the water this low in the past?

He started to catalogue the 'little things.' He wanted to recall every part of this experience. He noted the carvings on either side of the door. He could taste the dryness of his cracked lips. Somewhere in the distance, he could hear the baying of a coyote. All of his senses felt primed, attuned to this moment.

Stepping out of the hot sun into the cave's cool interior, he felt transported to another age. With his senses heightened, he had an acute awareness of sensory stimuli. His eyes feasted on a wide range of ancient images. The walls were covered with pictures. Men with tunics and heads like Pharaohs holding some sort of vassal which contained a snake. It was clearly Egyptian in design.

There was a woman, with a headdress of cow horns sitting on a throne. Before her were supplicants making cone-shaped offerings. Along both sides were flower blossoms, they looked like lotuses.

He lit a lantern from his rucksack and placed it on a stone table. Maybe an altar. There were chairs, tools, and a horde of artifacts. Many of them were made from gold and silver. There was a jewel encrusted urn full of white powder and next to it sat a sixteen-inch rod made of gold and covered in symbols.

All of his aches and pains were washed away with the elation of discovery. Of untold riches and vindication. His heart raced as he inventoried his surroundings and started calculating what he would haul away first.

"Definitely taking that." Next to it was another gold item, also covered in symbols. "And that." He began placing items in his pack.

The room was about fifty feet long. The walls were finished with rectangular blocks. Taking his lamp, he ventured in further. He was surprised to see images painted on the walls that looked like workers harvesting corn. Strange corn, but ears nonetheless.

He continued to explore. At the end of the far wall was an opening that contained a long row of corniches. With only the glow of his lantern, he saw dozens more of the jewel encrusted vases. Mired in cobwebs, he took one and wiped it on his sleeve. They were exquisite, crafted with precious stones recessed into solid gold embossed with fine filigree artwork. Each displayed detailed scenes of another age.

He was giddy with excitement. He had never seen so much wealth in a single place. And it was all his.

As his eyes feasted and his brain counted, he absentmindedly removed the lid hoping to find more jewels, more riches, more.... But like the one out front, it simply contained a mysterious white powder.

What is it?

He sniffed it, but it was odorless. He pinched some with his finger. It was granular like sand, but much finer. He put his fingers to his mouth to get some saliva, to see if the powder would dissolve. He noted the grains touching his tongue were tasteless. He had no idea what it could be.

Whatever it is, it must have been important to whoever built this place. Maybe at another time I will come back and take some.

He started dumping the powder into a single pile and putting the chalices into his bag. After emptying close to a dozen and placing them in his sack, suddenly he wasn't feeling right. Dizzy, he needed to sit down. His head grew heavy, and his breathing slowed to the point where he was no longer in this world.

◆〰ﾶ〰Ж♎♎ﾶ■〰♋■♎

"I do believe we are going to be rich," Carruthers said with a huge grin.

"No shit," Fottrell chuckled. "I'm gonna get me a different woman every day."

"And you'll still never run out of money."

Tim guffawed as they continued filling their sacks with treasure. Solid gold Pharaoh heads, jewel encrusted urns, dog-headed men, obelisks, cats, and winged goddesses. There were alabaster jars with various amorphic heads full of some unknown powder. They poured it out and took the jars, too.

When they first discovered this place, they had done a cursory exploration of the interior. But it was so large, with so many rooms and so many chambers, and seemed to go so deep into the earth, they had put their focus on their primary concern. Anything of value they could cart away.

Back again, it was not long before they had collected more than they could haul out on their six horses, so they decided to explore a little. They pushed beyond the initial room onto what could best be described as the main boulevard. Drools of bat guano caked the walls where spongy mushrooms grew out from some of the cracks.

"Well?" Mike asked, when they reached a four-way intersection.

"Forward. We can backtrack and explore the other areas later." They continued deeper into the mountain.

The air grew thick with an old musty smell. The light from their lanterns caressed brightly painted walls that were thirty feet on either side of the middle. The echo of their voices changed, and they found themselves inside a barn-sized chamber.

"Who the hell were these people?" Tim wondered aloud.

"And how many years ago was this place built?"

All around them, highly stylized coffins were tucked into wall openings like a crypt. The height of the ceiling was lost at the edge of the lanterns' glow, but it had to be over fifty feet. They pulled one of the coffins out and pried the lid open. There was an ancient body wrapped in gauze linen.

"Creepy," Mike said.

"No shit," Tim agreed.

The sound of prying coupled with their conversation, set off a flurry of bats. One minute they were roosting in the eaves and the next, a black wave had swarmed over them. Tim tried covering his head.

"Let's get the hell out of here."

◆〜♏〜⊁♎♎♏■〜♋■♎

Wynn found himself in a world like none he had ever known.

Am I dreaming? What's happening?

Before him was a raging river, but it did not flow of water, but images, like time was washing over him at a great speed. It seemed ancient. Portraying a land of milk and honey, safe, peaceful. Primordial.

Then the water began to roil and toss beyond the hem of its bank. The images flowed through him. They changed, he felt nauseated, he was

305

them, in them, watching them? Confused, they poured forth. Scenes of war, a dark cloud growing ever thicker. There were machines like he had never seen. Large treaded vehicles shooting fire from their trunks like elephants. Flying contraptions, like locusts, creating death from above.

He could not shut his eyes to the horrors, no matter how hard he squeezed them shut.

Am I awake? Or is this a nightmare?

He could not distinguish. There was a dread deep in his gut. The fear was consuming him, it was coming, he could feel it. Suddenly there was a large bright mushroom that spread across the land. Everywhere people were falling over, the world was on fire. A darkness was coming, closer, more dreadful.

"No!' Wynn screamed as this inalienable shadow blotted out all light from the sun. He was woken by the sound of his own terror. He was sitting inside the cave amongst the sprawled chalices that must have spilled from his bag when he passed out.

Shaken, scared, confused, he rushed to the exit, thankful the sun was still shining. He inhaled the sweet nectar of mother earth and squinted into the blue sky. From the corner of his eye, he saw movement.

Far below were two Indians, they looked to be tracking, picking their way along the water's edge. One of them looked across the river, but the other seemed unsure. Instead, he was looking down the side to where he had stashed Bessie.

Are they looking for me or the other two?

Fear ran down his spine, a guttural instinct that screamed danger.

Further behind was a long line of white men on horseback. They followed the guides to the other side of the river.

He was relieved, confident no one knew of his presence and by extension, his discovery. But he had a growing sense of foreboding. Wynn understood that the two men called Tim and Mike had trouble at their doorstep.

He retreated back into the cave, gathered the most valuable items he could carry, and practicing prudence, allowed a sizable gap of time to pass. He used the moment to make a few more drawings. Once the men were long out of sight, he made his way back to find Bessie just as he had left her.

He struck out for Yuma, away from the way the intruders had come. On the long ride south, his fear of being found out had vanished but the foreboding was replaced by the images he had seen.

So much death, disease, war, plague, and a darkness so terrifying and so great it blotted out the sun. But as hard as he tried to forget, the visions had been seared into his soul.

♦ ≋ ♏ ≋ ♓ ♎ ♎ ♏ ■ ≋ ♋ ■ ♎

The Story Continues

The story is not over, Book III of *The Manna Chronicles* will bring Maya and her team face to face with the UFO phenomena. Interstellar or interdimensional. Alien visitors or stalking demons who seek a pathway to physicality. End times, a global ruler who rises from the ashes…

The agents of Darkness have regrouped and are angrier than ever. Deception, chaos, promise, false hopes…. the world is being played. Will Maya Harrington be a lone voice in the darkness or a beacon of light?

But before this next chapter unfolds, those who have followed us on Facebook or at www.AuthorChrisReynolds.com will be able to receive a free copy of a prequel to *The Manna Chronicles* Due out in early 2022.

ALEX HARRINGTON – THE TIME MASTER
Prequel – The Manna Chronicles